THE VINEGAR JAR

THE VINEGAR JAR

Berlie Doherty

HAMISH HAMILTON · LONDON

HAMISH HAMILTON LTD

Published by the Penguin Group
Penguin Books Ltd, 27 Wrights Lane, London w8 5tz, England
Penguin Books USA Inc., 375 Hudson Street, New York, New York 10014, USA
Penguin Books Australia Ltd, Ringwood, Victoria, Australia
Penguin Books Canada Ltd, 10 Alcorn Avenue, Toronto, Ontario, Canada M4V 3B2
Penguin Books (NZ) Ltd, 182–190 Wairau Road, Auckland 10, New Zealand

Penguin Books Ltd, Registered Offices: Harmondsworth, Middlesex, England

First published 1994
1 3 5 7 9 10 8 6 4 2

Filmset by Datix International Limited, Bungay, Suffolk
Printed in England by Clays Ltd, St Ives plc
Set in 11½/14 pt Monophoto Garamond

A CIP catalogue record for this book is available from the British Library

ISBN 0–241–00258–3

For Alan, Erica and Simon

ONE

Rose Doran lay as naked as a peach on top of her bed and watched the moth that fluttered its dark and dusty wings down the wall. Maybe, she thought, Paedric will hear its whispery strumming between her room and his and think of her before sleep takes over. She closed her eyes and imagined the moth's lips brushing like velvet along her flesh.

From next door she heard the drawing-to of bolts and the rattling of keys that told her that he was still awake. Outside, owls shrieked. In the distance a night train drummed. She lay in the blue wash of the one street lamp with her curtains full open. She liked it best when her room was soaked in this gaudy, filmic light, when her pieces of furniture grew for themselves wholesome shadows. The bed that had been her grandmother's creaked as she turned in it, and she found no comfort in the toast-crumbed sheets. One foot rocked in a familiar ceaseless rhythm in the sole of the other, as it had done when she was a child listening in the night to what her parents did.

She heard then the sounds she had been waiting for. Voices rose and fell. A man spoke love, a woman cried, the man's voice bellowed grief. He has never lost that, Rose thought. Such a powerful voice.

In the small back bedroom upstairs Edmund snored like a donkey into his feather-spiked pillow. Ranged round the room like silent mourners at a vigil were his suits, hanging from the picture rails, and underneath them the right shoes and socks. On his bedside table lay his alarm clock with the time set as always for 6.30 and his diary opened out at tomorrow's date neatly listing in black fountain pen his day's duties, which began and ended with 'Make drink for Mother.'

Rose pulled her cover across herself. Soon nothing in the house stirred, nothing, except for Edmund's coloured fishes in the hall, arranging the pale stones at the bottom of their tank like tidy wives.

In the light of the morning Rose turned on her back and flexed out her fingers. For a time, before the early morning train passed through, the terrace was silent. The house on the one side of her where the Merlins used to live was empty, boarded up against vandals and a sanctuary for rats and field mice. On the other side of her, for a time, Paedric's house was silent. Underneath her fluttering and shredded dreams she had been aware of him, pacing and pacing, counting aloud his steps and the hours and the stars, calling out from time to time in a way that had startled her into full wakefulness. At last the morning train came through.

Paedric lay wide-eyed, listening out for the train. He half-dressed himself and went downstairs in his bare feet, padded across the stone floor and unbolted his back door. He went out into his garden, delighted and surprised to see it again, dewdrops on the marigolds and all that sweetness in the drizzle and the sunshine, snails on the walls, and his tree a shower of light, a glorious fire. It was just as he remembered it from yesterday, or was it twenty years since he had last seen it so?

He used the outside toilet because he preferred it still with its torn triangles of newspaper threaded on string, and where catastrophes came to him at odd angles and in ripped words to present their own surprises and chaos: IDDLE EAST CRI; SANDS DIE IN EARTH; KILLED IN HIS OW. A drowned insect floated in the pail of water that served to flush the lavatory. As he sat he scratched at peeling whitewash. 'Too soon, too soon,' he said aloud, 'too soon the ash of day will come,' the words rising from nowhere at the sight of the white powder settling on the stone floor.

At the door to his kitchen the night snails had left their tracks. He rubbed at them with his toe as he went back in. Already he was thinking about the marmalade he would have for his breakfast. 'Oh for the spiky zest of oranges,' he said aloud as he opened his cupboard door. 'The bitter zest. Fervent. Yes, the fervent zest.' There was a tilting movement in his head like the spill of water or the gushing of blood and he half-turned to see Helena entering the room, just on the last stair. She came to him like a child, her hair loose and pale, her eyes made big for him so he clutched a sob in his throat. That gushing in his head surged through his limbs as she came towards him, a pluck of nightdress in her hand so her feet were freed. 'Paedric,' coy as a pigeon, her face turned up to his.

'Down before day, my love?' He placed both hands on her shoulders while she tiptoed up to be kissed. He led her to the table and put breakfast things in front of her, put coffee in a jug and poured in boiling water for her, and turned back, expecting her to be gone.

'I have been thinking all night,' he told her, 'about the nature of night itself. What is it, night?'

He watched how she pouted her lips to sip at her drink. She held the cup at its rim, circling it with the thumb and first finger of each hand.

'You know, Paedric. Night is for bed.'

'Is it the other side of day, like the other side of a record? Is it just the absence of sunlight that makes the night? Or is it the presence of the stars?' As he bent down to put the coffee in front of her he saw how light caught in her hair, and put out his hand to touch it. 'Is night our acknowledgement of infinity? Is that why it scares the shit out of us? It scares the shit out of me. There is nothing about daylight that reminds me of infinity, but night is dense with it.'

'If you're scared of the dark you should come to bed.'

'I think I will.' He was roused, caught unawares by her. 'Will you come with me?' He watched the languorous way she had of sucking marmalade off her fingers.

'Now, Paedric?'

'Wasn't it always like this?'

'Oh yes, always. You have always been outrageous, squandering daylight in love-making.'

'Isn't it ours to spend?' He had forgotten her. For hours he had wandered through the night and had let his thoughts of her slip away like smoke. He wanted to carry her upstairs now, a child, with her gown flowing through his arms. He leaned towards her to watch how she would smile up at him. He put out his hand and felt how one by one she put her fingers into his palm. He eased her up, his free hand in the small of her back. He could smell sleep on her, in the pale tousle of her hair and on her breath and on her flesh. It was as arousing to him now as it had been all those years ago.

The bedroom was dark and stuffy. For a moment he let her hand slip away while he opened the window, and was afraid even as he turned that she might have gone away. The breeze sucked the curtains; they sighed and breathed like living things. On the walls her coloured silk scarves fluttered like the wings of birds. 'My Helena,' he said, and held out his arms for her to come to him, and eased away her gown to drape it over the bed. 'I love you still, after all these seconds and minutes, after the comings and goings of so many stars.'

*

4

Rose Doran heard his cry of ecstasy, and closed her eyes against the unbearable imaginings of day.

TWO

When she was a girl she was Rose Waterhouse. Her parents had a grocery shop in town. She was always afraid of her father, a big, noisy man who lost his temper easily and frequently shouted. Her mother never crossed him. She suited herself in a quietly rebellious way. She was a cold, withdrawn woman, who rarely smiled and never laughed out loud in all Rose's memory of her. There was an anxiety about her that never seemed to soften. Rose had an older brother, Desmond, and she adored him. He was the one who took her for walks to be out of the way of her father's tantrums. He told her stories at night, curled up with her under the blankets. They were about princesses locked in dark towers and wolves who ate children. She loved to be frightened by them, because then Desmond would put his arms round her and comfort her. 'You can have a magic wish,' he told her, 'before you go to sleep.'

She would screw her eyes up tight, so bobbing coloured stars danced in the darkness. 'I wish I could always have a magic wish,' she would say, knowing that was the right answer, and that nothing could ever go wrong then.

During the war it was Desmond who took care of her, bundling her down to the air-raid shelter when the sirens went off. Their father was a warden, and their mother never went into the shelter with them. She said she was more afraid of the rats in the shelter than she was of the bombers, and she would sit under the stairs on her own, with her hands folded quietly in her lap, waiting.

'Guess what!' Desmond told them one day, panting from

the excitement of having run a mile through a raid to get home. 'Rose – the school's been bombed!'

Rose could not be comforted, even by him. She loved school. She loved its quiet order and the progression of paintings on the walls, from springtime lambs and daffodils to haystacks and autumn leaves and winter snowflakes. 'Where will I go?' she sobbed. 'Where will Miss Cleary live now?'

'Silly!' Desmond said, bending down to her and putting his arms round her. 'Miss Cleary has her own little house. And I bet you'll be going there to have your lessons now. That'll be much better, Rose!'

He took her to Miss Cleary's house the next day and stopped to have a laugh and a chat with her. He liked to flirt with girls by now, and the teacher was very young, with long, loose red hair and a deep and thrilling voice. She taught the children very little, according to Mrs Waterhouse.

'I don't think you've learned a thing since you went to that school,' she told Rose. 'Nothing that's going to be useful to you in life. When you get in the shop, that's when you'll learn.'

'She tells us stories,' Rose protested.

'Stories!' Her father laughed in his abrupt and scornful way. 'When did stories ever do anyone any good!'

Every school day ended with a story, most of which Miss Cleary made up with the children or remembered from her own childhood. It was Rose's favourite time. When she was allowed to choose she asked for the story of the fisherman and his wife, who lived in a vinegar jar. Maybe it was because she lived in a grocer's shop that she loved that story best. She knew that the jar would be of belled glass, and that the liquid inside it would glow like wet gold. Even when she was told that it was a house that was shaped like a vinegar jar, she saw its amber light and the figures inside it floating like fishes.

'Well, there was a fisherman,' Miss Cleary would begin, smiling at Rose, who was her favourite child. 'And he lived with his wife in a vinegar jar. He was a little dreamy man, and happy. And oh! she was a nagging wife, a sour and spiky sort of wife. Well, one day he went out fishing and what should he catch but a magic fish! Such a beautiful fish it was, such a big and gleaming fish . . .'

Rose would sit cross-legged on the floor and sketch and crayon on the backs of envelopes and scraps of paper from the shop. Most of all she loved to be in Miss Cleary's house on dark afternoons when the teacher didn't put on the lamp but would let them sit and listen in the firelight, watching the flames and shadows dance across the walls.

She must have been about eight years old when Desmond left home. He came up to her room one night and told her that he was going away. He was very quiet, and she sensed in him a contained excitement and sadness.

'When will you come back?' she asked. She was drowsy with sleep, and yet she wanted to make the most of her last night with him.

'Are you sleepy? Close your eyes, Princess.'

She did as she was told. 'Keep them tight shut,' he said. 'I want to look at you. I want to remember you.' He drew down the covers and she lay in the thrilling darkness, aware only of his breathing close to her.

'Tell me a story.'

'Once upon a time,' he said softly, 'there was a princess, whose name was Rose.'

She smiled in her darkness. 'And she was very beautiful.'

'Of course. And one day a fairy put a spell on her, and she fell asleep. And she would never wake up again, the fairy

8

said, until a handsome prince came along. When he kissed her, she would wake up and open her eyes.'

Her eyelids fluttered.

'Ssh now,' he said. 'Keep your eyes closed.'

The next day her mother told her that Desmond had left to join the army and fight in the war.

'Why?' Rose asked her.

'Because he's a man, that's why,' her mother said, her voice tight and small.

'Then why didn't Dad go?'

'He's not well enough.'

None of this made sense to Rose. She longed for Desmond to come home again. Nothing was the same without him. There was no comfort for her now, not even in Miss Cleary's house. She wanted her brother back. She used up her magic wish, and still he didn't come. And then, one important day, a telegram arrived. What always brought it to mind, throughout her life, was the sight of cheese, because at the precise moment of the telegram being opened she was standing by her mother, who had the wire held taut in her hand across a slab of yellow cheese. Rose had reached out to peel off the thin shaving that was hanging loose, and ever since that moment slabs of cheese had looked like fat lumps of flesh to her, and had a sound that she associated with it, the gush of sound that had come from her mother's throat and which she would never have recognized. Her father stood in the dim bulb-light with a paper in his hand, and it was as if her mother had known what was in the paper before he spoke the words –

'Desmond's dead.'

Rose was quite sure her father was mistaken, and that he could simply undo the news by folding up the piece of paper and putting it up on the shelf where bills and receipts were kept. But instead of this he stood with the paper trembling slightly in his hand and said that he was proud that his son had died in this way. When he said that, just after closing-time with twilight coming on, Rose's mother moved away from the cheese counter and flung tea and sugar at him, their precious store of the stuff that he had been about to bag up for special customers, and it rained down on him in a shower of white and brown, flakes and grains in his hair and in his eyebrow tufts, layering the neck of his shirt. Her grief had rained with it. Rose had stood with her hands to her mouth and the cheese still fatty on her tongue.

'What good is this country?' her mother gasped at last. 'When all its boys are dead?'

'Don't think I don't care,' the grocer had roared then, his voice like a bull's, his neck red and ringed, his big hands held up and helpless. It had been a terrifying thing then, to see that big man crying.

Rose ran off to Miss Cleary, who drew her in to the warm room and folded her arms round her, and then Rose knew that it was true. Miss Cleary took Rose to the phone box on the corner and phoned the shop to say that Rose could spend the night with her. On the way back to her house she held the child's hand. Rose felt solemn and important.

'What does it mean,' Rose said, 'when you say he's dead? What does it really mean?'

Miss Cleary's hair was like a blaze of red gold around her sad face. 'You know what it means. You'll never see Desmond again, Rose.'

Rose tried to imagine this, and couldn't. She could no longer picture her brother's face. She squeezed her eyelids together but no tears would come. She couldn't imagine what she was supposed to feel, but she remembered the sound that had come from her mother's throat and the sight of her father's wet face, and that made her afraid. She wanted the teacher to hold her and comfort her.

'Will you tell me a story?' she asked in a baby voice. 'The one about the fish?'

'Oh, the magic fish.' Miss Cleary went to the cupboard next to the fire and brought out a knitted blanket and pillows. She drew the settee up to the fire for Rose to sleep on. 'For it was a magic fish of course, that the fisherman caught. "Let me go," the fish said to the fisherman, "and I will make your dearest wish come true." "I have no wish," the man said, "but I'll let you go all the same." And he flung the gleaming fish back into the sea, where it flicked its tail and whisked away from sight . . .'

'What's that picture?' Rose interrupted her. The painting was hung above the mantelpiece, and showed the inside of a cave, with brown and green and blue layerings on its walls. In the nervous shadows the layers looked as if they were encrusted with flowers. Rose opened and closed her eyes and watched how the flowers became bones; limbs and skulls all in a litter.

'Do you like it?' Miss Cleary stood behind Rose, just lightly resting her hands on the girl's shoulders.

'I don't know. It's got bones in it.'

'My young man gave it to me, Rose, before he went away.' She turned away to clear up the plates. 'It's good to have it, to remember him by.'

'Is he dead too?'

'It's only a cave, that picture. It's not about anything.'

'What did the fisherman's wife say?'

'Rose, you know what she said.'

'I can't remember.' Rose sat up, impatient for the next line of the story which the teacher told so well. 'Tell me.'

'For God's sake, Rose!'

For a long time after Miss Cleary had gone to bed Rose lay awake, her eyes wide open and staring. Miss Cleary had never shouted at her before.

The next time Miss Cleary held lessons in her own house she was white and drawn. She spoke in a quiet, weary voice that could hardly be heard. Her eyes were red.

'My daddy has killed three Germans,' one of the children whispered across to Rose, knowing about Desmond. Another child assured her that her father had killed hundreds and that there were more to come.

Miss Cleary laid down the book that she had been working from and without looking up asked Rose to fetch her the cane. It hung in the kitchen and as far as the children could remember it had never been used, either in Miss Cleary's house or in the schoolhouse that had been bombed by the Germans. Rose fetched it and Miss Cleary stood up, and as Rose was returning to her place on the settee Miss Cleary said to her, 'Come back, Rose, and hold out your hand.'

'Me, Miss Cleary?' Rose was astonished. 'But I . . .'

'Just do it, Rose.'

The children watched in a fearful, unbelieving silence. Rose held out her hand palm flat upward and watched while Miss Cleary raised up the cane with both her fists clenched around it.

'What about the little children of the Germans that your daddies have killed? What about them?' Miss Cleary demanded. Her voice was a strangle of sound in her throat. Nobody spoke. They watched in the same horror as Miss Cleary brought down the cane in an unwieldy gesture across Rose's hand. The ripped sound it made and the impulse of pain across the faces of the woman and child were separate happenings. Rose and Miss Cleary stared at each other, with the same unbelieving look, before Rose broke into bewildered sobs, her fists bunched at her sides.

'There now,' said Miss Cleary at last. She turned to the children. 'Did Rose deserve to be caned?'

'No,' one of the boys muttered.

Rose sobbed.

'No, she did not,' Miss Cleary confirmed. 'And did the little German children deserve to lose their daddies?'

No one spoke.

'I was wrong to hurt Rose. Hurting people is wrong. Killing people is wrong. It's always, always wrong.'

In the same fascinated horror the children watched as Miss Cleary hung the cane across the mantelpiece in the place where the cave painting had been. She stood with her arms outstretched across it and her back to them.

'Go home now,' she whispered, and, grinning awkwardly at one another, they went.

When Miss Cleary turned round Rose was still there. 'Go home now.'

Rose tilted up her face to her, wanting the teacher to see her distress and comfort her. Miss Cleary turned away from her.

'I'm tired,' she said. 'I want to go to sleep.'

Rose followed her into her room. The painting was propped against the wall by the bed. The curtains were still undrawn. Miss Cleary sat on the bed and unbuttoned her shoes, took off her blouse and, standing up, unfastened her skirt, which fell like a swathe about her legs. She climbed into bed and pulled the covers around herself, shivering. Still Rose stood there.

'Take off your shoes, Rose.'

Rose did so and climbed in next to Miss Cleary, who put her arms around her and hugged her. Rose could tell that her cheeks were damp.

'Are you too hot, with all your clothes on?' the teacher asked her.

'No,' said Rose.

'Good girl.'

Rose lay still while Miss Cleary kissed her neck and her cheeks and her hair. She was aware of the soft frish of the woman's underclothes and her smoother skin around it. She grew very hot in her woollen skirt and cardigan and Miss Cleary drew a little away from her. Rose turned over and Miss Cleary drew up her knees behind her and looped her arms across her chest, and although Rose felt she was swooning with heat she lay quite still, enjoying the sensation.

'Once upon a time,' Miss Cleary whispered, 'a long time ago . . .'

'There was a magic fish,' Rose began, giggling slightly.

'No, no, not a magic fish. You and your magic fish! Once upon a time, Rose, there was a mighty tree called Yggdrasil. It was the tree of the world. Its great branches sheltered all the men of the world, all the animals, all the elves and giants and dwarfs of the world. Now under its roots there was a dragon. But this dragon was not content with eating the corpses of all the dead, which is what dragons are supposed to eat. No. It gnawed and gnawed at the roots of the tree of life itself. And not only was the dragon destroying the tree under the earth, but stags were nibbling at its leaves, and goats were chewing away at its new shoots. The skin of its trunk peeled away and left sore, bare patches. They grew rotten and would never heal. There was nothing that could be done to save the life of the tree of life itself.'

THREE

Mrs Waterhouse never spoke of Desmond. It was as if he had never existed for her. If Rose's father mentioned him it was with a sigh of bitterness, as if his son had let him down. 'I could do with Desmond in the shop,' he would say. 'That's the sort of help I need.' Mrs Waterhouse would clench and unclench her hands, staring into some distant thought, and Rose would watch them both, bewildered and guilty. She knew they had loved Desmond best. She didn't know how to talk to her mother about him, and so she never mentioned his name either, afraid of stirring up her own grief. It seemed to Rose that her mother lived in her own thoughts, as if what was going on in her head had become more real to her than the routine functions of life around her. To speak into her silences was an intrusion.

As Rose grew into adolescence she found she preferred to be anywhere other than at home. She had one friend, Barbara, but they never had the sisterly sort of relationship that other girls had. Mrs Waterhouse thought Barbara came from a common family, and never welcomed her into the house.

'And I don't want you going round there, either,' she said.

'Why not?'

'I've told you. They're common people.'

'I don't think they are. Anyway, it's not catching.'

Mrs Waterhouse shook her head as though her daughter knew nothing at all about life. 'Oh, but it is,' she said.

Rose spent most of her time at Miss Cleary's, who had become more like a sister to her than a teacher. She loved to help her with the small children at the schoolhouse, and then to walk home with her after school, talking about the children as if they were equals rather than teacher and pupil.

'I've left school now, haven't I?' she said to her one day, watching the little ones as they set off for home.

'I should think school's left you, Rose, now you've grown so big.'

'So what should I do for a job?'

'Are you not expected to help out in your dad's shop?'

'I hate my dad's shop.'

If she had looked inside herself she would have known that it wasn't the shop she hated, with its sweet and spicy smells, but her father himself. She hated his brusque and hollow laugh, his loud manners, his busyness, his shining red hands. Her mother was a frail, dignified woman, quite different. It would never have occurred to Rose to wonder what she thought of him. Mr Waterhouse never let Rose serve in the shop, which she would have quite enjoyed. He made her fetch and carry for him, weigh and measure in the back of the shop, or traipse up and down the cellar steps for spare stocks. Most of all she hated being sent down to the cellar, for there was Desmond's bike, rusting now. She wanted to take off the handle-bar bell before it lost its shine, but she didn't dare touch it.

Now that she was working so closely with her mother she couldn't help drawing comparisons between her tightness and Miss Cleary's warmth. There were no smiles of reward for her work, or shared laughter about the way the day had gone. She just had to get on with it, as her mother did.

'I miss school,' she told her mother.

'Do you now.'

'It was fun. And Miss Cleary was always so lovely with us.'

She and her mother were working together in the back room, squaring slabs of butter on the marble table. They were plagued by wasps that year, and it was a pleasure to be in the cool away from them. Rose quite enjoyed working with her mother, who had a quiet, deft way about her, not at all like the hurried and clumsy style of her father.

'I have something to tell you, Rose,' Mrs Waterhouse said. 'We're going to close the shop.'

'Why?' asked Rose, surprised.

'We want to move,' her mother said. She glanced sideways at Rose. 'Out of the city altogether.'

'But aren't we going to have a shop any more?'

Her mother thumped the butter with the wooden pats. 'It seems not. Your dad's lost heart now,' she said. 'I think it was the war that kept him going. Now it's all over he's not interested in work any more, and that's the truth.'

Rose noticed how grey her mother's hair was becoming. 'What would you do with yourselves?'

Mrs Waterhouse spread out her fingers. 'I've always fancied living out in the country.' She smiled a little as though her wishes were frivolous things. 'And now your father says he doesn't mind. He's not a well man, you know,' she said quickly. 'He's ready for a rest.'

'I should think you are, Mum. You work as hard as him.'

'He's worked hard all his life, that man. He doesn't know what rest is,' her mother asserted. 'But he needs it, all the same.'

'Well,' said Rose. 'I don't want to come with you.'

'It'll be lovely out there. And where would you live, if you didn't come with us?'

'I'll find somewhere.' Rose turned away from her mother to hide her flush of excitement.

When the shop had closed for the day she went straight to Miss Cleary's. She hardly ever saw her these days. The teacher laughed with pleasure to see her and drew her into the house. It looked different, crowded with new furniture, and it smelt of cigarettes. Miss Cleary's cheeks were red and full, and she moved about heavily.

'My parents are selling the shop.' Rose felt awkward with her now. She didn't like to sit down at her usual place on the settee, which had been moved against one of the walls of the room.

'Oh, so it's goodbye?' said Miss Cleary.

Rose shook her head. 'I'm not going. I've told my mother, I don't want to go with them.'

'I see.' Miss Cleary's eyes were misty these days, Rose noticed. She seemed to have her mind on private things.

'I thought I could easily find someone to stay with,' Rose said.

Miss Cleary looked at her, a slight frown puckering her forehead. 'Could you? I'm sure you're right, Rose. I hope so.' She held out her hand and, feeling awkward and confused, Rose held out her own. 'I hope you do well for yourself,' the teacher said.

Rose went back home, bewildered now.

'I don't want to come with you,' she said to her parents.

'Where would you live, for goodness' sake?' her father shouted. 'You haven't got a job, you've no money . . .'

'That's because you never gave me any.' His anger made her brave. 'You owe me money for all the work I've done for you.'

Her father's neck flamed with rage. She watched the spittle froth at the corners of his mouth, the clumsy helpless movements of his hands. She felt quite distant from him.

'I've fed you and kept you. I've given you a home, isn't that enough?'

'Where will you live, child?' Her mother came between them. 'You're fifteen years old . . .'

18

'She's old enough,' her husband said. 'Don't keep her if she doesn't want to stay.'

'I wondered if I could live with Miss Cleary,' Rose told her mother. 'She'd let me help at the school.'

'That shows how much you know,' her father scoffed. He had his back to them, and was stuffing tins into boxes, forcing them together in such a way that they would be impossible to separate. That was his way. 'Your beloved Miss Cleary's getting married and giving up the school. She won't want you around now.'

Her mother nodded that this was true. 'It's a bad business,' she said. 'She's not a good woman, Rose. And I never liked you spending so much time with her, anyway.'

Rose watched her parents as they sorted the shop things into boxes. There was nothing she could do to help them. They worked in a vigorous, determined way, shutting her out already. She sat in her room and listened to the busy scuttling downstairs. She couldn't imagine living anywhere else.

'If they actually ask me to go with them, I will,' she said to herself. 'That would prove they really wanted me. But they can't just expect me to tag along.'

Shortly before they were due to move she went to see Barbara. Her house was untidy and always seemed to be littered with small children. Rose had never seen Barbara's father. He was always working or asleep, Barbara said. Mrs Gleadall and Barbara were working together in the kitchen, and called her in to join them. Rose hadn't seen much of Barbara since she left school.

'I came to say goodbye,' Rose blurted out.

Barbara looked up, surprised. 'Where are you going?'

'Nowhere,' said Rose. 'My parents are going away next week and they're not taking me with them.'

'What will you do?'

'I don't know. I'll look for lodgings, I suppose.' Rose felt close to tears of self-pity.

'Mum, couldn't she stay here?' Barbara suggested. 'Just till she finds lodgings?'

Rose ran home, jubilant. Now they would surely ask her to go with them, but she would still refuse. The shelves were bare now. The house things had been packed away completely. Much of the furniture had been given away or sold. She faltered as she went in, shocked to see her home reduced to this cold shell.

'I've been invited to stay with Barbara,' she told her mother. Mrs Waterhouse said nothing. 'She's learning to type, Mum. I could do that.'

'Maybe you could,' her mother sighed. There were deep lines around her eyes. 'You're one on your own, Rose. Always will be.'

Rose watched the rhythmic way she had of poking the fire, her powdery elbows jerking outwards. 'My dad won't care, will he?' she said.

'I don't suppose he will.'

And when her mother stepped down to the cellar to wheel Desmond's bike through for the boy next door to collect Rose leaned down after her with her head twisting in air round the square hatch hole. 'But you care, don't you?' she said, over the clattering of the door bolts. If her mother heard her, she said nothing.

On the morning of leaving she tried to be alone with her mother to say goodbye, but her father was always in the way, impatient to be done with it and to get his own move over. At breakfast her mother looked as if she had been crying.

'I'm sorry, Mum,' Rose said, at a loss to explain her own turmoil.

'So am I,' Mrs Waterhouse said. She reached over quickly

and touched Rose's hand. She seemed to be searching for words. 'I didn't want this to happen.'

Her father delivered her to the door and gave Barbara's mother an envelope with some money for Rose's keep. 'You can pay me back when you've earned it, mind,' he told Rose. She stood in the doorway with him while Barbara's family watched from the kitchen.

'Don't forget to come out and see your mother sometimes.' He was awkward with her. It was obvious to Rose for the first time what the effort of moving had cost him. He was not his ebullient self, but had turned morose over the past weeks. His bitter moods were even harder to take than his bursts of anger. Rose had no idea how to say goodbye to him. At the last minute her mother had scarcely seemed to notice she was going, distant with the last throes of leaving the home she had lived in now for thirty years or more.

'I'll come and see you soon,' Rose promised. She was afraid suddenly with the recognition of what she was doing. Her father bent down as if he might kiss her and when she flinched away he thought better of it. What she couldn't know was that she would never see him alive again. Maybe, if she had known this, she would have let him touch her, and would have forgiven him his roughness.

As it was he walked away with his head bowed and his hands deep in his pockets, and she thought, 'He's thinking about Desmond now,' and closed the door against him.

FOUR

She shared a bed with Barbara. At first she was very shy and kept herself rigidly awake on her own side of the mattress. She liked to watch Barbara when she was asleep, and to listen to the light rhythm of her breathing. It made her think of Desmond's story of the sleeping princess who would be wakened with a kiss.

'I miss my brother,' she said to Barbara, in a sudden rush of warmth for her. They often talked well into the night, telling secrets.

'Do you? And do you miss your mum and dad?'

'No. The only other thing I miss is school.'

'School!'

'Well, Miss Cleary really.' She was reminded of the teacher when her friend was combing out her hair under the light. It splintered away from her face in fine threads. 'Remember her stories? Remember that one she used to tell us about Pele?'

'I don't,' said Barbara, vigorously brushing until her hair crackled in its hot strands.

Rose was sitting up in bed with her arms looped around her knees. 'She was the goddess of fire, who lived in a mountain. You reminded me of her just then, with your hair all shining red.'

Barbara laughed, swinging her hair like a garment across her shoulders. Her face was plain. She had her hairpins like spines in her mouth, sticking to her dry lips. 'You know why she's getting married, don't you, Miss Cleary?' She removed the hairclips and licked her tongue across her lips. 'She's having a baby.'

'She never is!' Rose put her hands to her flushed face.

'Isn't it a disgusting thing! Specially for a schoolteacher. Don't you think so?'

'I do!' Rose lay back in bed, listening to the froof of Barbara's hairbrush.

'I'm never going to have babies,' Barbara went on. 'Are you? Imagine having a thing that size growing inside you, and then sucking away at you! No, I couldn't do it. It makes us animals, that's what it does. Why should women put themselves through all that, when men don't have to?'

'Maybe there's something nice about it though,' Rose said. 'Having something to love and cuddle. It would be nice sometimes.'

Barbara tossed back her hair, scornful. 'My mother goes on and on having babies and just look at her. All she does is look after babies. I think she ought to have more pride in herself than that.'

'I like her,' said Rose, picturing Barbara's plump and milky mother. 'She's very kind. She's not a bit like my mother.'

'Didn't your mother like having babies then?'

'I don't know. How would I know?' Rose felt uncomfortable. She had only just left her mother and already she was talking about her as if she were a stranger.

'Anyway,' said Barbara, 'we've got more sense, haven't we?'

About two weeks after she had moved in Rose was alone in the house looking after the younger children while Barbara and her mother were at the market. Barbara's father came home, filthy with the grime of his work. She was surprised and alarmed to see him at home in the daytime, and he was just as surprised to see her, seeming for the moment to have forgotten who she was. The household revolved around him in his absence; the water must be hot for his wash, clean clothes and food prepared for him. And when he was home the household crept around his sleeping presence. Rose rarely saw him. If he arrived home when the girls were still around she and Barbara went up to the bedroom so he could wash in the kitchen. The one thing she had observed about him was that he loved his children. She was always fascinated by his tenderness, which seemed an alien thing in such a rough sort of man. If the children were asleep when he came home he would go up to their room and wake them up with kisses and teasing. Rose loved to hear the laughter that came from their room then.

Now the youngest child ran to him with her arms held up. He opened out his own hands to show her that he was too dirty yet to lift her.

'Where are they?' he asked.

'They're shopping,' Rose said. 'They'll be back soon.'

He nodded, stripping off his top shirt and moving aside the dishes in the sink so he could wash himself.

'Would there be anything to eat in that oven?' He spoke over his shoulder as she was about to creep upstairs.

'I can do you something.' She hesitated. 'I could do you some eggs.'

He peeled off his vest and stood with his back to her, his braces dangling, while he dowsed his face, snorting with the coldness of the water.

'You could just give my back a scrub,' he said, gasping through his hands.

She was afraid to move.

'No need for fright,' he laughed. He turned round to her, his smile rueful. His black hair hung in damp coils round his forehead, making him young. He held out his arms in a helpless gesture.

'Let me wash you, Daddy,' the little girl shouted, and he

squatted down while the child reached up for the cake of soap and dabbed it across his back.

'That's it,' he chuckled. 'Rub it in. Maybe the lady here would reach you up to the tap for some water.'

Rose filled a pan with water and placed it beside the child. Kate squidged the soap and it flew from her hands and skittered across the tiles. Laughing, she tumbled after it, pressing it at the end so it shot out of reach again.

'Come on now,' her father said. 'Stop fooling, Kate.'

But the child was absorbed in her game of chasing the soap. Rose knelt down quickly and scooped water on to the man's back, timid and daring, marvelling at herself and at the silken touch of his skin. Kate ran to her again with the bar of soap and wiped it across his back.

'That soap is full of grit now,' Rose told her, taking the bar away from her and returning it to the sink. She was aware of the fire crackling, and of the slow hiss of the child's breath as she worked. Rose didn't dare turn round again to the man's nakedness.

At last he stood up and reached to the rack for a dry towel. Rose moved away from him to the cooker.

'You're a fine pair, you are!' he laughed. 'What is it they call you again?'

'Rose,' she said, clearing her throat and saying it a second time. She turned away to the cooker and slid a pan across to the heat. The fat began to sizzle. She broke three eggs in it, one after the other, dipping the shell to tilt out the membrane, intent on watching the clear mucus thicken to white. The man was shaving himself. Her hands were trembling. She drew the eggs away from the heat and sawed down the side of a loaf. She tried to butter it but the butter was hard and tore holes in the bread. She took it to the cooker, sidestepping so she wouldn't have to turn round, and tried to melt it over the heat. She dared not speak or look up. She could feel her throat clogging up again and dared not even cough to clear it. She heard him lowering the rack where his ironed shirts hung. He would be dressing. She closed her eyes in shame, hearing him unclipping his belt and stepping out of his trousers. Kate ran upstairs and fetched him the clean ones from his bed. All the while Rose stood with her back to him, not knowing what to do with herself. Tears began to blurt in her eyes. She couldn't hold them. Her cheeks were wet with them; they ran into her nostrils and she tried to sniff them back.

He came up behind her, bringing with him the warm smell of laundered clothes and of soap.

'Don't now,' he said, taking the plate of food and carrying it to the table. His chair shrieked like startled laughter as he pulled it to. Released at last, she turned to go up to her room.

'Stay here,' he told her. He was gentle to her unhappiness. She took the pan over to the sink and held it under the cold tap to let the heat spit up from it.

Before he had finished his meal Barbara and her mother came in, bringing cold with them. Barbara's mother cast her husband a surprised look, then went over to the fire, making the coals spurt flames with her vigorous poking.

'I see you've eaten,' she said.

He made a coarse, private remark to her and she swung round. 'Don't talk rough,' she snapped. She glanced at the girl's pale blotched face. Her husband scraped back his chair, sucking butter off his fingers, smiling across at her in his teasing way.

'I'm home early because there's been a fire at work, if you must know,' he told her. He bent down and lifted Kate up into the air. 'And this little one scrubbed me down as if she was trying to rub me away, didn't she? Eh? Didn't she?' Kate screamed with laughter.

Barbara took off her coat and stretched out her hands to the grate, palms forward, and turned them to warm the backs.

'Come on, Rose,' she said, looking up over her shoulder to her friend, who still stood away from the family by the sink. 'Come and sit round the fire with us.'

At Rose's house the fire had never been lit in the daytime. She stepped forward, made bold by her fear, and entered the ring the family had made.

'I like it here.' She appealed to Barbara's mother. 'In this house. I like it.'

That night she lay in bed next to Barbara. The thoughts of Mr Gleadall's back bared to her would not go from her mind, nor from her hands. In the darkness under the sheets she spread out her fingers and stroked herself where her own flesh was silky as petals.

FIVE

It was when Rose was nearly eighteen that she fell in love with the tap-dancer. At the typing pool where she worked with Barbara one of the girls was about to have an engagement celebration, and had arranged to have it at a night club. Neither Rose nor Barbara had visited such a place before. They marvelled together at the invitation.

'What will we wear to go?' Rose asked. Barbara draped a sheet around herself in the fashion of a Greek goddess.

'Oh yes!' said Rose. 'You look fantastic, with that hair of yours!' She piled it up with her hands and held it in place with hairpins. The strands streaked free, volcano sparks.

'What about you?' Barbara asked her. Rose took a towel and draped it around herself, tucking an end in just where her tight breasts rose.

'Beautiful, ain't I?' she laughed, wriggling the towel free so it slid loose. Deep inside her her own sparks arose, surprising her with their intensity. A little ashamed, she pulled the towel around her shoulders.

'You'd better not let Mum see you doing that,' Barbara said. 'She thinks you're a nice girl.'

'So I am. Sweet seventeen and never been kissed.'

'Is that so?'

'You know that's so, Barbara Gleadall. Where I go you go, so when have I ever had the chance of a wink, never mind a kiss?'

'Oh, I've had more than a few winks.' Barbara draped the corner of her sheet across the lower half of her face. 'The more you conceal, the more they want to see. That's the first lesson in sex appeal.'

'I can't hear you,' Rose told her, angry with her both for the beauty of her hair and for her smugness.

Barbara's mother helped them both to make dresses for the party. The little ones were allowed to stay up to see them dressed up before they left.

'Aren't we beautiful princesses?' Rose said to Kate. The child put her thumb in her mouth and nodded solemnly.

'What do you think, Mrs Gleadall?'

Barbara's mother stood eyeing them up and down, her arms folded, quiet, seeing how pale her daughter looked, demure in the grey that set off her fiery hair. Rose's dress was a deep red that made her own hair glow dark.

'Might it be a little overpowering?' Rose turned from side to side to view herself in the mirror, astonished at the transformation the dress made in her. She was beautiful, she realized. She was a woman now.

'It's exactly your colour,' Barbara assured her.

Rose laughed, glancing at Mrs Gleadall. 'It looks brazen to me.'

'On Barbara it would be,' Mrs Gleadall said. 'It takes a girl like you to carry it.'

'They look good enough to eat, both of them,' Mr Gleadall laughed.

His wife hugged both the girls quickly. 'I wish I was going,' she said. 'Off to my first do again!'

The group of eight young men and women went into the night club together. The air was thick with a grey mist of smoke. Each table had a wine bottle crusted with ripples of candle-wax. The room was crowded. Rose sat slightly apart from the others, glowing in her rich dress. She sipped slowly at her first glass of sweet sherry. The girl and her fiancé began to talk loudly about their wedding plans.

'We'll need a big house,' the girl laughed. 'I'm going to have ten babies at least!'

Her fiancé beamed round at the group to show that he was man enough for all this and they laughed. Rose couldn't imagine what her friend saw in him; she didn't find him at all appealing.

'Wouldn't you like ten babies, Rose?'

She remembered her conversation with Barbara. 'I certainly wouldn't,' she shuddered. 'I couldn't bear to have something growing inside me like that, sucking the life out of me. It's so primitive.'

'It's good fun though, making them. My mother seems to think so anyway!' Barbara said, and they all laughed.

Rose felt betrayed by her. 'I think I'd rather adopt,' she said, but they ignored her, intent on jokes. The voices faded away from her. Occasionally she would glance across at them and smile. All the time she was conscious that someone was watching her through the crowds and the smoke, though when she dared to lift her head to look there were no eyes for her to focus on. It was an unnerving feeling. It was one that she would remember for the rest of her life. She found herself becoming self-conscious in the focus of the hidden gaze, smiling a little too often, threading her fingers through her hair. A fat man in shirt-sleeves pushed his way from the bar and sat down at the piano and began to play ragtime. Rose put down her glass and leaned forward with her elbows on the table and her chin propped in her hands. She watched how his rings flashed, how his fat fingers danced and his small feet pumped the pedals, how with a lift of his shoulder or a satisfied rolling of his head the man spoke his music. She had never heard live music like this before. She had heard the organ playing and had joined in with desultory hymn-singing at church, with her father droning on one side of her like a lost ship out on a foggy ocean, and her mother's breathy piping on the other. Once she and Desmond had followed a group of carol-singers who had called to the house. She remembered how all the tuneful voices round her had seemed like coloured lights, how she had turned her young face from one to the other of them, trying to fit in the words that she knew. And she remembered being yanked away from them when her father had found them at last, how he had shaken her till she cried, and how Desmond had run on home with his father's hand-mark red on the side of his face.

The pianist half-turned to her and closed one eye just for her. She glowed with the fun of it. She glanced towards Barbara and away again. They were a laughing group, and she was outside them now. She didn't care. She was drawn in to the music, unfamiliar though it was, and it was like a spell that was being cast around her.

From the other side of the bar there came a pattering like steady rain. The talking round the table stopped for a moment; people looked up, surprised, and then there came the white flash of swinging shirt-sleeved arms and neatly through the grouped tables came the tap-dancer. His hair was as shiny as his shoes. She marvelled at him, at his leanness and dexterity. When his face turned her way she risked a smile at him, and when he turned again she leaned back easily in her chair. Soon the piano player stopped casting glances at her altogether and stared morosely at his jigging fingers, while the tap-dancer pattered and swanked across the floorboards.

When at last he swung himself down to a low bow Rose let out an Ah! of disappointment, not realizing till her friends laughed that she had done it. She turned to them, knowing that he was leaving the centre of the room now, placing him somewhere near the bar where he lounged with his back to her, and when she looked his way again he turned round slowly. He watched her over his glass while he took long slow draughts of his drink, and she knew now for sure whose eyes had been on her earlier in the evening. She felt herself flushing. He sauntered across to her group and pulled up a chair, sitting back to front on it, with his legs straddled across it.

'You're not even out of breath,' she marvelled. 'How d'you manage that?'

His brown eyes fixed her again. 'Enjoyed it, did you?'

'I'll say!'

'Will you come again?' He leaned right forward, addressing only Rose.

'I'm with my pals,' she faltered.

'So?'

'I daren't come on my own!'

'Not even to see me?' he smiled.

'My goodness. Why ever should I?'

'Why ever not?' he mocked.

But she did go again, coaxing Barbara to go with her, and the third time she went alone. In his dancing he swaggered round her table, finishing up with a flourish to kneel in front of her, one hand stretched out towards her. She held out her own hand and he pressed it to his lips. She felt as if the applause was for herself.

'I'll see you after!' he whispered. At the end of the evening she waited for him. He was in conversation at the bar and, seeing her waiting, raised his glass to her and smiled.

He walked her back to Barbara's house. His game was to kiss her under every lamp-post. Once or twice to begin with she protested, but his kisses were such gentle, fleeting things that she knew there was no harm in them, and as they drew nearer the house he seemed about to forget occasionally, and she would wait by the lamplight, tilting her face up to him a little and laughing to remind him.

'Haven't you ever been kissed before, Miss Pretty?' he asked her.

'Might have been.'

'But not as sweetly as this, I bet.'

'Might have.'

Near the house Barbara's father walked past in his work clothes, whistling, and Rose struggled to free herself from the tap-dancer's arms.

'Well, Rose,' Mr Gleadall said. 'I reckoned it must be you.'

'I'll be right in,' she told him.

'Who was that?' the tap-dancer asked her. 'Not your dad, I hope?'

'My friend's dad. My dad was a grocer,' she told him, proud of it. She couldn't understand the deep feeling of guilt she felt at being seen like this by Mr Gleadall.

'Well, it's none of his business then,' William said to her, pulling her into his arms again, sliding his hand inside her coat. But the evening was spoilt for Rose, and she ran after Mr Gleadall, head down, and when she was in the house she went straight past him and up to bed.

'Are you courting now?' Barbara asked her, drowsy with sleep as she climbed in next to her.

'Yes,' said Rose. 'I think I am.' She lay awake, rousing herself to the soft rhythm of his remembered kisses. 'Is this him, Desmond?' she whispered.

The entire family was interested in her progress with William. 'Don't rush things, whatever you do,' Mrs Gleadall warned her. 'But I'm pleased to see you looking so happy,

Rose.' She was pleased to be the centre of so much attention, but even so she complained about it to William.

'They're getting on my nerves,' she told him. 'They're treating me as if I was their own daughter. I don't like it.'

'I've got a room, you know, that's big enough for two,' William said. She pretended not to hear him, marvelling inside herself at his words, turning them over like coins. They were walking on the hill above her side of town, looking down at all the slanting rooftops. There was just enough wind to ruffle her hair without spoiling it. He slid his hands round her, up and inside her jumper, and she struggled free.

'You want me, don't you?'

Rose didn't know what she wanted. She wanted to peel off her clothes and lie naked with him, especially there, where they could see the rooftop of the Gleadall house and could even pick out the road where her father's grocery shop used to be. There, to lie naked with him and to look down on all those familiar streets would be a terrifying and thrilling thing to do. But she didn't think she wanted to wash his socks, which must get very sweaty with all the tap-dancing; or iron those smart white shirts he wore.

'So where is this room?' she asked, conscious of being a little ungracious.

'In my grandmother's house,' he told her.

So it would be his grandmother who ironed the shirts. That wasn't so bad. He fingered her bra and this time she didn't resist him but swelled her round breast to his touch and felt her nipple becoming as hard as a button under his fingers. He nibbled her ear, breathing into it.

'She wants you to come home one day for tea. Will you come?'

*

On Mrs Gleadall's advice Rose wore pale blue. Barbara walked up the road with her to the tram-stop, linking her arm tightly as though this was to be the last time they would do this together.

'What d'you think?' she asked Rose. 'If he asks you, will you marry him?'

'How do I know?' Rose's nervousness made her snappy, and she regretted it. It was Barbara's white handbag she was using, after all. 'Why? D'you fancy being a bridesmaid?'

Barbara nodded, delighted. 'I wouldn't wear pink, though,' she shouted as Rose climbed on to the tram.

Rose sat on the top deck and smiled down at her friend, and at the rows of houses with their matching tiles and their lace curtains. 'Ishy-wishy, magic fishy,' she thought suddenly. 'Here am I trapped in a vinegar jar, and all for the sake of a magic wish. A little house with flowers in the garden, that's all I ask for in this world . . .'

She leaned back and closed her eyes, conscious that a new life was about to begin for her. She thought of her mother, alone in the country cottage of her dreams which she shared with the memory of her dead husband. 'William will dance for me across soft carpets and silken sheets. His room will be scented with flowers and blazing with light. I will be dazzled by him.'

William met her from the tram. He walked her to his home with his arm casual across her shoulder. When they passed a small row of shops he flourished away from her and danced backwards and up to her again, watching himself all the time. He took her hand and swirled her round.

'Don't, William!' she gasped. 'People are looking at us!' All the same, she watched with pleasure the way her skirt swirled out in the reflecting glass.

He pulled her to him. 'Do I make you happy?'

'You know you do.'

'I want you,' he told her, serious suddenly, thrilling her with his earnestness. 'Do you know that? I want you very much.'

She nodded, solemn with the intensity of his words. He led her away from the shops and the wide road into a back street of terraced houses. It was not unlike the Gleadalls' street.

'This is where I live. At the moment,' he added. 'But I used to live by the park.'

'Oh, posh!' she teased, hiding her disappointment. 'I like it round there.'

'Well,' he said, 'we'll see what we can do. Come and meet the old lady.'

William's grandmother wheezed in a dark room in a house no bigger than Barbara's. It smelt of damp carpets.

'You've let the fire out!' William scolded her. 'You mustn't let the house get cold.' He crouched on his hands and knees to get it going again. Smoke billowed into the room. The old woman set up a pantomime of wheezing and coughing, flapping her hands across her face and across the back of his head as he crouched there.

'It's no good when it's windy like this. I tell him, and he ignores me, every time. It's freeze to death or choke to death in this house. I should know, I've lived here since time began for me.'

'The fire's all right if you don't sit so close to it,' William told her. 'It's too cold without it today.' He sat up suddenly on his haunches, alert to a sound in another room or another house somewhere, and his grandmother stopped her coughing and watched him.

'Excuse me a minute,' he said to Rose, and went out of the room abruptly, closing the door behind him. His grandmother peered at Rose, saying nothing. Rose sat down and gazed round her at the frayed carpet and bulging arm-chair. The fire cracked. The grandmother spat into her handkerchief.

'He's like a little monkey,' she said. 'Don't you think so, the way he darts about? I don't know where he gets his energy from.'

'He's a lovely dancer,' Rose said, wondering how such a graceful young man could be related to this sprawling woman, who sat with her legs apart and her feet swimming over the sides of her slippers.

'He was a real little monkey when he was a kid.' She stared at Rose, making her uncomfortable. 'You want to watch him, love.'

'I will.'

'His grandfather was a good man though. Just passed out on me.' Her breath fogged up. 'It only takes a second, you know. Alive one minute, dead the next, that was him. Make the most of what you've got, I'd say. You never know when you're going to lose it.'

Rose gazed round the room in despair, wondering where William had gone and how she could escape to him. She picked at the hem of her skirt, regretting the rushed stitching and the way it had caused the fabric to pucker. She heard the clink of crockery behind the door.

'Maybe I should help William.'

The grandmother ignored her. 'When I say you want to watch him, I don't mean he's a flirt exactly.'

'I'm sure he isn't.'

'He's glamorous. All the young women are after him. I suppose you know that though, you're not daft.'

Rose shook her head. She could hear William running up the stairs and down them again. The old woman, too, sat with her head cocked, listening.

'You don't meet many glamorous young men these days. Not like before the war. Oh my word, we had some swanks around then! They fall all over him, the girls.' The woman took off her spectacles and spat into them, polishing them on her knee. She stared at Rose, her eyes a sudden cloudy blue, not at all like her grandson's. 'I can see you like him. I said to him, if she's any good, grab her and have done. He needs a girl like you. He's had bad luck.' She closed her eyes. 'And so have I.'

Rose stood up to go out to the kitchen and at that moment William opened the door and came in again carrying a tray. His grandmother replaced her glasses and nodded at him. Rose knew then that she had just had an interview and that she had passed the test. In a painful silence they ate the sandwiches and drank the tea that William had brought in. His grandmother removed her teeth in order to eat the fruitcake and never wore them in Rose's presence again. Rose sat with a cup and saucer in one hand and the chipped plate balanced on her knee. When she caught William's eye he winked solemnly at her without smiling. He stooped to stoke up the fire and once again a billow of smoke shrouded the room. It was almost too stuffy to bear. Into the grandmother's coughing fit came another sound. This time all three heard it at once. William put down the poker and turned to look at Rose. It was an unmistakable sound, and it was not coming from next door but from a room of that very house. It was for Rose to speak.

'Did I hear a baby crying?' she asked.

William took her cup and saucer and plate from her and led her into the other room, and there in a makeshift cot lay Edmund, six months old, wide-eyed and smiling now, and stretching out his arms to her to be picked up. It was Edmund whom she fell in love with.

SIX

'Whose baby is this?'

'Mine,' said William. His grandmother was watching Rose keenly. 'At least,' he added, 'I look after him.'

'Oh, I see,' said Rose. Her heart was thudding as she leaned forward and lifted the baby out of his cot. It was a natural gesture for her. She marvelled at the firmness of his flesh and the way his small hands opened and closed to find her. She pressed him to her. 'I'm not sure what that means. Where is his mother?'

'Dead,' said the old lady. 'That's where she is.' She shuffled past them and back to the room, where she sank back into her chair. 'He's well looked after here,' she called out.

'Dead? You didn't tell me . . . Was she your wife then, and only just died, William?'

'No. She was never my wife.'

'She was a slut,' the old woman called again.

'She came here when she was pregnant, and told my grandmother it was my child she was having . . .'

'Was he?'

'He could have been, Rose . . . I'm sorry.'

She turned away from him, resting her cheek against the baby's. He was quiet in her arms. 'How did she die?'

'I don't want to tell you,' said William.

'I'm sorry.' Rose rocked the baby, pondering the horror of the situation, though she didn't yet know the half of it. Edmund slept, and at last she surrendered him to his blankets. There was a smear of saliva on his cheeks. She bent down and smoothed it away. She could hardly take her eyes off him. 'He's beautiful.'

'Do you think so?'

'I must go now,' she said. 'For my tram.'

'Like babies, do you?' the old lady asked her when she went back into the room. She twisted round in her chair to catch Rose's expression, and, satisfied, nodded to her grandson.

'She has to go,' said William.

They walked quickly down to the tram-stop.

'I wish you'd told me,' Rose said.

'If I'd told you, you wouldn't have come. Would you?'

'I don't know.'

'I'm sorry if he was a bit of a shock to you – but you do love me, don't you, still?'

She bit her lip.

'Because I love you. More than anything. I want you to live with me.'

'In that house!' She tried to speak lightly. 'It's not what I want, William, to live in a house like that.'

'It's only for a bit. We'll move into a flat by the park soon. That's what you'd like?' He tilted up her face in both his hands.

'I love to see trees!' she laughed.

'So you will. That's my promise.'

The tram was coming. Rose felt the bargain had to be struck before she left him. 'Would the baby be with us?'

'Would you like him to be?'

She nodded. She couldn't bring herself to speak. She looped her arms round his neck and closed her eyes. When the tram drew up William disengaged her clasp, kissed her lightly, and helped her on.

'You're my girl now!' he called after her, as the tram lurched along its track. 'My girl!'

'Well?' Barbara asked her as soon as she arrived home. 'Did he ask you?'

'What? Did he ask me what?' Rose teased.

'Did he ask you to marry him?'

'No,' she said, smiling. 'As a matter of fact he didn't.'

Secretly she was glad. She had no desire to commit herself to his grandmother by taking on the family name. It pleased her to keep her own name for herself. She knew that her mother would think she had defiled it in a most hideous way. She wrote to tell her that she was moving into another lodging house. And she disappointed the entire Gleadall family by simply moving in with William without a hint of celebration of any kind.

'Not even a party,' Mr Gleadall said. 'What a cheat.'

'Never mind parties,' his wife said. 'A party only lasts a few hours. I hope you know what you're doing, Rose.' She held Rose's hands, embarrassing her. 'I hope you'll always be happy, that's the thing.'

But she was not happy. Sometimes when she was lying in their bed she would think fleetingly of Mr Gleadall, and be shocked. William devoured her with his love-making, but she lay still in his arms, unable to respond to him, aware of the old woman listening in the room next door to the creaking of their bed.

'You're like a fish,' William said to her one night, rolling away from her and spreading out his limbs. 'A cold fish.'

To Rose a fish was a leaping, lively thing, sparkling and sinewy and deft in its element.

'What's up?' William said. 'Cold fish, what's up?'

She stroked him. 'I don't like your grandmother to hear us,' she whispered. 'I'm embarrassed, William. It'll be different when we live by the park.'

She put on his shirt and went over to stand by the window, drawing back the curtains.

'What's up now?' he asked her from the bed.

'I can't breathe.' The baby stirred in its cot and she went to him immediately, lifting him out in his warm and drowsy state. She knew this made William jealous.

'Let him sleep,' William told her. 'There was no need to waken him.'

'I like to hold him,' Rose said. 'And he likes to be held.' She climbed back into bed with the baby in her arms. 'Tell me about his mother.'

'It's not a nice story.'

'Tell me all the same. I want to know.'

'Her name was Ella. We had fun together a few times. That's all I know about her.'

Rose shuddered and he laughed, turning away from her, stretching luxuriously. 'She knew how to have fun, though.'

'You mean she wasn't a cold fish.'

'She was cheap. Gran was right. She was a slut. She meant nothing to me. But she turned up here one day and told the old lady she was having my child. They ganged up against me. Women are like that. By the time I knew about it she was installed, bag and baggage.'

'But how did she die, William?'

'Topped herself, if you must know. It wasn't my fault. Walked in front of a train, that's how she did it.' She could see that he was lying with his mouth open, his eyes gleaming. She put out her hand to him and he drew into her side, crouching himself up.

'She must have been very unhappy to do that,' Rose said at last into the long silence.

'I don't know why she did it. I tell you, I was nothing to her, and she was nothing to me. You have a bit of fun with someone and they put all this on your back.'

'You mustn't feel guilty.'

'She could have just walked out of my life and neither of

us would have felt a thing. I was nothing to her. It was him she was running away from.'

Cold to the bone now, Rose lay back against the pillow with Edmund still sleeping in her arms. 'That was a terrible story.'

'Don't ask for stories if you don't like unhappy endings,' said the tap-dancer.

Shocked as she was, Rose had to admit that Edmund had been given a home by William and his grandmother, and that the older woman had cared enough for him in her slovenly and haphazard way. Once she knew his story Rose was frightened to let Edmund out of her sight, fearing for him as if he was in danger of being spirited away. But William was often out, especially in the evenings, and she hated to be at home alone with the old woman. When he was setting off for the jazz club Rose would walk with him to the end of the street and kiss him goodbye there. He would dance away from her then as if he was tossing away the burden of his home. Rose would go back to the house and the smoky room, to share the long, quiet hours with the grandmother.

'You should go with him, you know,' the old woman surprised her by saying one evening. 'A young girl like you doesn't want to be stuck in like this, night after night.'

'What about Edmund?'

'I can look after my own great-grandson.'

'Maybe I will go, now and again,' Rose said.

The old woman leaned forward, searching her out with her smoky blue eyes. 'If you want to keep him, go with him,' she warned her. 'Men are all the same. I'm telling you, Rose.'

Rose loved the atmosphere of the bar. At first, when she had just started going back to the jazz club, William danced only for her, just as he had done that first night, fixing her with his eyes out of the shadows before ever his dancing started, making her glow for him and long for him. It was never the same when she was in bed with him. She pretended not to be looking and then found she could do nothing else with her eyes after all. Watching him was a way of possessing him. They were linked for everyone to see, and she was part of his act, glowing in the attention of the audience. But other women would be smiling at him too, and he would flash smiles at them, or bow gravely to them at the end of one of his dances, his way, she thought, of dedicating his dance to them. Sometimes he would swagger cheekily up to one of the women in the audience and, hidden in his role, wink or kiss her hand before turning away.

'I don't like the way you flirt with those women,' Rose found herself saying to him one evening. She couldn't help it. He took her hand and pressed it in his, and she warmed to him immediately.

'It's part of the act,' he said. 'It's only show. If they feel I've left them out they'll stop watching me.'

'Is that all it is?' she asked doubtfully.

He stopped to kiss her as they were walking. 'What do I need to do to prove that you're my one and only for ever?'

'I suppose you have to stay with me for ever,' she said.

'Which is exactly what I mean to do,' he told her. 'So stop fretting.'

Even so, he left her one gale-ridden evening in late October, and she knew exactly who he had gone with. It was a red-headed cinema usherette who had let him into all the Hollywood musicals free so he could watch the American tap-dancers. On her night off she started coming to the jazz club and he would sit her and Rose together so they could talk to each other. Rose was pleased to have company. Then one day she caught the secret glances that they exchanged and which had nothing to do with William's dancing. After that he stayed away from home overnight a few times. At last he turned up with a new suitcase and packed up his tap-dancing clothes. Rose discovered him in the bedroom.

'It's Eileen you're going away with, isn't it?' she said to his busy back. 'And what about Edmund?'

He turned round to her. His face was white, and the bones were sharp angles. He spread out his hands. 'Must I be responsible for him for the rest of my life? I'm twenty-one years old, Rosie.'

She knew how wretched he felt. She turned her back on him.

'I'm an artist,' he called to her as she walked out of the room. 'I need to be free or I can't work. I can't live!'

She went to the room where the baby lay passive on the settee and she picked him up and held him with her face pressed against his until she heard the door close. Then she woke up the grandmother, who was dozing in the armchair, and told her. Mrs O'Brien gasped back a glass of whisky and stared at the ashes of the fire.

'I warned you,' she said. 'He's a glamorous boy.' She clutched out at Rose, whimpering suddenly. 'You won't leave me, Rose, will you now?'

Rose knew then that if she stayed another day she would be trapped in a tyranny of pity from which she would never be released, ever. She would be rubbing the woman's back and chest with goose-grease every winter, queuing down at the market-stall for her tripe, and doing jigsaws with her in the quiet evenings. She would be listening out with her for William to come home.

That night she filled three brown paper carrier bags with her clothes and crept out of her room. She listened in the passage for the sound of Mrs O'Brien's wheezing and heard nothing. Maybe the old woman was lying wide-eyed in the dark, awake to her. She crept to the baby and he sighed in his sleep, fluttering his fingers. She knelt down and picked him up, snuggling him to her.

'I can't leave you. I can't leave you,' she whispered to him, crying about to come at last, hurting her. She wrapped his blankets round him and crept from the house, pressing his face against her shoulder. When she closed the door she leaned against it, taking in huge draughts of air. She had no idea where she would go. Edmund woke up and began to sob in alarm. The strings of the carrier bags cut into her palms. Wind rushed at her as she began to walk, tugging the bags and banging them against her calves, dragging her back. In the end and in despair she lined the bags up in a shop doorway and left them there. She wanted to run then with the freedom of it. She wanted to shout out into the wind.

SEVEN

Rose took a tram to town and on a sudden whim caught the last train out to the village where her mother lived. She was the only one to get off at that station, and when she stood alone on the strip of platform her courage left her. The train rattled away into the night and she was left in the darkness, with the wind chasing leaves around her and huge trees shuddering. She walked down the long dark lane that led to the house, which was itself in darkness. It was past midnight. She knocked at the door several times before she saw an upstairs light being switched on and heard the creak of the stair.

'Who is it?' came her mother's voice, nervous.

Rose felt a rush of remorse. It was over a year since she had last been to the house. Her mother knew nothing about William.

'Mum, it's me, it's all right,' she shouted. She shifted Edmund's weight in her arms. The bolts were drawn back and the door opened just enough for her mother to peer through the crack.

'Good gracious. Rose, is it? What's that you've got?' And it was only then that Rose cried properly while her mother stood in her open doorway with her hands clasped in front of her. She understood nothing of her daughter's sobbed words but at last drew her in and bolted the door behind her, and then took her into the kitchen where the last ashes of the day's fire glowed.

'Thank God your father isn't alive to see this,' she told her. 'You'd have been turned away, late as it is, you know that, don't you? You would never have been allowed into this house with that child.'

Instinctively Rose kept the even worse truth from her mother. She unfastened Edmund's blankets and sat down with him on her knee. His eyelids fluttered open and he searched the room, a little afraid of its unfamiliarity. She put out her hand to him and he grasped it, laughing up at her. If he was anybody's at all, he was surely her child.

'Well,' she said to her mother, calm now, 'he isn't alive, is he?' In her head she could hear her father's booming voice, chiding her in that unrelenting way of his.

Mrs Waterhouse made up a bed for her while she fed Edmund a little bread soaked in boiled milk. Both the women were too anxious and tired to talk that night. In her room Rose put together cushions and blankets as a bed for Edmund. Her mother found a rubber sheet to cover them with, saved from Mr Waterhouse's last illness. She boxed the makeshift cot against the side of her bed with chairs. The baby slept soundly, but Rose lay wide awake, listening to the unfamiliar voice of the wind in the trees outside, feeling herself jostled by harsh elements.

The next morning she told her mother about William. She kept the story of Edmund to herself. He was her child now. Her mother listened to her story in anxious silence.

'What about this William? Can't you find him and make him come back to you?'

Rose shook her head.

'Surely you want him to come back to you, Rose?' Her mother was a little embarrassed to be asking such an intimate question.

'I don't know.' Rose looked away. Edmund was standing up on the couch, clinging with both arms to the back of it, swinging his leg round to try to lever himself up. Both women leaned forward instinctively to check him, and he tumbled back, laughing, on to the couch. She thought of the old woman and the dark house, the traitor bed, the winks and smiles of the dancing man. 'If he came back he'd only go away again, Mum. I know that.'

'Better off without him, then.' Her mother had registered the hurt in her voice. 'But you can't stay here, Rose. Not with that child.'

'No,' said Rose. 'I might have known you'd say that.'

'Mind you. What's done is done.'

By the time the week was over Mrs Waterhouse was showering Edmund with a grandmother's affection. He was a beautiful child. She fancied she saw Desmond in him.

'Is he at all like his father?' she asked Rose, hoping she would say no.

'Well, he's a charmer all right, if that makes him like William,' Rose admitted. 'But he's much calmer than ever his father was. Much calmer. I wish he would be a bit sparkier, just sometimes.'

Her mother was astonished. 'You should thank your stars he is like this,' she said. 'What would you want? Crying all night, demanding attention, fussing? You don't know you're born.'

Rose stared at the child's eyes, at his hands, his smile, searching for traces of William there. When she closed her eyes she could see William dancing across the room towards her, his hair as smooth and black as ice, his smile quick and full. She wanted to howl into the night for him to come back to her. Instead she cradled the child so tight that she felt she could squeeze the breath out of him.

'I have an idea for you, Rose,' her mother said to her. 'I think you should go back to town and find work for yourself.'

'How can I?'

'I'll look after your baby.' Rose's mother tried to keep the greed out of her voice, the nuances of comfort. In all those bullying years she had spent in the service of her husband the best part of it had been when her babies were small and had allowed themselves to be loved. Desmond had ruined the memory of all that by dying. She had scarcely allowed herself to take comfort from little Rose for fear of rekindling her grief. But Edmund was different. He allowed her to experience her babies again.

Rose was jealous of the way her mother took possession of the child. 'I don't know,' she said. 'I don't know what I want to do.'

'You want money for a start,' her mother reminded her. 'Where would you find work round here? I can't keep you for ever. And you never know. You might meet someone and want to start again. A good man, this time, not a fly-by-night. Someone who could be a father to this little one.'

So Rose went back to town. She found work in an office and took lodgings with a woman called Kitty. And there she waited for a father for Edmund to come along.

EIGHT

All that was long ago. Now Rose Doran lies in her swampy bed and listens to the rise and fall of voices behind her wall. High and low they come, light and dark, like the strike of water on stones; eroding years, bringing grief.

Edmund put away the last of the dishes in the kitchen. He rearranged the plates that Rose had stacked in her random and dreaming fashion on her last foray into the kitchen, poured bleach down the plug-hole and mopped the kitchen floor, backing out across the dry part till his feet touched the hall carpet. He looked at his watch. Rose was tucked up in bed in a pink and cosy pile, sleeping off her Sunday roast. Because she slept in the only other downstairs room there was nowhere for him to retreat to except his own bedroom. He tiptoed up to it now.

'Time for a lie-down,' he told himself. 'You've earned it now.'

He eased his tie and took off his jacket, hung it up from the picture rail and placed his shoes underneath it. Then he lay on his bed, pulling only the top cover over himself. He would rest till four, his diary told him. After that he would talk to Mother and they would have a light tea of cheese and tomato sandwiches. He'd already made the jelly. He ticked off the rest of the day's duties in his head. The days wind on for ever, he thought, Heyho! and rising up on that came another thought. In two days' time he would be forty years old.

'Such is life Without a wife And I without a lover,' he said aloud. 'What a misery you've turned into, young man. "What would you like for your birthday, Edmund?" "A pound of cheese, please."'

And there he was, without even trying for it, riding high on his father's shoulders along market alleyways, tall as a crane and a little afraid of the naked upturned faces smiling at him, and realizing that just by tilting his head he could make lights spangle on the pyramids of fruit heaped on the stall below him.

'I'm a withard!'

'The Withard of Oz or the Withered Arm?'

'Jutht a withard.'

'Don't cry now, little boy. There's no need to cry.'

'Edmund!' Rose was standing at the bottom of the stairs, calling up to him. Edmund sat up smartly as though he had been caught sleeping on duty.

'What is it, Mother?'

'Where's Paedric gone?'

Edmund lay back on his pillow, smiling. He crossed his arms behind his head and drifted off to sleep again.

By late afternoon Paedric and his dog David had had enough of sleep and darkened rooms. It was the dead of the week, a still Sunday afternoon with no weather to speak of and the birds gone quiet.

'Come on, David,' Paedric said. 'Let's find some bitches.'

They walked away from the railway bridge and towards the canal, and took the towpath that led away from town. Derelict buildings of failed industries plunged in on themselves into the greasy brackish water, as though here at last they could give up their ghosts without shame. Wooden spars hung like dismembered and blackened limbs among the reeds. A rubber glove floated near the bank, fingers upwards, like a green hand grasping out for help. Paedric was excited and troubled at the thought of it. He squatted down and reached out for it, almost overbalancing.

'God, I can't reach him,' he told the dog. He sat back on his haunches, his breath heaving with the effort he'd made. He felt round for a stick and his dog jumped up, panting with attention. Three boys on mountain bikes swerved past, jeering. He knelt on the towpath and reached out with his twig, this time just touching the glove. He teased it towards himself with little nudges, cursing when the thing spiralled in slow circles away from him again. At last he had it. He put his finger and thumb round one of the digits and trailed it in. He stood up, draining the canal water out of it.

'Doesn't that look vulnerable now, David?'

He put his hand inside it. It was cold and slimy, large for him. Residual water bubbled up inside the fingers.

'To die with rubber gloves on,' he said, 'can only be to die in shame, wouldn't you think now? Such a vulgar and naked death too. Such a heroic and domestic death this has been!'

He grasped David's lead with his ungloved hand and walked on, temporarily alarmed by the call of geese on a distant allotment. 'They fill me with fright, David, with their obscene cackle and all. If they would fly away free, that would be one thing.'

Then he spotted something in the water ahead of him and recognized it with delight.

'It's the other glove, David! The left hand!' He knelt down on the towpath, took off the glove he was wearing and, absorbing himself in tender ritual, dipped it carefully. He shifted it around till water began to plump it up and of its own accord it came to rest at last. The fingers of the two gloves met, tip to tip.

He was dribbling with the effort of leaning so far forward.

As he straightened up the mountain-bike boys swerved past him again, nearly overbalancing him for good.

'I would not have allowed my son to do that!' he shouted at them, rage and dislike making his voice as full as a young man's. The boys grinned over their shoulders at him, jeering and safe.

'Come on, David.' Paedric and his dog walked along the towpath till they were away from the industrial dereliction and into the country. They crossed the lock gates and carried on where the towpath gave up, scraping through brambles and ferns till they came out into broad fields and along a sunken lane. They had reached a small town. They trudged through the streets without stopping, Paedric with his head down and unaware of anything except the need to walk. When dusk was beginning to fall they turned and made their way back, groping unsteadily now along the side of the canal, hearing the hushed whisperings of night, the clutterings of pebbles that their feet tipped into the water, the hollow echo of their own passage under the bridges. Stars were up, clouds swept across them like the billows of flimsy curtains. At last they came to the row of three small terraced houses, and saw that theirs was in darkness.

That afternoon there had been no sunlight in Rose Doran's room. She slept pleasantly and woke to the cup of tea that Edmund brought. He tiptoed into the room in his socks and stood smiling by her bed.

'Wake up, Sleeping Beauty.'

'Is it that time already?'

'It's that time, Mother, and it's chocolate ginger biscuit time, too.'

'I like them.'

'I know you do.' He helped her to sit up and perched next to her on the bed. 'And I thought to myself, they're dear, but why not? I know a little lady who'll be very happy when she sees these on her plate.'

'Once in a while. What did you do this morning, Edmund?'

'You know very well what I did.'

'Tell me though,' like a child eager for a story. Her toes curled up under her sheets.

'I went to church. And then I cooked your Sunday roast, which I must say you gobbled up pretty fast.'

'In between?'

'I read the papers.'

'Where?'

'In the park.'

'Did you see anyone?'

He sucked the loose crumbs of biscuit off the back of his hand, which he held tucked under his chin like a bracket fungus. 'Lots.'

'Anyone you like, Edmund? You'll drive me mad one of these days. Anyone you like?'

He sucked at his tea.

'Well?'

'I can't say that I liked anyone that I saw.'

'There must be someone. You're not trying.'

'Except Molly.'

Rose let out a deep, satisfied sigh. She put down her cup and saucer and wriggled down under the sheets. She patted his knees and he swung up his legs to tuck his feet under her quilt. He leaned back against her propped-up pillows.

'Tell me about Molly.'

'I don't know anything about her. She goes to church.'

'Well, that's a start.'

'And she's about . . .' His eyes searched the room. 'About as tall as that cupboard.'

'As tall as a cupboard.' She giggled and closed her eyes, groping out to touch his hand.

'And she wears good shoes.'

Rose laughed out loud.

'Well, she does.'

'So she should suit you.'

'And she has grey eyes.'

'Now then.' Rose squeezed his hand. 'Pretty?'

'You're a naughty girl to ask such cheeky questions.' He gave her hand a small squeeze and slid his own away. 'I'm not telling you.'

'Shall I have to wait and see for myself?'

'Of course you will.'

Rose Doran tucked her arms behind her head and smiled at Edmund.

'Are we going to walk about a bit?' Edmund asked her. 'We don't want your bones to seize up. You're not an old lady yet, not by a long chalk.'

He slid out of her bed and leaned over her, his breath warm on her cheek, his arm sliding into the small of her back until its pressure eased her up. She laughed up at him, tossing back her white hair in a girlish gesture.

'It's a wobbly world, isn't it, my lady?'

'Pass me my gown, just in case.'

He lifted her gown from the hook behind the door and placed it round her shoulders.

'I don't know who we're expecting.'

'You never know,' she said. 'Molly might take it into her head to pop round and see you.'

'And you wouldn't want to let me down.'

He propelled her into the narrow hall with its blue-faced

clock and its fish tank, and along to the kitchen. The back
door was wide open.

'How about the patio, young lady?'

'Dressed like this?'

'Dressed like a princess.'

Rose stepped tentatively into the garden, grown wild and
thick with brambles now. She liked the way the thin air
stirred her hair. She turned her head slightly towards Paedric's
house.

'Anything going on there?'

'Nothing at all. It's as quiet as the grave.'

'I see the Merlins haven't mended the fence yet.'

'It's a long time since the Merlins left, Mother.'

'Is it? I used to have a pond there, by that bit of hedge.'

'I know you did. I remember it.'

'Of course you do.'

A few weeds straggled through the cracks where the pond
used to be. As she peered down into it a train approached and
she turned away involuntarily, gathering her gown around
her as if she had been discovered naked. Whatever it was that
Edmund said to her was lost in the engulfing roar. She let her
gown fall loose and held up her hands to her ears and pressed
them there, head back, eyes closed, and long after the train
had passed and the roar abated she held them there, as
though she was savouring something, as though she was
afraid now not of the din but of the silence.

At six o'clock Edmund brought in the sandwiches and a
pot of tea. Soon it would be time to draw the curtains a little,
though not enough to shut out the light of the street lamp,
which Rose loved. She loved best of all this end of the day;
night drawing in. She read the paper out loud to herself,
hearing in the sound her own mother's voice, seeing her face
now puckered with concentration, her first finger curled

under her lower lip. Edmund went into the kitchen to polish his shoes over a sheet of last Sunday's newspaper. At ten o'clock he would bring her a cup of cocoa, and then he would switch off the light for her and open the curtains fully. And there she would lie bathed in lamplight listening to her old blue clock creaking in the hall, and waiting for the passing of the midnight train.

Paedric did not go straight to his house. He released David from his lead and walked on past the terrace and up the embankment that led to the railway tracks. He could hear them zizzing and knew that a train was coming. Soon he could see its lights as the body of carriages snaked through the towers and gantries of a distant building site. He braced himself, feeling in that instant like a butterfly pinned in tiny ecstasy, as if his life was an exposed and beautiful thing. He took a step forward and straddled the lines, arms held up high so he formed a black X in the light that flooded up from the far town's sodium dawn. The frisson of the oncoming train shuddered through his flesh and his limbs, deepening to a dull ache the downbeat of his heart, and he stood steadfast and open-mouthed as the train lumbered like a beast towards him.

Instinct rather than imagination took hold of him then and swung him round and off the tracks, so he stood facing the train, knocked backwards by the wind of its passing. The slats of light from the carriages poured stripes on him, black on yellow on black on his outstretched arms and his upturned, sweating, weeping face. Long after the train's sound was only a hum on the earth he stood gazing after it.

At last he turned to go back down towards the terrace. Still he walked. During the night his footsteps could be heard circling the three houses, binding them as surely as the bumping links of a chain would have done. Rose turned her head towards the street lamplight and listened to the scuff of his shoes. The footsteps dragged.

'Make him stop. Please God make him stop,' she said in her ragged dreams.

At last Paedric came to rest. Rose opened her eyes and saw him spread like a crucifix against her window. His black shadow fell right across her bed. His eyes were closed, she knew that. He was in sleep, and in his sleep he bayed out like a dog in pain. In response to his bellowing came another voice, a girl's.

'Paedric?'

'Helena, is that you?'

'Where are you? There's nobody here. Don't leave me alone.'

Gradually his voice weakened into sleep. Rose heard the front door of her house opening.

'Come on, old chap.'

Paedric slumped away from the window and on to Edmund's shoulder.

'You must be worn out with all that walking.' Edmund half-dragged, half-carried the man into his own house, helped him up the stairs and into his bed, and covered him over with blankets. The dog whined up the stairs after them. Rose listened out for the last closing of doors and turned over in her bed. At last she could sleep.

NINE

When Rose had left her mother's home again she could hardly bear to leave her baby behind. He was a beautiful child with dark eyes and long lashes in a face that was almost girlish. But unlike William he was big-boned and clumsy.

'This one will never make a dancer,' said Mrs Waterhouse with satisfaction in her voice.

'It's just as well,' Rose agreed. 'I wouldn't want him to turn out as skittish as William.' But she longed for her dancer again. His voice haunted her, his face shining in the smoke-filled pub room, the light swing of his arms as he danced.

Her mother came to the station to see her off. She carried the baby in her arms, and he slept. Even when Rose took him from her mother on the platform he refused to open his eyes but hunted for his food, his lips sucking.

'I can't leave him,' she told her mother. 'Don't you think I should take him with me?'

'I do not,' her mother said. 'You're lucky. You can start your life again now.'

'I don't feel lucky.' The train was coming, and she wanted her baby.

'I wish I'd had your chance.'

Rose stepped on to the train and found her seat. She leaned out again to wave goodbye, and the train gave out its shriek. Edmund, startled, began to cry. She wanted to lean forward and snatch the child from her mother's arms, claiming him for her own, abducting him.

She found herself cheap lodgings and took up her old job at the typing pool. The routine of work became so familiar to her so quickly that she soon found herself being pulled back into her old way of life, meeting up again with old friends. Barbara was married now and had moved away. Rose avoided the jazz club, but toyed with the idea of going to see William's grandmother. It was just possible that William might be back there, and the thought of maybe seeing him there half-thrilled and half-distressed her. She fantasized about what she might say to him. He might draw her back with promises of a new flat by the park. She thought of the damp-smelling house and of his wheezing grandmother. She couldn't bear to go back there. More and more as the weeks passed by thoughts of William preyed on her mind. He must want news of his son. She would never return Edmund to him, not to that house. She panicked at the thought of it. What if they had set up a police search for him? What if they imagined the child to be dead? She knew she must go to the house and tell her story.

One evening after work she made up her mind. At the top of the familiar street she almost turned back. She saw again the shop doorway where she had left her bags of clothes. She remembered the anguish she had felt when she had run out of the house with Edmund in her arms. William must not be there. She must not go back to him, to be betrayed again. She took shelter in a shop doorway and wrote a hurried note to say that Edmund was quite safe and well. That was all they needed to know. As an afterthought she wrote down her work address in case they wanted to see the baby again. It was the best she could do. It was more than she wanted to do. She ran to the house and was relieved to find it in darkness. She glanced up and down the road to make sure that no one was looking and pushed the letter through the flap. Immediately the door was pulled open. William's grandmother presented herself there in her dirty nightdress, her hair in loose grey coils around her neck.

'I've been watching you,' she told Rose. 'Standing over there in that shop doorway. Too much of a coward to knock on the door, were you?'

'I thought you were out,' Rose said. 'There weren't any lights on.'

The old woman snorted. 'I never go out. You know that.'

'Away then. How was I to know that you'd be standing there spying on me?' Shock and distress made Rose angry. She was sorry about that. It was not what she had meant to happen, to be standing out on the doorstep shouting like that.

'I had an attack the night you went. I could have died. I don't suppose you would have cared.'

'Blame your grandson, not me. He deserted us both, remember.'

The old woman flapped her hands at Rose. 'I'm better off without any of you. Don't bother coming back.'

'I won't,' said Rose, relieved.

Tears of self-pity welled up in the old woman's eyes. Rose couldn't bear to look at her. As she turned away she heard the door close. Not once, she realized, had the old woman mentioned Edmund.

Every time she went to her mother's, which was most weekends at first, Mrs Waterhouse quizzed her about her search for a husband.

'It's not that easy, Mum,' Rose told her. 'Most of the men I meet at work are so infantile.'

'You don't have to ask for much. Just someone to provide a home for you and Edmund. That would be enough. Love's a fickle thing, anyway.'

'You're right there. I'm sure it's something I can do without.'

'I'm sure you can. I did.'

Rose cried every time she had to leave Edmund. He was learning to walk, and it thrilled her to loop her hand around his loose fingers and guide him. This was the only kind of love worth having, surely, she said to herself. All the rest was shock and heartache. She knew it all, and would never go back to that dangerous territory. When she married it would be for the child's sake. That was all she wanted now.

So as soon as she met Gordon she recognized him as the man she wanted to be Edmund's father. She decided she would bide her time and nurture him. She realized that she would have to do all the work, and she found the idea pleasing. After all, William had wooed her mercilessly when all he had wanted had been a mother for his son.

Gordon was the brother of Rose's landlady and was staying in town while he was doing some research work about the railway. He was old enough to be Rose's father, and yet he was nothing like Joseph Waterhouse. He was a shy man with a taste for pickled herrings, and he had a slight deafness which caused him to tilt his head in a thoughtful, listening way when other people were speaking. This kind of attentiveness was very flattering to Rose. His hair was grey, nearly white. She liked that. Like his sister he enjoyed telling stories at mealtimes, though hers were funny anecdotes about previous lodgers while his were rather tedious recollections of railway journeys, recounted in meticulous detail. But he had a gentle and courteous manner which Rose liked from the start. She knew that he and Edmund would get on well together.

'How long will you be staying, Mr Doran?'

For some reason he glanced at his watch. 'Two or three

weeks,' he told her. She would have to work fast. Panic made her bold.

'And whereabouts do you live? When you're not in town?'

'Just below a railway line,' he told her. 'Out in the country.'

She closed her eyes and shuddered. How safe would a railway line be with a small child? She opened her eyes again and noticed with satisfaction that he had half a digit missing on his left hand. For some reason this endeared him to her more than anything else might have done. He noticed her looking at it.

'My big sister bit it off,' he said.

'I never did, Gordon,' Kitty puffed. 'I never did.'

'And swallowed it whole.'

Rose smiled at him, noticing the tiny crease lines around his mouth. She lowered her eyes as his smile fixed hers and watched how his hands moved as he spoke, how square and strong they were, like labourers' hands. Under the sleeves of his shirt cuffs pale hairs curled.

'Must drive you mad, that rattling of trains going past,' Rose's landlady said.

Mr Doran leaned back in his chair. He swallowed his food slowly, thinking out his response in a way that was to become very familiar and in the end irritating to Rose. 'D'you know, Kitty, I like it. I miss them while I'm here. It's comforting, in the night, to hear the trains. Every hour or so a bit of life flashes past. I stand in the back garden and I look up at all those strangers rushing past, speeding somewhere, and I feel as if my own life is standing still. You're outside it all, real life.' He glanced at Rose, who looked like a child to him. 'Do you know what I mean?' he asked her.

'I feel the other way round,' she told him, eager to be included. 'When I'm sitting in a train, just sitting and daydreaming, I think it's the people in the back yards who are getting on with real life, while I'm just watching it.' She stopped, confused. 'I often go on the train,' she said. 'To see my mother.'

'Does she live in the country?'

'She does. It's so quiet there, you could hear a mouse breathe.' And she added carefully, 'I like it.'

It was impossible for her to carry on eating. She put together her knife and fork. Something was taking place that was fine and symmetrical, colours in a kaleidoscope sliding together, endlessly patterned and complementary and absorbing. She saw herself again as a little girl in her father's shop, running a dampened cloth over the neatly labelled jars of fat colourful fruits. She felt again in her palms the pressure of the gleaming brass weights, and saw herself precisely balancing them into their lovely gleaming pyramid. She took one of them in her palm before she spoke again, the smallest one perhaps, her favourite, nursing it gently. It was cold and smooth and fitted exactly. 'And do you live on your own?'

He looked at her steadily. His eyes were pale grey and flecked with blue, just so, woodsmoke blue, calm and very still. They told her, yes, he did.

'Well then,' his sister said, breaking a silence which she felt to be uncomfortable, shuffling plates together, edging crumbs with the wedge of her hand, while loose thoughts skittered in Rose's head. 'Gordon is no stranger to loneliness. Nor am I, for that matter.'

'Gordon,' said Rose quietly, practising the sound.

One day towards the end of that week he asked her if she would like to come and see his house. He said it as though the thought had just occurred to him, though he had sat absorbed throughout the meal, hardly noticing his sister's good fish pie. He snatched at the question as soon as Kitty left the room, and then looked immediately embarrassed, regretting his boldness. When Rose said yes he pushed back his chair and went out of the room, and didn't mention the matter again.

Rose went home for the weekend and told her mother that she thought she had found someone she could be happy with.

'Don't rush it now!' her mother warned. 'It's for life, remember. God knows, life's long enough without spending it with the wrong man.'

'I suppose you're telling me you did spend it with the wrong man?' Rose asked, but her mother picked up the child and buried her face in his hair.

Towards the end of the next week, which was to be Gordon's last week with Kitty, Rose told him again that she was looking forward to seeing his house. His face lit up. Inside she was trembling, knowing fully what it was that she was suggesting, and he gave her such a concerned look that she faltered. 'If you'd still like me to, that is.'

'Oh, I would, of course I would. I feel honoured, Rose.'

On the journey there they sat opposite each other. They had nothing to say to each other until he leaned forward and touched her lap.

'That's it,' he said. 'That's my house.'

The touch of his hand startled her. Below her she could see a short terrace of houses and then three, apart from the rest.

'The middle one!'

He smiled and she smiled too, both pleased. She craned forward to keep the house in sight. She was excited. Maybe, she thought, this is where I'm going to spend the rest of my life.

TEN

Edmund fastened his tie in front of the mirror. Behind his own reflection a train was flashing past. Beyond the railway line lay the squat and ugly buildings of light industry that had grown up along the canal in the past few years, linking the terrace to the town. But you couldn't see it even so, the railway embankment rose up so steeply from the back yards. Trains rocked the terrace as they hurtled past. They excited him with thoughts of worlds beyond worlds that he would never know, trapped as he was between Paedric and Rose and their particular nightmare. Yet he loved to hear the comfortable rumble of the trains. As a child he used to wave to them from his bedroom window. Sometimes he would gaze out at the lit squares and try to focus on a particular face, a particular arm, perhaps, raised in salute, and try to imagine his father there. Now, of course, he would be an old man. Edmund would never recognize him.

He went downstairs with his black shoes in his hand. The smell of cheap vinyl rose to meet him as he opened the kitchen door. He made two cups of tea and went into Rose's room backwards, dancing round to face her, holding up her cup and saucer like a stage magician.

'Is it that time?' she grumbled.

'It's always that time.'

'Well, I haven't slept a wink, with his carrying on.'

'Didn't you take your sweeties?' he tutted. 'Naughty girl.' He perched on the edge of her bed, swinging up his legs as he did so.

'Is this the usual tea?'

'The only thing that's different is the price. It's up 5p on last week.'

'Daylight robbery.' She sucked at her tea through closed teeth, a habit she had picked up from her father, long ago, and which Edmund now copied.

He winked at her without smiling and went back into the kitchen, made himself some toast and sat down to eat it, holding his left hand flat under his chin to catch the crumbs. Then he tiptoed down the hall and tied on his shoes outside her door.

'Bye, Princess!'

As soon as he stepped out into the morning he saw again the child that he had been, creeping into her room, which had been downstairs even then. His father's room had always been as neat and ordered as Edmund kept it now. Rose's was always a higgledy mess of story-books and cigarette ends and fascinating undergarments draped on chairs. She used to slide out of bed and come across the carpet to him, her brown-eyed breasts swaying under her loose gown.

'Another bloody day,' she used to say. 'Oh my God!'

And he would run from her embrace, delighted to be free, into the outside air. In those days he had always loved his father best.

He remembered, too, the day Gordon had left. Edmund had come downstairs first that day, wretched from the disturbances of the night before. A spider had made a long line across the kitchen, and there it was, looping from the top of the door to the fridge and across to the table. It must have worked all night to have done that. Edmund stood watching it, and when Rose came down the hall to him he turned to her with his finger to his lips. 'Don't break it!'

'I want a cup of tea, Edmund,' she had said, but she

followed him, ducking under the web. And they stood there on the other side wrapped in its silence as if they were locked in a spell. When Gordon came down they were whispering together, Edmund giggling. They had made their tea and were drinking it on their side of the web. It was some time before they noticed he was there. 'Come on in,' Edmund had said. 'But don't break the web, will you?'

Gordon had just stood there, saying nothing. Nothing in the world would have made him crawl under that web to join them. Rose knew that. And in the end Edmund had ducked back under the web to join Gordon. Gordon opened the back door then and just stood there looking out at the rain sweeping across the yard, and said, 'I'm leaving.'

'Yes, I know,' Rose said, and Edmund knew years later when he remembered it that he had known too; in the way Gordon stood, in the way he had been watching them, apart. He had never forgotten that moment or those words, but the incident of the spider's web was something he couldn't recall. It was Rose's interpretation of the day, and because she had retold it in that way so many times to Edmund he recognized it as the truth. But then, he no longer knew what was truth and what was fantasy in Rose's mind. It was only the story that mattered.

ELEVEN

In those early days Rose felt that Gordon was unlike any man she had met before. That morning when he had led her down from the station to see his house she felt herself to be cherished and protected for the first time in her life. She felt very close to him, and sure of herself. As he guided her he touched her hand. It was only a fleeting and furtive touch, as if it had happened just by chance, but she glowed inwardly with it, not daring to look at him.

'That's a beautiful tree,' she said as they came up over the embankment and looked down at the terrace.

'Oh, that one. It's not in my garden, that. It's Paedric's tree. He planted it when he was a little boy, and just look at it now.'

'Does Paedric live in the house next door?'

'I haven't seen him for a year or so, but it's his home, I suppose, still. His parents are dead now. I've never had much to do with Paedric. Strange child, strange man.'

'Paedric's tree.'

'You're right. It is a beautiful tree. I hadn't thought about it much. Do you know what sort it is, then?'

'I don't.'

'Neither do I, I'm afraid.'

'Then it's a wishing tree.'

He unlocked the door and let her into the house. She liked it. In the narrow hall there was a blue-faced clock that had suns and moons painted on it.

'That's lovely,' she said, pausing in front of it. He stood behind her, close enough for her to lean back against him. She could hear how he was steadying his breath.

'I made it, in a way,' he said. 'Not the clockwork. But I made the cabinet, painted the sky on it.'

'I love it. What a shame, if no one else sees it but you.'

He moved away from her. 'How old are you, Rose?' he asked her.

'I'm twenty-three.' She gave herself nearly three years. 'How old are you?'

'About twice your age.' He cleared his throat. 'That's awfully old.'

'Of course it isn't. You could be much older. And . . .'

'And what? I could be much older and what?'

'And I wouldn't mind,' she said, quietly. She knew still that she would have to do all the work.

'I'll make us some tea,' he said. 'And then . . .'

She followed him into the kitchen. Something lusty bloomed inside her. She risked everything. 'And then what, Gordon?'

He looked up, surprised, from the teapot. 'And then it'll be about time for you to get your train home again, I should think. Though maybe you would stay a little longer next time. If you'd like to come again, that is.'

She took a slow breath. 'Why did you want me to see your house?'

'Oh dear,' he said. He filled the teapot with boiling water and put the lid on it. She pointed out to him that he hadn't put any tea in.

'It's very difficult,' he told her.

'Then let me do it.' She took the tea-caddy from him and spooned in the tea-leaves. She saw her mother, bent over the deep wooden bins in the shop. She could smell the dark tea-leaves in them, kippery and sweet. 'I think you ought to know,' she said, refilling the kettle, 'that I have a little boy.'

For a long time she didn't dare to turn round. Behind her Gordon Doran was absolutely silent. He has gone out, she thought. He has tiptoed out of my life for ever, and I wouldn't blame him. She waited until the kettle had boiled and tea was made. She lifted cups and saucers down from the shelf, busying herself.

'I just thought you might want to know,' she said.

When he spoke at last his voice was steam in his throat.

'Is he a nice boy?'

'I think so!' Rose laughed. 'I hardly know him, and that's the truth. He lives with my mother, and I hardly ever see him.'

'And what about his father?'

'His father? His father hasn't seen him since I brought him away. His father is not interested in him.'

'Or in you?'

'Or in me. I'm not married to him, Gordon.'

'I see.'

He was silent again, and then they spoke at the same time, words colliding in mid-air, he saying, 'I always wanted a son,' she, 'Perhaps you'd like to meet him some time.'

I will tell him the truth one day, she thought, smiling to herself on her journey home, but not yet. It's enough that he's accepted without shock or recrimination the fact that I have a son. I will save it for the wedding night.

The following week she took Gordon out to the village where her mother lived. Edmund was by now a sturdy two-year-old, big-boned and solemn-eyed, quiet, and it was quite obvious from the start that Gordon would cherish him. He took the child by the hand and told him about the trains where he lived. Edmund watched him with wide eyes.

'Would you like to see them one day?'

The child nodded, turning his face away then and hiding in

Mrs Waterhouse's shoulder. When she saw Gordon and her mother together, white heads bent over the boy, it occurred to Rose that they were nearer in age than she and Gordon were. She was closer to Edmund's age than she was to her future husband's. Gordon looked up at her as she was thinking that, and smiled at her. She blushed, warmed by him.

'He'll be good to you,' Rose's mother said as they were walking to the station. 'But don't you go spoiling it.'

'What do you mean, spoiling it?'

'He's a lot older than you.'

'I know that, Mum.' Rose was impatient with her. Gordon had stopped some way ahead, whistling, quite happy to wait for her. He was not a man to put pressure on her.

'But he loves you, I can see that.'

'I know.'

They walked along in silence. Gordon walked a little in front, pushing the child in his pushchair, knowing the women had things to say to each other.

'I didn't love your father, you know,' Rose's mother said tightly. 'Nor did he love me.'

Rose said nothing.

'But it was a good marriage, all the same, Rose. I have no regrets.'

On the train home Rose longed to touch Gordon's hand, but didn't dare. His hand and hers were inches apart. The air between them burned. At last she could stand it no longer. She moved her hand across to his. He squeezed it slightly, and released it by putting it back on her knee and patting it.

'You look very nice,' he told her.

She looked at her reflection in the darkening glass and smiled.

'Would you like to come out with me next Saturday? Do you like the countryside?' he asked her.

'Oh yes,' she said.

'There's rather a pretty little town we could visit. We could have tea there.'

She looked forward to the outing all week. He had gone back to his house. It pleased her to imagine him there, pottering about in his kitchen in that slow and thinking way of his. She borrowed Kitty's sewing-machine and set to work on some dresses for a trousseau. She knew that they would get married.

He came over on the Friday evening and they talked throughout the meal about their week. Kitty watched them both, morbid with memories. The next day they set off early. The village they were to visit was pretty and crowded with tourists. Its feature was a series of limestone caves which undermined it, and which were quite an attraction.

'Could we go in one?' she asked.

'If you like. They're dark and cold, mind you. Very cold.'

In the darkness of the cavern tunnel she had an engulfing sense of terror. She felt for Gordon's hand and pressed it tightly, took it in both her own, and wanted him to bend down and kiss her. Her thoughts flew to William, to the way his kisses had caressed her flesh. 'Oh, William, William,' she wanted to cry aloud. She felt faint with the terror of loneliness. The blackness in the cave was like water that would one day drown her; she wanted Gordon to reach out to her and haul her up into the light. When they were outside the wind rushed at them, spanking her back to wakefulness and then to a bright exhilaration. The entrance to the cave was at the top of a pass; its green and bony sides reared up on either side of them.

'Oh look!' she said. 'It's wonderful!'

She took Gordon's hand and pulled him after her, scrambling up the steep side of the pass, stumbling over boulders to reach the top. Her breath was bursting in her lungs; she clenched her teeth together and hauled herself up, hand over hand over the boulders, clutching at the sharp grasses to gain purchase. Sheep in alarm skittered away from her, scattering loose pebbles as they ran. When she reached the top she flung herself down and waited for him. He stood over her, heaving for breath, puzzled by her mood. She held up her hand and arched up her body to him. She wanted him, and had no words to tell him. He sat down next to her and opened up the rucksack with the picnic that Kitty had prepared for them.

'You didn't like it in the cavern?' he said.

'I didn't know how much I need this,' she said, spreading out her arms. 'Under the ground I was a piece of rock, a stalagmite. I couldn't move, I couldn't breathe. And up here I'm drops of air. Aren't you?'

'I can't tell.' He was amused. 'I wouldn't like to drop off here, I know that. I'd soon know how solid my flesh was, then.'

'What's the mountain behind us?'

'I don't know what it's called. It's not really a mountain, Rose.'

'He's like a sleeping giant.'

Her hair escaped from its loops and tousled round her face. She knew by the way he looked at her that she was beautiful to him. She was full of him. William rose in her, and away. She must drive him away. His frittered passion was, after all, a spent dream.

'Do you know the story of how this pass was made?' Gordon asked.

'No,' she said, anticipating magic. 'Tell me.'

'Well, it could have been a cavern, like the one we went in, and it caved in. Or it could have been glacial. An ice-melt would have come this far, and it would have formed this, pushing up the sides like this.'

'I thought you were going to tell me a fairy story,' she said.

'Oh, a fairy story. I'm not very good at things like that.'

'Does space frighten you,' she asked him, 'or darkness?'

'I really haven't thought about it,' he said. And later, when she thought he'd forgotten the question, 'Loneliness, that's what frightens me. I think I've had enough of that.'

'I know,' she said. She felt very close to him then. She lay back on the grass so her side was pressed against his leg. 'Long ago,' she said, shielding her eyes with her hand, 'there was a beautiful woman, a giantess.' She looked sideways at him. 'Shall I tell you the story of how this pass was made?'

'All right,' he said. 'Are you making it up?'

'No,' she laughed. 'It's true, every word of it. Lie down.'

He put out his hand to hers, smiling across at her. 'You look like a little girl,' he said, 'with your hair loose like that.'

'For thousands of years the giantess slept, and the wind made sounds around her hair, and the birds flew above her. Sleeping near her was a giant, and he was alone too. His limbs were like rocks. One day he woke up. He heard the sobbing that the giantess always made in her sleep. He rose up out of the earth, and boulders thundered away from him. He saw her sleeping below him and he fell in love with her. When she opened her eyes they were as blue as the sky, her breasts and her belly were like small hills, her forests were mysterious.' Rose stopped, shy suddenly. 'Shall I go on?'

'Another time, perhaps,' Gordon said. He was sitting up now, turned slightly away from her. Rose moved her hand closer to him but he didn't take it. He lay back on the grass and propped himself up on one arm, looking down at her. She wanted to take his hand and put it on her breast. She closed her eyes, afraid to look at him. In the groin below them jackdaws were fighting, their sharp cries ricocheting along the rocks like pistol shots. She was afraid, thinking that she had made him angry.

'Perhaps you don't like fairy stories,' she said at last. He shook his head at her, standing up. It had gone cold. He put the rucksack on and waited for her to stand up and brush herself down.

'You're a clever girl, to make up stories like that,' he said. 'I didn't know you had thoughts like that in you.'

They walked back down to the village, cold to the bone now. She longed for the comfort of his arm round her, but he kept his hands up, thumbs tucked into the straps of his rucksack.

'It's only a story,' she told him, hurrying to keep step with him. 'It doesn't mean anything.'

He stopped and looked down at her, placing his hands on her shoulders so that she had to turn up her face to him like a child.

'I should like to ask you to marry me,' he said. 'But I don't know if I have the right.'

'Please,' she said.

So after all it happened very easily. They were married within three months. Her mother and his sister came, and Edmund wore a little grey suit that his grandmother made and a pair of shiny black shoes that he loved. He kept bending down to peer at his reflection in them, and rubbing them with damp fingers to make the shine go away and reappear. He cried when his grandmother went home without him. 'Be good to your mummy,' she had told him, hardly able to look at him.

The present from Rose's mother arrived in a removal van. It was her own mother's bed, with black rails and a heavy mattress. As soon as Rose saw it she remembered seeing her parents in it, and heard again the suppressed and frightening sounds that had come from their room at night. There was a note with the bed, flung carelessly on the floor by the delivery men who brought it. 'I hope you'll be very happy in it' was written in her tidy shopkeeper's print.

But Gordon never slept in it. He liked the little bedroom, he said. He'd always slept there. He liked to watch the trains. And he liked to sleep alone. He told her this sorrowfully but firmly on the night of their wedding, leaving her no space for protest. Then he kissed her gently enough and went into his own room, closing the door quietly behind him. Rose was trembling. She had never even undressed for him. 'With my body I thee worship,' she cried to herself in her grandmother's bed, and wondered whether anything in life was worthwhile after all. She consoled herself by dreaming that the tap-dancer danced into her life again and took her cheekily into his arms. In her dreams she was voluptuous and abandoned with him, in a way that she had never been in real life. Little Edmund slept next to her and cried too, and sometimes they snuggled up together in those first few weeks, for consolation.

TWELVE

It was on an extraordinarily cold day that Paedric returned to the terrace. Ice had filled in all the cracks of the earth. Peewits haunted the fields in search of food. It seemed that for ever the land had been grey and iron-hard. Edmund was now nearly five, and was a big, clumsy boy for his age, docile and contented and, Rose feared, totally dull in imagination. She fed him at night with stories of goblins and bewitched trees, jewelled serpents and hares that turned to herons, magical and half-remembered tales hatched from Miss Cleary's early story-tellings. But he liked just as well to hear Gordon's anecdotes about trains, which weren't so much stories as lists, details of gauge and weight and colour, which he copied down laboriously long before he understood what the letters and numbers on the page represented. He was far more Gordon's son than her own, these days.

That morning Rose had gone with him, as usual, to school. She preferred to leave him at the gates and walk quickly away, because she didn't like to see the way he hung back near the railings, mutely observing the other children in their shrieking, routeless running round the playground. Today she needed to speak to his teacher. He held her hand all the way to his classroom and went straight to his desk, taking out his coloured pencils and arranging them neatly in rainbow shades. Rose wanted to tell his teacher that she was now sure he was ready to eat with the other children. Edmund listened, keeping his head down. He rearranged his pencils, this time according to length.

'He doesn't like butter beans,' Rose smiled, remembering her promise to him. 'But he's to eat everything else.'

She walked home quickly, enjoying now the smart of cold on her cheeks, wondering whether it was the first time she had walked alone since she and Edmund had come to the terrace, and how she was going to fill in her day till it was time to fetch him home again. The long walk to school four times a day had left her with little time to herself these past few months. When she crossed the railway line and looked down the embankment towards the terrace she stopped in surprise. There was smoke coming from one of the neighbouring chimneys. She ran down to the cottages, alarmed and a little excited, wondering whether someone could have broken in next door. Boards had been removed from the downstairs windows. She hesitated at the door, wondering whether to go up and knock, then changed her mind out of shyness. She heard no sounds from next door during the day, though she listened keenly. Self-consciously she made house sounds herself, deliberately pulling heavy furniture about and clattering dishes in the sink so that whoever was there would know there was someone to talk to if they needed anyone. The two neighbouring houses in the terrace had been empty since she came. It was wonderful to think of someone living next door at last. She brushed her hair before she went out again to fetch Edmund, and as a last-minute thought rooted out a bright scarf to wear. When she told Edmund they were to have neighbours he skipped along eagerly, aware of her excitement and happiness.

'Are there any little boys there?' he asked.

'I don't know,' she told him. 'I've not heard a thing, Edmund. All I know is that this morning there was definitely a chimney smoking, so someone must have lit a fire in there. They must have let it go out again though, because when I left the house just now the chimney wasn't smoking. They've taken some boards down from the windows.'

'Did they burn the boards?'

'They probably did, Edmund. I never thought of that.'

'Can we look through the windows, then, and see what it's like inside?'

'Edmund! It would be very rude to do that!' She giggled. 'I must say, I'm very tempted!'

That day Rose and Edmund went out in the dark to meet Gordon from the train.

'We've got some neighbours,' Edmund shouted out to him.

Gordon bent down and kissed him. 'Neighbours! Well that makes a change! Which side?'

'Paedric's side,' Rose told him.

'Oh, let's hope it's not him,' Gordon said.

'Why not, Daddy?'

'Because he's an odd-bod.'

'What's an odd-bod?'

'Never mind.'

Later that evening Edmund asked the question again. 'I'll tell you what his job used to be.' Gordon sat at the table and opened out his arm for the boy to come and sit on his knee. 'He used to work the signals in the box up on the bank. He made sure the trains came and went at the right time.'

'Is that what an odd-bod does?'

'No, that's what a sensible person does. He gave up his job because he wanted to see the world. That's what an odd-bod does.'

Rose, washing up the dishes at the sink, gazed out of the window, at the room reflected back on itself, at the child and the white-haired man at the table and the young woman with her hair wisping round her face. And beyond the blackness outside reared the dark wedge of railway embankment, blocking out the lights of the distant village. Her knuckles were white.

A little later they heard the sound of singing from next door. Rose and Edmund both looked at Gordon.

'That's Paedric, all right,' he said.

'He's got a funny voice,' said Edmund.

'Well, he's a funniosity,' Gordon insisted. 'I never had much to do with him, though I got on fine with his father.'

'Shouldn't you go round and see him?' Rose suggested later. 'Ask him if there's anything he needs? He could have a bit of supper with us.'

'Don't start that. We'll never get him off our backs.'

Rose knew Gordon's shyness. It was hard for him to get on with anyone. He had everything that he needed in herself and Edmund. She made a private resolve to get to know the neighbour, funniosity or not. He would tell her stories of the outside world. That would be all she wanted. She saw that Gordon was watching her, reading her thoughts, maybe. She went up to him and sat by him, put her hand in his. Surprised, he let her keep it there. Edmund was in bed. In their downstairs room the curtains had been drawn to. They sat in firelight, quiet for a time.

'Gordon,' she said, roused by him, as she often was just by being near to him, 'let me come to your bed tonight.' She stroked his hand, sliding her fingers under his cuff where the hairs curled. 'I just want to lie next to you. You needn't touch me if you don't want to.'

His voice was gruff in his throat. 'I don't want to hurt you.'

'You won't hurt me. You hurt me more by leaving me alone.'

He closed his hand round hers. The flames in the grate purred. From next door they heard the comforting sound of Paedric in his kitchen.

'Tell me a story.'

Gordon laughed. He freed his hand so he could smooth away the hair around her face. He liked to see it fastened back. 'You're the one who tells stories. I'm no good at it.'

'Tell me about when you were five years old.'

'Five years old.' He closed his eyes and let his head loll against the settee back. In the firelight his skull shone through his thin hair, his cheek bones were sharp. Rose thought to herself that he would look like an old man soon. He had that sort of face. 'I only know one story from when I was five years old, and it isn't nice.'

'Tell it me though.'

'When I was five years old I went with my sister into the woods.' He kept his eyes closed. 'Kitty was seven. We went into the woods.' He swallowed several times.

'And the trees were high and deep,' Rose prompted him, but his voice cut into hers.

'I can smell them. They were pine woods. I can see the tall trees. I can hear the silence.'

'You scattered breadcrumbs behind you so you wouldn't lose your way.'

'We heard something like an animal moaning. I wanted to run away but my sister held my hand, very tightly, and we went forward together in the direction of the animal sounds.'

'It was a big bad wolf.'

'It was a man. He was crying, but it didn't sound like a man's voice.' Gordon made the sounds, crushed in his throat. 'And he was bending down. He had his back to us, so we couldn't see what he was doing at first. He was scooping pine needles up and spilling them over something. We went a bit nearer. It was like treading on a carpet, the ground was so soft. Pine needles, they melt down into a fine dust. He was scooping pine needles up and spilling them over something. We wanted to see what it was he was doing with the needles. He scooped them up in his hands and just let them rain down on something, and then he scooped more up, and more. We could see something white. It was a big white doll. That's what it looked like. She had baby yellow hair. Her skin was like candles.'

'Did that really happen?'

'I don't know.'

'Did you dream it?'

'I don't know.'

'Haven't you asked Kitty?'

'No. I never asked her about it. I never spoke to her about it. We held hands and ran home.'

'You dreamed it, Gordon.'

'I don't know.'

After all, Rose and Gordon did not lie in the same bed that night. He went up on his own, and for a long time she sat till the fire burnt itself out. She was just aware of Paedric next door going up his stairs. The sound comforted her. It made her aware of how chilled she had grown. She thought she heard him speaking to someone, but she couldn't be sure. The night train was coming. Its thunder shook the house and drowned all sounds, and when it had gone there was only stillness. Rose pulled Gordon's work coat across herself and slept where she was, curled up on the settee, too disturbed by his story to go up to her bed.

THIRTEEN

Rose heard Paedric leave his house the next morning. She was in Edmund's bedroom, changing his sheets. Edmund and Gordon were washing in the bathroom together. She could hear the boy's high voice raised in laughter as Gordon splashed him with cold water. When she caught the sound of Paedric's door being closed she ran to the window to peer out, but she was too late to catch sight of him. She was disappointed. She opened the window wide, feeling stifled. She leaned out into the wash of cold air.

'I've made a terrible mistake,' she whispered. 'I should never have married this man.'

Gordon was good to her, he made no demands on her. He looked after her. To her mother it seemed a perfect marriage. But to Rose it felt as if her real self was in a deep coma and was waiting for something else, the kiss of life, perhaps. 'Just if someone would touch my body, that would be enough,' she thought to herself. 'Just if someone would tell me I was beautiful.' She had upset herself. She went down to get breakfast ready.

'Tell me about this Paedric,' she asked Gordon when he came down. 'It's a lovely name, Paedric, don't you think? A bit gypsyish.'

'He's odd.'

'You keep saying that. How odd?' She had her back to him, pretending to be only half-listening.

'He thinks odd. And he looks odd. I don't know where he gets it from. His parents were ordinary, simple people. His mother was a beauty.' He sat down to begin his breakfast.

'Am I a beauty?' Rose asked him lightly. Gordon didn't look up at her. He didn't always hear what she said.

'On Saturday,' he told her, 'I'm going to take this little lad fishing.'

Rose pulled up her chair and sat opposite him, breaking open a cob of new bread. 'He's too young for that.'

'He won't fall in,' Gordon said. 'I'll choose a safe place.'

'Too young for that brutality, is what I meant.'

Edmund looked anxiously from one to the other of them. He was more aware than Gordon of the undercurrent of pain in Rose's voice.

'He wants to come,' Gordon said.

'Please, Mummy?'

'There was once the wife of a fisherman who lived in a house that looked like a jar of vinegar,' she said. 'And her husband caught a magic fish and threw it back into the sea without asking for a wish to be granted, though he could have had anything in the world.'

'"Oh husband, husband," said the wife in the vinegar jar,' giggled Edmund, remembering the story. '"You could have wished for me a beautiful cottage instead of this old brown vinegar jar. Go back and catch the magic fish again and ask him to grant me just the one wish . . ."'

'So the husband went to the sea's edge, and oh, it was a rough sea that day, and he cried out . . .'

'"Ishy wishy, magic fishy . . ."'

'Stop it,' said Gordon, excluded from all this. 'You'll be late for school, Edmund.'

Edmund slid down from his chair. '"My wife doesn't want to live in a house that looks like a vinegar jar,"' he whispered, laughing up at Rose. '"She wants a lovely cottage in the country."'

'"With roses around the door,"' she whispered back to him.

'And the magic fish said, "Go back to your wife, and you'll find her waiting for you in a cottage with roses around the door."'

'I said stop it!' Gordon was roused to anger now by the child's spluttering laughter.

'But the wife still wasn't happy,' said Rose, bold to his face.

'She wanted a big house with lawns all around it. She wanted a mansion, and servants, and a coach and horses. She kept sending her husband out in tempests and storms to catch the magic fish.' Edmund pranced round the table, delirious with the excitement of remembering the story and with the challenge of making Rose and Gordon watch him instead of each other. 'Ishy wishy . . . And there was a tempest out at sea . . . Ishy wishy come to me.'

'But she was never happy,' Rose said quietly. She pushed her chair away from the table, denying all prospect of the story being told to its end. 'Come on, Edmund, get your shoes ready now.'

Edmund was disappointed. He stamped up the stairs to get his things together, remembering that he was again to spend the whole day at school, crying a little about it. Gordon put on his overcoat and picked up his bag as if nothing had happened.

'I may be late tonight,' he said. 'Don't wait up for me.'

Rose listened out all day for her neighbour to return, but it wasn't until night-time that she heard him again. He seemed to be in conversation with someone, and this was comforting to hear in her own quiet house after Edmund had gone to sleep. He sang from time to time, which made her smile. She wanted to join in. She would have liked to think of him hearing her voice, too. She wondered whether he was at all aware of her presence. When she worked in the kitchen she moved things around noisily, sure that he would hear. She listened out for him when he went to make a late evening drink and she tried to synchronize her own sounds to his: turning on the tap, fetching a cup down from the cupboard, closing doors. She wondered if he was as aware of her. In bed, just as she was drifting to sleep, she heard voices again. She heard a light laugh, and knew it was a woman's. Then she heard Paedric call out a name, as if one of them had left the room. Helena, it sounded like. A nice name.

When Saturday came she knew exactly what she wanted to do. The plot had been hatching over the last few days, over the comings and goings of Paedric and his Helena. She packed up a lunch for Edmund and Gordon and sent them off on their fishing trip. Edmund was anxious before he left, remembering the hostility of the other morning, but Rose had forgotten about it. She wanted them to go. It would be good for Gordon and Edmund to spend time alone together. She was gay with excitement as she waved them off. The day would be fine and cold. Edmund clutched Gordon's hand as they went up the embankment together. She could hear his piping voice. As soon as they had disappeared over the bank Rose went straight upstairs and changed into another blouse, a special one that her mother had given her and that she had never worn. She watched herself in the mirror as she dressed. Her flesh was creamy and full. 'It's not fair,' she said aloud. 'Someone should cherish my body.'

The blouse, when she put it on, was too dressy. She was not herself in it. It would not do for strangers to meet her like this, in a fine garment of silk and lace, with its small pearl buttons. Edmund loved the blouse. He would stand in her cupboard stroking it, holding up the sleeve to his cheek, his thumb in his mouth. She would save it to wear for his birthday, that would be the thing. They would go together to her mother's house for tea and she would wear the blouse for him. She hung it back up, put on something less extravagant, and went out to Paedric's yard. She had heard no house sounds that day. She knocked on the door and looked round at the yard, with its huge spreading tree and the tumble of weeds sprouting beneath it. The one rose-bush was thick-limbed and unpruned. She put out her hand to touch one of its late flower heads and as she did so the petals tumbled free, reminding her of the way a woman unpins her hair.

Paedric opened the door to her. He was not at all what she expected. He was swarthy and squat, with a large ugly head sunk into his shoulders. He was unshaven and the stubble was dark on his face. His hair was long and untidy. His shirt was unbuttoned and his feet bare. Rose was embarrassed.

'I came to introduce myself,' she told him. 'I live next door.'

Paedric ran his fingers through his hair. She noticed how long and thin they were, belying the squareness of his body. He stepped back as if he were bowing a little, gesturing her to come in. The smell of the sweat of his body was pleasing to her. She stood, awkward in his bare kitchen, as he continued to stare out into the yard, absorbed in some motion of sparrows out there.

'I thought I might come and say hello to your wife.'

'My wife?' Still he didn't turn to her.

'I thought . . .' she faltered.

'I have no wife,' he said. His accent was thick and deep. She had heard singers with this kind of speaking quality, which had a resonance that was quite thrilling to her. He was a half-clothed man in the kitchen with her, with the smell of sleep about him. She noticed the gleam of his flesh under his loose shirt as he turned towards her. He gestured to a chair but she remained standing, feeling she should leave now. She had no good reason to stay.

'You married to Gordon Doran?' he asked.

Rose nodded.

'Is that kid yours then?'

'Yes,' she said.

'I've heard him about. Good to hear a kid laughing in this God-forsaken place, this desert. I'd forgotten how it is here. It's the beginning of nowhere, that's for sure. And the end. If it wasn't for the railway you'd think there was no life left in the world.'

'Gordon tells me you've been travelling.'

He shrugged. He was a curious ungainly figure in his small kitchen. 'Hiked about a bit.'

'It must have been wonderful.'

He gave her a sideways look. 'Like travelling, do you?'

'I've never done any. Never will, I don't suppose.'

'The world goes out there,' he nodded up towards the railway line, 'and all most of us ever do is watch it.'

'Why did you come back home?' she dared.

He shrugged. 'Time to come back, that was all. Can't shift your roots for ever. Fancy old Gordon Doran getting a wife and kid.' He laughed. 'That gets me, that does!'

'I'd better go,' said Rose.

He bowed his head a little, in a way that was half-mocking, half-courteous. She went back to her own house, curiously elated. She went straight to her room and brushed out her hair, remembering how the tap-dancer had loved to see it loose and floating. She washed it and rubbed it dry, brushing it out again till its fine strands were separate and gleaming. This was the way William had loved her best.

During the morning the sky began to cloud over. Rose decided to make a hot drink in a thermos and go in search of Gordon and Edmund. Rabbits were playing on the railway banks; they scudded away from her as she approached them, and she laughed aloud to see them. The sun of the morning had cleared away most of the frost. It would not be long now before spring came. For the first time in weeks she began to believe that it could really happen.

Before she reached the river she had to walk down a lane next to a farm. Cows came over the tops of the fields towards her, holding out their heads and bellowing. As she walked on past them they gathered alongside the wall. Their lowing voices were threatening and powerful, beast voices that were half-human in register. Their intensity built up a tunnel of sound. She hurried through it, half-afraid of them in spite of the wall that separated her from them. She was not afraid of their bulk, as she would have been if she was in the field and they were nudging round her. It was their voices that frightened her: their human voices, bellowing after her like wounded men. She hurried on out of the cold sun and into the wooded darkness of the river bank, anxious to find Gordon and Edmund and their familiar comfort.

FOURTEEN

It was days before Rose saw Paedric again, though she heard the house sounds he made from time to time, and learnt to match her sounds to his. She loved best to hear his bouts of singing, bursting as they did into the silence of her own house when Edmund was at school. Twice she was sure she heard Helena. She had a coquettish and wooing voice. His responses were murmurs or sometimes shouts, and their voices would rise up in a crescendo of staccato exchanges that ended always in a frightening silence. It was as if, suddenly, they forgot to talk to each other. Rose was fascinated.

'It must be the radio or something,' Gordon said when she told him about it. 'I've never seen a woman there.'

'Neither have I. And he did tell me he hasn't got a wife.'

'There you are then.' But Gordon looked at her quizzically. 'I didn't know you'd spoken to the man.'

'Only once,' she told him. 'He's a funny little person, isn't he? But I thought he was all right,' she added.

The next morning she heard the talking again, this time in the kitchen. She decided to go straight round. Edmund was off school that day with a cold. She took him with her as an excuse for the visit. He wasn't used to other adults, and didn't like the idea of visiting the odd-bod. He hung back while Rose knocked on Paedric's door. She looked down at him, frowning. He had cupped his hands round the one late rose and as she pulled him away it collapsed. All the dusty petals drifted down.

'Now see what you've done,' said Rose. His eyes filled up, and she crouched down to him.

'It was dead anyway,' she said. 'There'll be a new one soon.'

Paedric opened the door and Rose stood up, staggering slightly as she caught her skirt under her shoe. Paedric made her feel foolish; she was unaccountably nervous of him, yet her nervousness made her bold.

'You said to come round again. I've brought Edmund to meet you.'

The three stood silent in the kitchen, where the tap dripped a sullen monotone into the sink. There was a bowl on the table, and a plate with a slice of bread, half-buttered.

'I'm sorry,' said Rose. 'You're having breakfast.' His kitchen sounds had made breakfast some time ago.

'Sooner or later,' he said. 'You can have some coffee, if you want. What about the youngster? Would he like a banana?'

Edmund nodded, mesmerized. This gnome-like, bright-eyed man was unlike any adult he had met before. Paedric half-peeled the fruit and crouched down to hand it to him, and Edmund took it from him solemnly. Rose felt suddenly protective towards him, aware of the small child's timidity in the face of a totally new situation.

'He's just turned down a perfectly good breakfast,' she laughed, 'because he's sick, he tells me.'

Paedric brought two cups from the cupboard, and hesitated.

'One for Helena?' Rose prompted him. His hand hovered, then drew out a third cup.

'Indeed,' he said.

Satisfied, Rose pulled back a chair and sat down in it. Edmund leaned against her, sucking rather than biting his fruit. Paedric filled up the three cups and pushed one across to her.

'Will she come down for it?' Rose asked.

'No. I'll take it up.'

'I'd like to meet her.'

'I'll tell her.'

'Good.' Rose sipped at her coffee, which was very strong. 'Did you meet her abroad?'

'I did, yes.' Paedric made vigorous sweeping motions across the table with his arm, scattering breadcrumbs and then imagined breadcrumbs on to the floor. The movements were obsessive. Rose wanted to reach across and hold his arm still. 'She gave me a lift one day.'

They sat in silence. His sweeping stopped. Edmund plucked at Rose's sleeve. Rose found it hard to look at Paedric. She pointed out that Helena's coffee would be going cold, and Paedric agreed with her that it would.

'When can I meet her?'

He puckered up his face, trying to make sense of her question. 'Today?' he asked.

She shrugged, feigning carelessness.

'You could come back later today,' he nodded. 'You could do that.'

'Do you do the signals?' Edmund asked suddenly, and Paedric raised his eyebrows at him, making the boy laugh.

'Do you like trains?'

Edmund nodded.

'All little boys like trains, I think. I used to help up there, Edmund. In another life it was. Not now.'

'Tell me about Helena. How did you meet her?'

He poured more coffee out for her. 'I'll tell you the story of how I met Helena,' he said, 'if you first of all tell me the story of how you met Gordon.'

Rose blushed. 'Oh, there's no story there. I was just lodging at his sister's house and he came to stay for a few weeks.'

'And you fell in love with him?'

Rose laughed and instinctively put her arm around Edmund. 'And that was the end of the story.'

'Tell your story now,' Edmund said.

'Once upon a time . . .' Rose prompted, whispering into the child's ear.

'Not very long ago I was hitching through France. It was a time of year when the fields were full of sunflowers all with their faces turned up towards the sun. Heliotropes. And I'd been set down in this pastoral place. Burgundy perhaps . . .'

'Or was it Transylvania . . .'

'Ssh, Mummy,' whispered Edmund. 'You always do that to stories. Anyway, this is true.'

'All stories are true,' said Paedric. 'One way or another, they're all true. So I decided I'd had enough travelling that day and that I'd find somewhere to have a wash, you know, and pitch my tent. A river bank, maybe. I was walking down a lane, whistling, and enjoying my own company, and a car drew up behind me. I didn't want a lift. I was in the mood for walking. But I looked round anyway and I saw that it wasn't an old farmer with a face like an onion but a young woman, so I began to think about changing my mind. Well, it turned out she wasn't offering me a lift, she was asking the way somewhere. I had a good map, of course. I love maps, don't you?'

Rose was surprised. 'I don't think I've ever looked at a map in my life, not since geography classes at school, anyway.'

'Well then, I must show you some. It's a way of possessing the earth, to see all the parts of it named and to read it like a book of poems. I'll show you a map of this county. You would like that, to see the hills and the rivers drawn on it, and to know the names of them like you know the names of friends. And think what it would be like to see your own house mentioned there.'

'Our house!'

'In the middle of the world. That's where it is, your house. It's all a matter of perspective.'

'Was she very beautiful?' interrupted Edmund.

'Of course she was. Women in stories always are, unless they happen to be the ugly witch. Anyway, Edmund, we looked at my map and found where she was wanting to go. There were two routes to it. One was to follow the road, a long, easy route with no danger of getting lost. A bit of an idle route for a summer day that was full of butterflies and heliotropes. And the other was through the forest at the side of us, a tricky route because the track was only dust and would disappear at times, and there were many cross-roads and junctions made by the log-men; and dangerous too, because if her car broke down she would be without help of any sort.'

'Were there wild animals in the forest?' Edmund asked.

'Without doubt there were wild animals. Stags and foxes and hares there would be. Snakes, for sure.'

'So she won't go that way.' Edmund shook his head as he spoke.

'Ah, but it was a much shorter route, Edmund, and would have got her there quicker. And forests are beautiful places, holding their own secrets in their dark hearts.'

Rose stood up, remembering the story Gordon had told her. Apprehension chilled her. She wanted to leave, but now it was Edmund who slid into her chair and leaned towards Paedric, willing the story on.

'I made a vow in my heart. If she chose to go by road, then she would go alone, and our paths would never cross. If she chose the forest I would go with her, and our future together would be decided. "I'll take the road," she said. "I'd get lost in the forest."'

'Ah!' said Edmund.

'"Very well," I said. I felt quite light-hearted, because fate makes decisions for us, that's how life is. But I felt sad, too, because I'd made a vow to myself and I couldn't break it. Anyway, while we had been looking at the map together we hadn't noticed that her car had blocked up the road. A tractor had drawn up and was waiting to pass us. The sun was shining on it, and it looked as if it was piled with gold. Its load of hay was spilling out from it like splinters of gold, and all down the lane behind it was a golden trail. That was the route she was to follow.'

'So it was a lucky road,' said Edmund, 'if it was paved with gold.'

'This child knows a lot of stories,' laughed Paedric. 'And I can't imagine Gordon telling him stories.'

'He talks to me about trains,' Edmund told him.

'Ah well, he used to talk to me about trains, as well, when I was a little boy.'

Rose looked at him quickly. The eyes in the gnomish face were clear and very young. He was perhaps not much more than thirty.

'Was that the end of the story?' Edmund rolled the banana skin into a ball and flicked it open, bored now.

'No. But I didn't want to influence her in any way. As I began to move away she said, "It looks very cold and dark in the forest." "Goodbye," I said. "And mysterious," said she. I set off to walk up the track. I could hear her manoeuvring her car to let the tractor pass. Before long she was drawing up behind me. I raised my hand to her but kept on walking, and she drove on ahead of me. And at the first crossing of tracks she stopped and waited for me. "Can I help?" I asked her. "You have the map," she said. She was laughing, you know. She was young and laughing and beautiful, and there was no sunlight in the forest, and only silence.'

'And had she made the right choice then?' asked Edmund. 'Even though she'd given up the road of gold?'

'Oh yes. She had made the right choice for me. That was how we met each other.'

'Where is she now?'

'In bed,' Rose reminded him. 'Come on, Edmund. I think we should go now. Thank Paedric for the lovely story.'

'And didn't the snakes come?'

'Later,' Paedric promised him. He poured the cold coffee from Helena's cup down the sink, threw Edmund's banana skin into the bin and tidied around. They followed him out and waited while he locked the door. He saluted them casually and went off up the embankment, and Rose walked back to her own house, her hand in Edmund's, letting his chatter spill over her. She gave Edmund crayons to draw a forest picture, which he peopled with gleaming snakes. In the centre of his forest he drew a tall fairy-like creature with long yellow hair that flowed away from her like a cloak of gold.

Throughout the day Rose listened out for the sounds that would tell her that Helena was about, but she heard nothing. She would not go round again, she decided. If Paedric wanted her to meet his Helena then he must bring her round. But she listened out, all the time, for him. Everything about Paedric himself and about his house intrigued her. Most of all she wondered about Helena. At times, when she heard the two voices, she tried to listen in to the conversations. She lost the thread when their voices dropped. Once when she put her ear to the wall she realized that she was listening in on the conversation of lovers. She was ashamed of herself. But when Helena cried out for Paedric and he didn't reply to her, there was such loneliness in her voice that Rose felt a sister's need to comfort her. Hearing her made her realize how lonely she was for female company. Yet something that was more than shyness stopped her from going round to the house again. Two or three times she was on the point of knocking on the door, yet turned away, afraid. He was odd. There was no doubt the man was odd. And Gordon didn't want her to have anything to do with him. She used that as an excuse for not calling in.

'Mummy, I've got a friend,' Edmund told her one afternoon when she was bringing him home from school. 'He's called Simon, and we're drawing a train together. I've always wanted a friend.'

'Aren't you lucky,' Rose said, pleased for him. 'I've always wanted a friend, too.'

'Ishy wishy,' said Edmund, pointing at the house. 'Look!'

There was a young woman walking towards the terrace.

'Helena!' said Rose, more to herself than to Edmund.

But the woman did not go into Paedric's house. She shouted something as she was walking, and a man's voice shouted back. The door of the third house opened; a man and two children came out. The woman picked up one of the children and they all went inside.

'We've got more neighbours,' Rose told Gordon that evening. 'A whole family this time.'

'I've been used to being alone on the terrace,' he said. 'When Paedric's parents died and he went away I thought I'd have it for myself. I can't remember how long it is since anyone lived in that house.'

'It'll be lovely for Edmund to have children next door to play with! Won't it, Edmund? And I'm pleased to have a woman neighbour. I can't see that I'll ever get to meet Helena.'

Later the young couple came round with their children to introduce themselves. They came hand in hand. Rose was embarrassed to see how the couple, who introduced themselves as Joan and Pete, fondled each other as they were talking. They sat squashed together on the settee. Every now and again he would slip his hand out of hers and put it across her back, kneading her. She would protest and giggle and then lay her head on his shoulder. Edmund watched them solemnly. He backed away from their exuberant children and had to be taken up to bed by Gordon, who stayed upstairs with him.

'How long have you been married?' Joan asked over her third cup of tea. She was a thin, wide-eyed woman swollen with another pregnancy.

'Five years now,' Rose told her. She wished they would go. They distressed her.

'And how old is the little boy?'

'He's nearly six.'

'I thought he was big for his age! You were married before then?'

'Yes,' Rose said levelly. She hated the way the man took possession of his wife. In the same way he took possession of Rose's house. When she stoked up the fire he took off his jacket and slung it over the back of Gordon's chair. He rolled up his sleeves. His flesh was pink and fluffed with ginger hairs. He reminded Rose of a pig. She hated the plumpness of his hands, and the way Joan and he melted together as if they were one body. He laid his hand on Joan's belly and kept it there. Rose closed her eyes and wished for Gordon to come down again, but she knew he wouldn't.

'Your children are doing well,' she said. 'Staying up till this time.'

When at last they left she heard Paedric and Helena again next door. It was a taunt to her loneliness. By now it was dark, late evening. Her house was asleep. She went upstairs to Gordon's room. She could hear the drone of his breathing. She opened his door slowly and went in. His suit for tomorrow was hanging on a coathanger from the picture rail, his shoes placed side by side beneath it. He lay with his mouth slightly open, one hand clenched up on the pillow. She stood by him and touched his cheek. He opened his eyes and stared up at her, surprised. He looked very child-like in that instant and she smiled down at him, her anger gone.

'Hello,' she said. He took her hand. 'I just came to see you.' Her throat was thick. She wanted him, and dared not say so. He always refused her.

'That's nice,' he said.

'Will you hold me?'

He sat up in bed, struggling into wakefulness. She sat on the edge of the bed and he put his arms round her awkwardly. They sat for a while like that in silence. In the house next door, the Merlins' house, there were scufflings and creaks. Rose realized that it was the movement of bedsprings that she could hear.

'What's the matter?' Gordon asked her.

'You know very well. It's over six years since anyone touched me, Gordon.' She unbuttoned her blouse and guided his hand to her breast, keeping her own hand lightly over his, a mating butterfly. 'Touch me. Just touch me.'

His hand stayed, quite still, where she placed it.

'Don't you desire me?'

'Desire's a quaint word for a woman like you to use, Rose.'

'What husband is it who doesn't desire his wife? Fancy me then. Love me. In the carnal sense.'

He drew away his hand and held hers in it.

'I do know what you want,' he said, and his voice had the hollowness of an old man's. 'I can't do it, Rose. Not with you or with anyone.'

'Then for God's sake why did you ask me to marry you?'

'I worship you.'

'You love Edmund, don't you?'

'Of course I do.'

'Well, he's mine, remember that. He's my son. Not yours.' She fastened up her blouse. A train was passing and she went over to the window and stared out at it, her head against the glass. She was weary. The house seemed to rock with its motion. When she turned back again Gordon was asleep. She crept downstairs, taut and hurt, and lay in her clothes on top of the settee. During the night Gordon came down to her and, seeing her like that, put his heavy coat across her and left her to sleep.

FIFTEEN

'In a dark, dark forest, long ago, there lived a woodman. He looked after the trees,' said Paedric. He was sitting at his kitchen table with Edmund leaning against him. Rose was standing apart from them both by the window, looking out at the dark spread of the tree, watching for the return of Gordon's train. After all, it had been impossible for her to stay away from Paedric's house. She told herself it was because the coming of the Merlins had aroused in her such dislike and disappointment, and also that she was concerned for Helena's loneliness. When Edmund asked if he could give Paedric the forest picture it had seemed such a simple thing to do, after all, and Paedric had greeted them just as simply. He gave them tea and toast with marmalade, and he told them that Helena was sleeping. It was Edmund who had asked for a story.

'This woodman planted new trees where none had ever grown before, and sometimes he culled the biggest trees so the saplings could see a little sunlight. He lived alone. He was very lonely, but he didn't know it. He knew all the creatures of the forest, the snakes and the foxes, the bats and wild pigs.'

'What was his name?' asked Edmund.

'Let's say it was Gondor. But this story isn't just about him. It's also about a woman who lived a long way outside the forest, on the banks of a river.'

'She was beautiful, wasn't she?'

'Of course she was, but she didn't know it. No one had ever told her, not even in her dreams. She was a weaver. She used to collect grasses from the river bank, and wool that the sheep had rubbed against hedges, and webs that spiders and moths had made. She used to weave them into pictures. And her pictures were like stories.'

'Give her a name.'

Rose turned around from the window. She had her hands clasped together like a child. 'She had no name,' she suggested.

'One day she needed something blue for a picture she was weaving.'

'Was it about the sky?'

'Ah no. It wasn't about the sky itself, Edmund, but about the reflection of the sky in her river. That was how she saw things. She wandered all along the river banks looking for something that was just the right blue, and then she climbed up the meadow towards the forest . . .'

'Gondor's forest!'

'So it was. And when she peered into the forest's darkness didn't she see the very colour she wanted, like a mist under the trees, like the creeping of blue smoke? They were bluebells. Hundreds and hundreds of bluebells. She was afraid of the forest because it was dark and treacherous and because she'd never been in there, but now that she'd seen the bluebells she knew she must have them. So she crept in.'

'Did Gondor see her?'

'He heard her. All the creatures of the forest set up their clatter of alarm when she entered, and then they scurried into their trees and holes and dens and watched her in silence. It was like the silence of sleep. Gondor came out of his hut and went in search of the thing that had caused the creatures of the forest to slip into such a well of silence.'

'Was he carrying his axe?'

'He might have been, Edmund. As for the woman with no

name, she heard the silence too and was very frightened of it. It made her blood as cold as her river when winter ice was upon it. She felt that there were eyes all around her, in the earth and in the air, in the trees, watching her. But she needed the bluebells, didn't she? She picked them quickly, afraid all the time that they would lose their colour and their scent, that they would die in her arms before she could weave them into her picture.'

'And did Gondor see her then?'

'He did. He just wanted to look at her. But suddenly, just as surely as if his shadow had fallen across her in sunlight, she knew that she was being watched. She was so startled that all her flowers spilled down from her arms. She looked up at Gondor and she saw two things. She saw that his eyes were the bluey-grey of woodsmoke, and she saw in them that she was beautiful. But she was afraid even so and she ran out of the forest, and it was at that moment that he knew that he was lonely.'

'Gordon's back,' said Rose quickly. The train cruised with its flashing panels of light behind the tree branches. In ten minutes Gordon would be home. Paedric pushed his hair from his face, focusing back on the room and the child there, the woman by the window. His long fingers drummed on the table top.

'You go,' he said. 'Get your husband's meal on the table.'

'Was that the end of the story though?' asked Edmund, disappointed.

'No, it wasn't, Edmund, but your mammy wants to go.'

Edmund twisted his face round to her, pouting.

'Tell him,' said Rose. 'I can wait.'

The child leaned against him again, his thumb in his mouth.

'Well. Gondor and the woman who had no name thought

about each other all day, and at night they dreamt about each other. They each decided to make the other a present. He chose some trunks of trees that he'd felled in the winter and he began to plane them down and soon, before you knew it, he'd fashioned them into a good strong bed. Along the four posts of the bed he carved the creatures of his forest, the bats and the crows, the snakes and wild pigs. Never before had he made such a beautiful thing. And in her cottage she wove a quilt for him. The story she wove into it was the story of her river, its song and its reflections, the colours of night and the colours of day, the loneliness of the river and all its loveliness. In a way it was the story of her life. They finished their presents on the same day and they set off in search of each other. They met half-way between the forest and the river, in a meadow, and they decided to make a home there. And at night, Edmund,' he leaned forward and took the boy's thumb from his mouth, 'when they lay in their bed with the quilt wrapped around them, what could they hear but the sighing of the trees in Gondor's forest, and the singing river of the woman who had no name?'

'And they lived happily ever after.'

'And that's what you'll have to ask your mammy, because she knows the ending of the story. I don't.'

'I can hear Gordon coming now,' said Rose. She took the boy's hand, and, reluctantly, he went with her.

That night Gordon cooked the meal. He told Rose and Edmund to wait in the room for it. She could hear his slow and careful movements in the kitchen, and sorrowed for him. She knew that he was distressed. He brought the meal in to them on a tray. The overcoat that he had put over Rose still lay discarded on the floor, where she had thrown it when she woke up that morning. He picked it up without saying anything and took it upstairs to his room to hang up. Because she had still been asleep when he had left the house that morning he had gone without it, midwinter though it was. He came back down again and sat with them, putting his hand over Edmund's.

'I'm going to stay at Kitty's for a while,' he told them both. Rose was silent, watching the way his hand stroked her child's. 'I can get to work just as easily from there. I think it would be a good idea, so we can decide what we should do.'

She couldn't answer him. Edmund understood nothing but the slight faltering in Gordon's voice.

'Don't go,' he said.

Gordon kissed his forehead. 'I'll come back.' He leaned across to Rose, just touching her cheek, an unfamiliar gesture to them both. 'It's for the best.'

She nodded. As soon as her husband had left the room she put her arm round Edmund's shoulders. Horror gaped like a pit inside her. The door closed. They listened to his footsteps. He was moving quietly in his room. He would be packing his case. He was humming in that tuneless, gentle way of his. Edmund began to eat the soup that Gordon had brought in for them and that had gone cold and skinned in the bowls. It contained small pieces of vegetable. The child sucked the liquid noisily from the spoon, using his teeth as a sieve, chomping the vegetables with his mouth open, shovelling more in and more till the tomatoey liquid dribbled down his chin and the vegetable pieces spilled out with it. She wanted to scream at him to stop. She wanted to slap his hand and send the spoon clattering across the room. She wanted to run upstairs to her husband and put her arms around him and plead with him to stay.

She did none of these things. When Edmund had finished eating she wiped his face clean and took him upstairs to his bed. The door to Gordon's room was open.

'When are you going to Aunty Kitty's?' Edmund called through to him.

'I haven't quite decided,' Gordon replied lightly. 'I expect it's a bit late to go now.'

Rose sat with Edmund on the edge of his bed.

'Tell me the end of the story. Paedric said you knew how it finished.' It was as if nothing had happened.

'I think I'm too tired,' Rose said. She was listening now to the silence from Gordon's room.

'Is it a happy ending or not?'

'Stories can have all kinds of endings.' It was growing cold. Rose swung her legs on to Edmund's bed and hoicked up the blankets so they were covering them both. 'How would you want it to end?'

'I think the lady missed the river and Gondor missed his trees,' said Edmund. 'And so one night they both ran away.'

'They might do. But what about the beautiful bed that Gondor made? And the quilt she wove? Whom did they belong to?'

She spoke the words as though she was chanting a litany that made no sense to her. Her thoughts were in the room on the other side of the wall, on her husband sitting with his head in his hands on the edge of the bed, his suitcase packed. She wondered whether she would ever see him again.

'They set fire to them,' Edmund giggled. 'Then nobody can have them. And they run away to their own houses and watch the flames from there.'

They heard Gordon going down the stairs, and the opening and closing of the door. So he had gone, as simply as that. He had made up his mind about it and without properly consulting her or even saying goodbye he had gone. She had no idea what she should do. They sat without speaking, and soon from the station they heard the whistle of the train. Edmund slid out of bed with his hand pressed across his mouth and ran to the window. He stood with his hand raised. Rose imagined Gordon's troubled face, his white hair, his hand just lifted maybe, his lips parted. She heard the mountainous rush of the carriages and pulled up the bedclothes like a tent over her head to stifle the sound. Edmund ran back to her and together they curled down into its darkness; into its airless comfort.

When she brought Edmund home from school the next afternoon Rose knew that he was grieving for Gordon. That morning he had not mentioned him, and neither had she. But when he walked back home with her his mouth was set in the pursed way of hurt that she knew he had picked up from her mother. She didn't know what to do to console him. She had spent the day herself in a strange kind of release, moving furniture and bringing in wild flowers, a thing she had never thought to do when Gordon was at home. It felt as if it had become her own house, in the way that it had felt that Edmund had become her own child the night William had left her.

'I've thought of an ending to that story,' she coaxed him as he walked silently at her side. 'D'you want to hear it?'

He nodded, sniffing.

'Well, there they were, stuck in that meadow, weren't they? And they began to realize that they didn't like being together all that much, after all. The lady with no name was grumpy and wanting her river back. And guess what? One night the quilt turned back into water and ran all the way home to the river bed! There was no stopping it, no turning it back or stemming its flow. Don't you think that might happen? And of course she ran after it, didn't she?'

'I suppose so,' Edmund agreed. 'But what about the man?'

'Gondor. Well, he would lie there twisting and turning because he couldn't sleep without the sound of the wind in his trees. He tossed so much that he woke up all the animals that he'd carved around his bed – the bats and the hares and the snakes and the crows. They scuttled back to the forest one by one till there was no bed left, and Gondor picked himself up off the ground and scuttled after them.'

They both laughed. 'And they lived happily ever after,' Edmund said, triumphant, running ahead of her down the track to home. 'Because people always do in stories, don't they?'

SIXTEEN

It was strange that with Gordon's going the voices from Paedric's house stopped completely. She heard no house sounds, and she was quite sure that Paedric had gone away too. Strangely, she felt she would miss him more than she missed Gordon. She had grown used to listening out for him. The house sounds had become some kind of communication. But the people on the other side, the Merlins, made more noise than ever. They kept their distance from Rose, either because they were so wrapped up in each other that they didn't even notice that Gordon had gone, or because they sensed her dislike of them so much that they didn't care. But it seemed to Rose that their daily household clamour was a challenge to her to get on with her own life.

She was surprised to see how quickly the days passed without Gordon. His leaving seemed to make no difference to her at all. But she missed Paedric's story-telling, and so did Edmund. She went to his house one morning and tapped on his door, and returned home quite sure now that he had gone too. Well, she must settle into her solitude, she thought. It was the night sounds that distressed her most. The drifting voices of Paedric and Helena had seemed to be part of her dreams; but what Joan and Pete did at night had the raw intrusiveness of nightmare. She lay awake night after night listening to their bursts of shrill laughter. Sometimes, when she had just drifted off to sleep, she was awakened by what she thought was the sound of a sudden carillon of bells, only to realize that it was the creaking of their bed that she could hear. She would lie in a state of taut distress, unable to block out the sound of their love-making.

One weekend she took Edmund to see her mother. She hoped that while she was there Gordon would come back. She liked the thought of his finding the house deserted. She also liked the idea that when she came home again she might find him there waiting for her. She took with her as many of Edmund's clothes as she could manage, and told her mother she would like to leave him there until the end of the holiday.

'Is anything the matter with you and Gordon, Rose?' her mother asked. 'I hope not.'

'I don't know.' Her mother's surprising tenderness was almost more than she could bear. 'He's gone away for a bit, that's all.'

Her mother nodded. 'You know, I always thought that man was too good for you,' she said. 'Taking a child in like that.' As she was speaking she was dabbing up crumbs from her plate, licking her finger from time to time. Rose thought she would never look up from this task. It was as though every crumb needed to be accounted for. 'You were the wrong person for him, though he was the right person for you. That's what I always thought.'

'You should have had him yourself then,' Rose said. 'He's more your age than mine.' She crossed over to the window. Children were playing in the lane outside, four red-headed girls shrieking like birds. Their mother was coming up to them. Rose could see how like them the woman was, and how age had turned the blaze of her hair into the powder of ash.

'Sex isn't everything, you know,' her mother said, suddenly astute. 'I was happier when your father decided he didn't want it any more. It's not an enjoyable thing for women.'

'It is for some,' Rose declared. Longing for William rose up unbidden in her.

She went back alone on the train, leaving Edmund to spend his Easter holiday with her mother. And it was during that week that the incident with the eel happened. It upset her deeply. She thought at the time that it was done deliberately to hurt her, because people could see that she was a woman without love.

She hated the thought of being cooped up in the house. It was early spring, and she decided to spend some time working in the back garden, planting seeds for summer flowers. She had never understood her garden enough to make anything of it, and it was grossly overgrown. She decided to work on a tangled patch of brambles over in one corner. As she cleared away the runners till she could at last get down to the roots and heave them out she discovered that they were lodged in a shallow shelf that had been concreted. She pulled away the rest of the roots and the top soil and realized by the shape of the basin that it had once been a pond. She was excited and pleased at this discovery, and decided to reinstate it. She imagined sitting with Edmund in the summer, watching goldfish and frogs and water-boatmen. She would fill it with water-lilies and she would nest forget-me-nots and irises around it.

It took her three days to get it cleaned out and filled up with water, which she carried by the panful from her kitchen, slopping it down her legs and her skirt. She knew how Edmund would have loved to help her to do this, and yet she wanted to get it ready for him; a surprise. She was being watched all the time from next door's kitchen. She was aware of that, and ignored it. They knew she was alone; why didn't they just get on with their lives and leave her to get on with hers? She placed boulders from the back of the garden, where there had once been a rockery, round her pond, and sat staring into it. She watched beetles diving into it, and the clouds rolling like smoke across it, and allowed herself to daydream.

'You want to get some fish for that pond, Mrs Doran.' The voice was Pete Merlin's, coming at her through the hedge which separated their gardens. His hair was a froth of ginger above the hedge-top.

'I will. I will.'

'And get it stocked up with taddies. I'll get the kids to fetch you some frogspawn from the park in town.'

'I'll do it, Mr Merlin.'

'No trouble. Pete, my name is.'

She stared into the pond, willing him to go away and leave her alone. At last she heard his wife calling him in. She watched the froth moving along the top of the hedge to the house. They stood in the kitchen watching her. She could hear them laughing. She could always hear them laughing, especially at night, through her bedroom wall.

They came out later to bring in the washing. 'She wants to get some taddies for that pond,' she heard him say. 'It must be nearly ready for hatching out, frogspawn. I think I'll take the kids down to the park for some.'

'I'll do it myself!' she called out sharply, hating him. She could hear Joan spluttering, imagined her face red with contained laughter.

That night when she went to put out the milk bottle she found a jar on the step, with a label stuck to it. She stepped outside and glanced at their house out of habit. The lights were out, the bedroom curtains drawn to. Paedric's house too was in darkness. She picked up the jar and carried it inside. The label was a note. Like an abandoned child, she thought. She locked and bolted the front door and carried the jar into the kitchen where the light was on. It was a large jam-jar, and its lid was punched with holes. The note said 'For your pond.' As she placed it on the table she saw with a jerk of horror that the jar did not contain frogspawn but a long live thing that seemed to waken when she moved away from it. It spiralled slowly. It was an eel. With something like distaste she pushed the jar away from her, then went to sit on the stool by the kitchen door, where watching was safe.

The thing was coiled on itself three times, like a muscled spring on some tight pivot, unwinding, and hobbled head to tail. It inched itself round in this clench. As it circled its dark hooded eyes hooked hers, like a lover's, she thought. Was it snake or fish? Would it wind itself round like this for ever, and never take its eyes off her?

She knew who'd sent the thing, all right. She thought of him lying in his bedroom next door to hers. She thought of his plump hands sliding over his wife's body. 'Well, he's a fool,' she said out loud. 'I bet eels eat tadpoles and fishes.' But he would know that, of course. He'd be laughing at her now. They'd be laughing together at the joke. His obscene joke. 'Anyway, how would an eel stay in a pond?' she said aloud to it. She imagined it sliding across her grass in search of a river that would take it down to its spawning seas. She imagined it coiling its way up the embankment, its slow and surely impossible journey across the railway lines. She shuddered. Of course he would know. She closed her eyes against the movement on the table. 'I'll see to the thing tomorrow.'

She put the kettle on for her bedtime drink, and all the time she was aware of the eel trapped in its slow tight circle behind her. She wondered if she could transfer it to a larger jar for the night. She hunted through the cupboards but there was nothing large enough to contain it. She imagined the thing dying on her. The sink perhaps. But she knew she would never bring herself to wash dishes in it again once the eel had been sliding round in it. At last she found an old deep pressure cooker. She put it on the table next to the jar. The eel would be much freer in that. Very carefully she unscrewed the lid of the jam-jar and, holding it at arm's length, dolloped the contents into the pressure cooker. The eel swam lazily round it, now only inches longer than the circumference if its container.

The kettle had boiled. She took down her mug and quickly spooned cocoa, sugar and powdered milk into it. She glanced behind her. The eel's stubbed head bobbed above the rim of the pan. Her heart jumped. The head bobbed down, then up again, down, and up again, higher this time. 'No,' she moaned. 'Don't.' Her hands were beginning to shake. It's only an eel, she told herself. She stirred her cocoa rapidly and glanced round again, and again the head bobbed and ducked, bobbed and ducked. She couldn't take her eyes off it now. She watched in fascination and horror as the searching head poked higher and higher, faster; she heard the eel fling itself against the side of the pan, heard it splash back down into the shallow water. 'Please stay there,' she whispered. She half-ran across the kitchen. As she went through the door she heard a wet thud behind her and turned to see that the eel had swung itself over the side of the pressure cooker, off the edge of the table, and on to the floor. It slithered towards her. She ran into the front room, slopping cocoa on to the carpet. She stood in the dark, watching. Only a stupid eel, she kept saying to herself. She imagined it wriggling across the carpet towards her. She listened out for the froof of skin on fabric that it would surely make. Her cocoa went cold in her cup as she waited, but she heard nothing. She focused into the dancing darkness but could make out no definable shape or movement on the carpet. At last she forced herself to reach across to the light switch. The eel wasn't there.

She tiptoed across the hall and into the kitchen. A wet trail snaked across the floor, but the eel had vanished. Panic rose up in her then. Must she search the house for the thing? It could be anywhere. She might tread on it, or sit on it even. Could an eel climb stairs? How long could it live out of its element? And when she did find it – must she pick it up?

She thought of that crude man, laughing in his bed next door. She ran down the hall, unbolted the door, and ran to the Merlins' house. She had to bang on their door again and again, and the sharp pulse of her knocking echoed in the silent terrace, and still they didn't come. Far away a train rumbled. A small child cried, and at last the upstairs light went on. She heard him coughing, coming down the stairs. She breathed deeply to steady herself. Pete Merlin stood in green striped pyjamas on the step and yawned at her. Froth bubbled from the corners of his mouth.

'I've come about your eel.'

'My eel,' he repeated stupidly.

'I think I've lost it.'

'Pete?' his wife called from upstairs.

'Could you come and find it? It is yours, after all. I didn't even want it.' She controlled her voice with difficulty.

'Tomorrow, love,' he promised.

'Now.'

Without saying anything he turned and trudged upstairs, leaving the front door open. She hovered on the step, wondering whether to go in or go back to her own house. She watched the black shadow between the two lit squares that the windows cast. She could hear an argument going on upstairs, and then Joan's familiar laugh, and he came down again, grinning at something he'd just shared with her, his shirt unbuttoned, trousers pulled on over his pyjamas, slippers on his feet. He followed her into her house and they stood together in the hall. She knew that he could see that she was trembling.

'I've no idea where to look,' she said, helpless. 'It's vanished.'

'He's probably gone upstairs,' he laughed, in his rough way trying to joke her out of her fear, maybe. 'You'd be all right, Mrs Doran. With an eel in your bed.' His vulgarity appalled her. It was an affirmation of everything she'd ever felt about the man. He was a brute, and this crude joke of his was a triumph over her. She thought again of the dreadful dividing wall and the animal sounds that came from their room in the night; the obscene laughter.

Suddenly he dropped down on to his hands and knees and crawled towards the kitchen. His large pink hands padded along the fabric of her carpet, one paw forward, one knee dragged, another paw, another knee. He lay on his belly, cheek pressed into the pile, and gently poked the kitchen door so that it swung slowly back. Stretched under, straight as a ruler, lay the eel.

'Dead?' she breathed.

The big man hoisted himself back on to his knees and with infinite delicacy placed his thumbs and forefingers near the tips of the eel and picked it up. His large builder's hands cradled it, so it looked tiny; a frail and harmless thing. She noticed the scatter of freckles on his arms, and the fine fleece of ginger hairs.

'Fetch me his jar, Mrs D.,' he whispered. She tipped the water from the pressure cooker back into the jar, and he tenderly lowered the eel back in and screwed the cap back on. Flecks of carpet fluff floated away from the eel as it wound itself round the inside of the glass. They both watched it, and the eel with its dark eyes watched them.

'I'm sorry you've been upset, like,' he said.

She resisted the comfort of his voice. They didn't look at each other but at the eel in its slow spiral, and she could see now that it wasn't the sinister black rubber hosepipe eel of her imaginings, but that its skin had in it the colour of rivers, and that its inexorable movement was slyly sensuous; more snake than fish, and woman-eyed at that.

'It is a beautiful thing,' said Rose softly.

The knot unfolded in its jar; the wheel turned. Pete Merlin stood in the doorway with his jam-jar held tight in the crook of his arm. He was uncomfortable, now. They could see the light from the patterned square of his bedroom window.

'Looks as if Joanie's still awake.'

'Go home to her,' said Rose, releasing him. When he had gone she locked and bolted her door again, made herself another drink, and went to bed. But she didn't go to her own room. She took her bedding down into the front room and spread it across the settee there. Tomorrow, she decided, she would bring down the bed that her mother had given her; her grandmother's bed. This would always be her room. She liked it. She lay in the light of the streetlamp and could hear the peaceful ticking of the clock that Gordon had made. She was out of reach of the sounds from the Merlins' bedroom. After all, they had nothing to do with her. When Gordon came back there would be no embarrassment about going upstairs together, and parting on the landing, no hurt. That nightmare, that failure, was over for good.

SEVENTEEN

Rose woke up late to the sound of singing from Paedric's kitchen. She surprised herself with the delight she felt. She got up readily and set herself the task of moving her bed downstairs. It was impossible, but it gave her an excuse to go round to Paedric's. When he opened the door to her his ugliness was a shock. She had forgotten what he really looked like. He bowed to her and ushered her in.

'I've come to ask you to help me, if you wouldn't mind,' she said, glancing round at the new untidiness of his kitchen. 'I'm trying to move a bed downstairs and I've managed to get it stuck. I had to climb over it to get downstairs!'

'I would have dismantled it first,' said Paedric. 'Didn't Gordon think of that?'

'Gordon's away.' Rose was surprised to realize that Gordon and Paedric had left the terrace at the same time. It seemed ages ago. And so it was, when she thought about it. It had been before Easter. Now it was late spring. Edmund was still at her mother's.

'I'm cursed with a child's strength,' Paedric told her. 'This body is an egg-shell.'

'I'm sorry,' said Rose.

'Never mind. Between us we should manage.'

Rose went back to her own house, pensive now about Gordon. She wondered whether she ever would see him again. She stood in her hallway looking up at the bed lodged in its odd angle there and could have wept for herself. When Paedric came with his spanners she was embarrassed suddenly at the thought of what she had asked him to do. She went into her kitchen, uselessly moving objects about. After that it was a simple matter to carry the bits of bed down and to sprawl the mattress over the reassembled frame.

She made tea and they went into the garden to drink it, sitting by the pond.

'This is a grand thing to have,' said Paedric. 'A pond is an eye in the earth.'

'I'm glad you're back,' she said.

'People are usually glad to see me go,' he told her. 'Wrinkled toad that I am.'

'I've missed your stories.'

'Tell me your story.'

'What d'you mean?'

'The pond. There must be a story to that.'

'No, there isn't,' she laughed. 'It was here already. I found it when I was weeding and I decided to clear it out and get it going again, that's all. But I suppose there is a story though.'

She told him a little about the eel, laughing as she remembered it. She was pleased to think that the Merlins would see her out there, sitting in sunshine with a friend, enjoying herself. 'I was silly,' she said. 'Fancy being scared of an eel!'

'We should all be afraid of wild creatures. We don't know them.'

He is a strange gnome, she thought. He is so solemn and earnest, like a child.

'Have you been far, Paedric?'

'Far enough.'

'Did Helena go?'

'Helena goes everywhere with me.'

'I really do want to meet her.'

'Your eel,' he said, 'reminds me again of meeting Helena.

But it's a story I promised Edmund, and he isn't around to hear it.'

'I'll tell it to him. Was it the story of the forest?'

'I think you like stories as much as your child does.'

'All children like stories.' She laughed at herself and blushed. 'You took the path through the forest . . .'

'And that night she slept in a farmhouse. We ate together and then she went into the farmhouse, and I pitched my tent in a near-by field and waited for morning to come. Do the crickets never sleep out there? Something in the sound the breeze made on the canvas brought a memory from long ago. I opened my eyes to it in the darkness and let it swim through, folding over images the way you fold over the leaves of a book, and the story that the images were telling me was not the story of my past but the story of my future.'

'Your future with Helena.'

'Next morning I was frightened of this dream. It was as if I was never going to be in control of anything any more. It was just like that moment before I went into the forest. It was your story of the eel just now that made me think of this. Fear catches us by surprise, but we should take note of it. I decided to go away. I set off very early walking for the station. I found myself whistling. I was free. I had chosen freedom. That's the excellent thing.'

'It is,' said Rose.

'Yet when I heard a car behind me and I knew it was her I couldn't help smiling. I didn't look round. I let her pull up in front of me and then I walked up to the car. "You might at least have stayed to say goodbye," she said. I climbed into the car and we drove through to the mountains. I couldn't take my eyes off her. I wanted to touch her, to put my arm round her or something, and I didn't know when the right time would be. I didn't want to frighten her away, I didn't want to influence my future. I decided that I would wait for a sign.'

The Merlin children had tumbled out into their garden and were now standing by the hedge, staring at Paedric.

'Did you have to wait long?' Rose asked.

'I knew it exactly when I saw it. She saw it first. I had walked past without noticing it, but Helena was drawn to it, and as I came back to see what it was she was looking at I knew this was the sign and so I put my arm round her.'

'So what was it?'

'What she was looking at was a jar of snakes. A big bottle, the sort you might have boiled sweets in, perhaps, or pickled eggs, but bigger than that, a belled jar; maybe you could have plants in it. Anyway, this jar was filled with snakes.'

'Dead?'

'Oh, a long time. It was a kind of Victorian curiosity. They were perhaps in alcohol or vinegar.'

'A vinegar jar!'

'They were twisted round each other so you couldn't tell where one ended or where another began, and yet you could see heads and eyes, you know. They were ropes of flesh. Ugly, dead, beautiful things.'

Later, it was all Rose could do to get the thoughts of the snakes out of her mind. She made up her bed in the front room and arranged the room as she wanted it. For the first time since her arrival at the house she unpacked her box of treasures and arranged them around the room. Many of them were things that her mother had given her from her childhood, fans and feathers to splay out across the walls. She liked the look of it. She had a photograph of the tap-dancer, and in defiance she put it on the mantelpiece. He was handsome. His dark hair gleamed. When Edmund came back she would tell him that William was his father, not Gordon. The child would have to cope with that. He ought to know. She heard Paedric in his kitchen and went through to be closer to the sounds, which were comforting and intriguing to her still. Like him, she filled the kettle. Then she heard again the woman's voice, a low, beguiling, coaxing voice, and it made her flesh creep as though small moths were brushing their wings along her spine.

'Don't leave me,' she heard her say.

Rose went back into her new room. She could just hear the voices still. She had fled from one kind of persecution to another. She had no resources of her own. She must leave this house.

She closed her eyes. Immediately she imagined the snakes, twisted on themselves like a torque of gold. In her mind they were not dead but alive; fleshy, gleaming restless things trapped forever in their jar of vinegar.

EIGHTEEN

During the night the voices from Paedric's house woke her up. She sat up in bed. Strange shadows loomed around her. She had no idea at first where she was, but the unfamiliar light from the terrace's single street lamp cast an eerie, theatrical gloom. It was as if she were taking part in a drama of some kind, and had suddenly become illuminated by the spotlight. She had no idea what her role in it might be. Gradually she realized that all the action was taking place next door, behind the walls. At first she couldn't make out the words at all, but the tone she recognized in them was fear – Helena's voice was a wail of terror, and his, close on hers like wave on wave, seemed to be begging her to stop. There was an unearthly chill about them. She almost longed for the sound of Pete and Joan's homely laughter again. When at last the voices stopped she found she was clutching the sides of her pillow and that she was trembling. She could hardly bear the silence.

She went into her kitchen and made herself a hot drink. Tomorrow, she decided, she would fetch Edmund home. He would love the pond. She would take him to a garden shop and they would choose fish and pond weeds for it. She would contact Gordon and ask him to come home again. She would rebuild her family. And she would brave the house next door and ask to see Helena.

At last she slept again, and she awoke next morning to the sound of Paedric leaving his house. She ran round and banged on the door. The house was in silence. She climbed up the embankment so she was on a level with the upstairs window, but she could see no movement. She felt sick. A train came past, temporarily distracting her. She wondered whether Gordon would be on it, and whether he would see her gazing at the window of her neighbour's bedroom. She would like him to come back to her now. There was nothing about him to surprise or dismay her. He would always act in the same way. She was just about to give up her vigil and go back to her house when she saw Paedric coming up over the other side of the embankment, picking his way over the still humming tracks. He had his hands deep in his pockets and his head down. He barely seemed to be aware of her, even when she went right up to him.

'I want to see Helena,' she said. Fear for Helena and for herself made her weak.

Slowly he brought her into focus. He looked dog tired.

'Come later,' he said.

'No, now. I want to come in now.' She didn't know what she was afraid of.

'All right.'

She followed him to the back of the house and he opened the door to her, nodding her in. The bones in his face were set in tense angles.

'What is it about Helena? Is she ill?' Rose asked him. She felt as if the air was swimming around her. She held on to the back of a chair for steadiness.

'All right. Come up now, if you must.' He took her upstairs. She clung on to the banister at the top in a kind of half-swoon, afraid of what she might find and what might happen to her. She knew he sensed her fear.

'It's all right,' he said.

'Then where is she?' She hardly recognized her own voice.

He pushed open the door of a darkened room and indicated that she should go in. Rose hesitated at the doorway. It was undoubtedly a woman's room. Though it was in darkness the windows were open and the curtains were breathing, letting in light as though it were a live and leaping creature, closing it out again. There were trailing scarves on the walls, lifting too in the draught, and they were all of rich colours, plum and turquoise, peacock blues and greens. Sequinned cushions scattered the floor and they too gleamed from time to time like the lights of eyes, winking and shutting. The air was perfumed.

Rose's heart was beating with a slow and dreadful drumming. She tried to back out of the room but Paedric closed the door behind her and sat down on one of the cushions. He bent forward to light a candle and from that one lit several more. The glow diffused in the room, softening its angles. He loosened his hair. It fell like a woman's round his face. He leaned back on the cushion and with his fingers trailing lifted down one of the scarves, letting it drape across his shoulders like a shawl.

'Wouldn't you rather sit down?' It was Helena's voice. Relief made Rose calm again.

'You wanted to meet me.'

Rose nodded. She was afraid to take part in the game, and just as afraid to break the spell. She was quite sure that at this moment Paedric believed that he was Helena.

'I'd like to tell you now what happened next, after the day of the jar of snakes. After all, it's your story.'

'Why is it my story?' asked Rose.

'You began it. You chose to talk about snakes.'

Rose sank back against the cushions. Her fear was beginning to leave her. She felt curious now, and only slightly apprehensive. After all, she could run for home from here.

'Eels,' she said. The cushions were real enough, the curtains, the candles. She half expected to hear Paedric's light laugh and to see him lounging against the door-jamb, watching her. But he was ridiculously draped in a woman's scarf, with his hair loose about his face and his eyes concentrating on something inside his head. He was miles and miles away.

'We were together, after the jar of snakes. I had a car, and he didn't. We decided to drive round France together. Do you know France?'

Rose shook her head.

'We chose country roads. They stretch on for miles, and you scarcely pass another car. There are tall trees each side of the road, and the sun comes through them and lies in black stripes, gold sunlight and black shadows; they flash across your eyes, blinding you with stripes. I was singing as I drove. I was in love. I felt as if I had known Paedric all my life. And there was the sun pouring like liquid through the branches, striping the road, and I was singing to him.

'And suddenly Paedric shouted out loud, threw up his hands. I slammed on my brakes, dreading to know what had happened. I sat with my head in my hands. I didn't dare look up. Paedric opened the door and ran from the car. I was too afraid to move. What had I done? "Didn't you see it?" That was all he could say, shouting at me from the side of the road. "You must have seen it." I climbed out of the car so I could see what it was he was looking at.

'It was a snake, striped black and gold, stretched along the patterns of the road, the sun and shadows. How could I have seen it? It had yielded itself to me and I had crushed its body twice. I wanted to touch it, and I was afraid. Paedric was crouched over it like a mourning child.

'And then this happened: the snake gathered itself and

wound away into the dry grasses on the verge. Like a trickle of gold it poured itself into black and out of sight, out of sound. But I tell you, I had killed that snake.'

Rose realized that the story was finished. She stood up and felt for the door, not wanting to break the spell of silence. The full daylight made her gasp. It whipped her eyes. She stumbled downstairs and into the yard. The sun was like a benediction.

And there was Gordon, coming down the embankment towards her. He stretched out his hand to her, and she ran to him.

NINETEEN

'Have you really come back, Gordon? To stay? I can't tell you how much I've missed you!' Rose was childish with happiness at seeing him again.

'I've missed you too,' he said in his steady way, smiling down at her. 'I've missed my home, and Edmund. And Kitty has finally kicked me out. She said my place was with you, not taking up the room of a homeless lodger. She was right of course. My place is with you.'

'And are you glad to be back? You will stay, won't you? Come and see what I've done to the garden!' Eager as a child, she led him through to the back. She clung to his arm, hoping to be seen by the Merlins or Paedric. 'Will you look at my pond!'

'You've been busy, Rose. Now I can fish in my own back garden!'

'You will not! I'm going to take Edmund with me to buy some pretty fish for it. Koi carp, or goldfish.'

'Where is the boy?' Gordon looked round. 'Has he missed me?'

'He was missing you badly. So I took him to my mother's soon after you left, and he's still there! He has friends there now. He doesn't like those noisy Merlin children. I didn't mind keeping him away from school for a bit. But he'll be all right again, now you're home.'

'Shall we fetch him today?'

'Could we not have a day or two on our own first, maybe?' She was shy of him, anxious to please him. She stood on her toes to kiss his cheek.

'All right. I'd like that.'

It felt like a holiday, having Gordon home again. They sat in the kitchen for a long time pouring out to each other the great and the small events that had happened to them over the last few weeks. He had been made manager of his firm. He might buy a car, he said, and take them for runs to the seaside.

'Oh, you'd miss your beloved trains too much!' Rose told him, and he agreed with her that he would.

Their talking eased into silence. Rose looked round the room, searching for new things to show him. They both spoke at once.

'I've brought my bed downstairs, Gordon.'

'Was that Paedric's house you were coming out of just now?'

They faltered again into silence. She told him about having coffee with Paedric. She didn't tell him what had happened there. It was her secret now. She had not yet decided what to do with it.

'He's a strange man,' she said warily. Gordon laughed, and she laughed with him.

'He was a strange child. His parents used to say he lived in storyland.'

'Most children do, don't they? I did.'

'I felt quite sorry for him, when he was a kid. He was such an ugly, gnomish child. I don't suppose there's any harm in him.'

'I'd rather have him for a neighbour than those Merlins. At least he's quiet.'

'What about that woman of his?'

'No. There's no woman there,' she assured him.

'I didn't think there was. He's not much of a catch, after all.' They both laughed again. 'I got the feeling the man was talking to himself.'

'I think he does.' Rose felt easy now. 'I do it myself, Gordon. It's awfully quiet, being in the house on my own. Awful creepy.'

While Gordon was unpacking she went down to the village to buy some food. She had let stocks run down so there was barely enough for herself to eat. She would make him a feast, she thought. A wedding feast. It was a long walk along the canal path, but she enjoyed it. Coming back she met Paedric. It startled her to see him. He was leaning against a tree, watching her coming. She had the feeling that he might have been waiting for her.

She felt awkward, not knowing what to say to him. 'Have you nothing to do today?' she asked him, in the way she might speak to a child. It occurred to her that she had no idea how he spent his time or how he earned his living.

'I've plenty to do,' he told her. 'I was watching a flock of finches there, but you scared them away.'

'I'm sorry.'

'They'll be back. It's their land.'

'You're not a writer, or an artist, or something like that?' she laughed.

'Nothing like that. Mother State pays me to do nothing. They say I'm disaffected, but the truth is everything affects me.'

'So you're on the dole.'

'Temporarily. I'm waiting for the man in the signal box to die so I can have my old job back again, tell Edmund.'

'I shouldn't depend on it.'

'Everybody dies in the end.'

'I suppose they do.'

They began to walk towards home together.

'You were pleased to come to my house this morning,' he said.

'I was. I was very pleased. Thank you.'

'But I see he's back.' Paedric jerked his head in the direction of the terrace. 'You won't want to come again.'

Rose felt a blush creeping across her face and neck. She knew that to go to his house again would be to play his game with him. 'I might.'

'Come now.'

'No. I couldn't do that.' Rose started to hurry away from him. 'I want to be with my husband.'

Next day Gordon set out for work as usual. She walked with him to the station. All the time she was with him her head was busy with the prospect of going back to Paedric's house. The image of Helena's room bloomed and faded like a room in a dream, disappearing as soon as she tried to recall it. 'I will go,' she was thinking, 'and this time I'll tell Paedric that I don't believe in Helena. She doesn't exist.'

She realized then that Gordon had asked her something and was watching her quizzically, waiting for an answer.

'I said, when shall we go for him?'

'For Edmund? Saturday, shall we? That gives us two more days on our own, Gordon.' She put her hand into his. 'I want us to be better.'

'We are better,' he told her.

'I want us to have a child of our own.' The words blurted out of her, surprising her with their boldness. But it was true. Edmund wasn't enough.

Gordon drew in his breath. He released her hand. 'There's no time to talk about that now. Not here, Rose.' He was brusque with her.

'We don't have to talk about it. I just wanted to say it.'

They were both silent. There was a well of pain between them. Up on the track the signal clicked into position.

'I'm late, Rose,' Gordon said. 'I have to run now.'

Rose walked blindly back towards the terrace. Paedric had

left open his door. She hesitated as she came towards it, and then she went in.

'Paedric?' she called.

'Come on up.' It was Helena's voice.

The bedroom door was ajar, the candles already lit. Again Rose hesitated in the doorway.

'I hoped you'd come.'

Rose sat down. She was tense and disappointed after her conversation with Gordon. She felt she had let herself down by speaking out too soon. She had let him down. She had opened herself up again to pain. She closed her eyes. She needed to cry. She had made a mistake, after all, coming to this room with this ridiculous man draped in scarves.

'I could tell you a story,' Helena's voice interrupted her silence. 'You might think it's not a very nice story. You might think it's beautiful.'

'I'm a bit upset just now,' said Rose. She couldn't help herself. Grief welled up in her. The soft light of the candles made her think of Miss Cleary's room again. She longed for the child she had been then.

'Is it because your husband has come back?'

Rose could feel the scald of tears on her cheeks and in the back of her throat. 'He treats me like his daughter,' she thought. 'Not his wife. He takes Edmund for his son, and me for his daughter.' She would have liked to curl up on top of the cushions and sleep. She wanted Desmond again, telling her stories into the night. She wanted William's caresses.

'This story is of Africa. Have you been there?'

'No,' Rose said. 'This is the furthest I've been from home. But this is the end of the world. You said that.'

'You must imagine how the night drops into full dark, cutting out the sun. You must imagine how the frogs set up their singing. Fireflies are sparks of blue light.'

Rose closed her eyes. 'Is this a story about yourself?'

'It's a story about longing. Imagine the smell of Africa. The rich, dark smell of Africa. It was a long time ago, when this happened. I'm telling you about a certain tribe. The man and woman who were the leaders of their tribe, the king and queen, were very wealthy. They were very much in love with each other, and they wanted to give each other children. No child came. They didn't know whether it was his seed or her seas that failed them, and they hid their disappointment from each other. He would go alone along the sandy tracks that took him up the pointed mountain, and he would look down on the plains and valleys where his people lived, and there would be a kind of loneliness, you know, an emptiness. And she would follow the river down to the swamps. She would sit hidden in the rushes and she would be heavy with sadness.

'Then one day she knew that there was a child inside her. Imagine this joy! When her time came at last all the people of the tribe came to wish her well, and the elder women stayed with her. But it was terrible news that they had to take to their king. He was praying in the mountains, and they came to him and told him, "Your wife has given birth to an egg." He came hurrying to see, despair and disbelief in his heart. When he saw that it was true he had the egg taken away and smashed.

'She found it the next day. She saw a hyena crouching over it. In the far trees she heard the shriek of a jackass's laughter. It happened again and again. Every time, the king made the servants smash the egg. He wouldn't even come to look at it. His wife would go down and find the fragments of shell, sucked clean in the night, and she would grieve over it.

'Next time, she thought at last, I'll make him let me keep it. So, because he loved her, he let her keep it, but he wouldn't look at it himself. Day after day in the mud hut that was her own she nursed the egg. She felt it growing warm in her lap, and she knew then that there was a live thing inside it after all. Then the day came when the shell began to splinter. Cracks appeared on it like threads of maize hair. Calm inside herself, she cradled the egg in both her hands and watched it open out. A long body oozed out of it. It was the body of a snake.

'She went to her husband then, and told him, and in rage and horror he went to kill it. She pulled him away. With all her woman's strength she dragged him away. "He's our child," she said. "He must live. And besides, a snake is a holy thing."

'Every day she nursed the snake in her hut, and she grew to love him. When he grew to full size he was a beautiful, jewelled serpent. He asked for a wife. So, heavy in her heart, she went in search of a wife for him. None of the women she came across would have been right for him. Far away from home she came across a valley that was like her own, with green swamps and purple mountains. Here a young woman was being courted by the sons of many tribe leaders. They brought all kinds of cattle and riches with them. She went into the hut where the young woman sat and knew as soon as she saw her that she wanted her to marry her son and to come and live with them. This is the way women love each other. As soon as the young woman saw her, she loved her as a daughter loves a mother.

'"I'd like you to marry my son." The girl agreed at once. They set off together burdened with wedding gifts and as they walked the two women talked and laughed, enjoying each other's company. In the dark they slept close to each other near the fire, listening to the night prowl of lions, and it was at these times that the queen worried deep inside herself, knowing what she was going to have to tell the girl.

'She waited till they were in sight of her own village. The tribespeople had all gathered to wait for her, and when they saw how young and beautiful the bride was they turned to each other with knowing looks. The king was too ashamed to greet her. Dread slowed down the queen's footsteps. At last she turned to the girl and told her the truth. They put their arms around each other and wept. They couldn't help it.

'The next day she was married to the snake. She went into the hut where he had spent his life, and rushes were piled around the entrance. The people didn't sing their wedding chant; they had no heart for it. They sat in silence around the hut and waited for the young woman to come out again. At last the dark came and the frogs started to sing and the fireflies were like sparks from a flame. The people slept and woke again, slept and woke again. They left food at the entrance of the hut for her but she didn't come for it. It became dark again. The frogs started to sing and the fireflies sparked. The maize crinkled as the beasts of the night came down from the mountains and returned again. The villagers woke, and saw that the rushes were being moved to one side.

'Out came the girl, and she was lovely and smiling. At her side was a tall young man. They went straight to the king and queen and asked permission to build for themselves a big hut from the red earth, where they could live in joy and raise a family.'

'But what happened to the snake?' Rose asked.

'Oh, but you know, Rose.'

'The queen goes into the hut,' Rose suggested. 'And there she finds the skin of the snake.'

'Exactly. It's a flimsy thing. Like a scarf.'

'Helena,' said Rose unexpectedly, 'I want Gordon's baby.'

'Of course you do. I wanted Paedric's child, once,' said Helena. She blew out the candles. 'You have to tempt him, Rose.'

Bewildered, Rose opened the door. Paedric followed her downstairs, tying back his hair. Rose made herself turn round to him. He looked tired. She stood in the kitchen, not wanting to leave yet.

'For a moment I almost believed,' she said.

'The only power we have is the power of our imagination.'

'I suppose it is.'

'And I had imagined that Edmund was Gordon's son.'

'He's neither Gordon's son nor mine. But nobody knows that.'

'Nobody will, if there's nobody to tell.'

She went to the door, and looked out at the thrust of the embankment behind Paedric's tree, and the billowing dove-grey sky.

'I hate this place, Paedric. Don't you?'

'I hate this place that I live in, yes.' He touched his face. 'But it's only a shell. Nothing is what it seems to be. That's what I've learned.'

She went back to her house. There was an aching inside herself that she had never known before.

TWENTY

That night Rose amused herself by thinking up ways of 'seducing' Gordon. She could hear him snoring comfortably in his bed upstairs. She could come up with no ideas. In the early hours of the morning she went up to his room. He lay with his fists tucked up to his face, like a child. She crept away again, a little ashamed of herself. After all, she didn't hunger for him. She hungered for William.

'My mother will be really pleased to see you,' she said on Saturday morning. 'If you're back for good, that is. Are you really back?'

'I think so,' he said.

If only he could have touched her then. If only he could have turned round and put his arms around her, as any husband might to his wife.

'Shall we go this morning?'

'Tomorrow,' he said. 'I'd like to fish today. It's Saturday.'

She sighed, impatient with him.

'You can't change your habits, can you Gordon? Not for me. Not even for the child.' He was becoming an old man already, governed by the comfort of ritual. There was no impulse in him, except for the day he had left her. He had only come back because his sister had turned him out. 'All right,' she said. 'Go fishing. I'll come with you.'

He laughed, looking round at her with fondness.

'Why not, Gordon? It's a lovely day. There's nothing else for me to do.'

'You'll be bored, that's all.'

'I'm bored in the house. I've been alone here too long. I

want to be with you.'

The day had become glorious. It was late May. She wore a new pink two-piece that she'd made, and white sandals. She knew she looked good in them. Gordon went ahead of her along the river bank, nodding to the men already fishing there. She wondered if he felt proud to have her with him. He chose a jutting tree stump and laid his pieces of fishing tackle round him. She'd never really looked at it properly; it was a mysterious part of him that she had never wanted to enter, like his obsession with trains, like his job. She opened a tin and found it was writhing with maggots. He laughed across at her as she jammed it shut.

'What on earth are they for?'

'Bait.'

'Where d'you keep them?'

'Our shed. I'm surprised you've not seen them, Rose. Edmund finds them fascinating.'

'You've never let him play with maggots!'

Gordon took the tin from her and opened it up. She remembered now how the hair on his wrists used to excite her.

'I don't know how you can do that,' she said. 'Sticking your hand in the tin like that.'

'Some of the lads hold them in their mouths,' he told her.

'Only a man,' she said, 'could do a thing like that.'

Gordon cast his line so it landed with a slight plop on the water, and rings spun out from it. He leaned back against the stump, tilting up his head, closing his eyes. Insects jingled in the undergrowth. As the water settled again, water-boatmen danced on its surface. Rose stretched out her legs and sighed.

'Are you bored, love?'

'No. I'm not bored. I'm enjoying myself.'

He opened one eye and smiled at her. 'Well, you look bored.'

The sun was warm on her. She held up her face to it, like a child anticipating kisses. Next time he asks me if I'm bored, she thought, I'll go for a walk. She fanned herself gently with a leaf, enjoying the stroke of air on her cheek.

'It could be a long wait,' came Gordon's voice, sleepy.

'All right.' She didn't mind. She stood up, brushing leaves and twigs from her skirt. 'I'll go for a bit of a walk,' she said.

He nodded, shifting his position slightly. She wandered along the river bank, away from all the men. After a time the path became overgrown and twisted with the river right away from the road. The men were out of sight now. She could hear the distant rush of cars on the road, and then silence; wind ruffling the trees and grasses, a bird chanting steadily behind her, the plash of water, the odd cough from the men round the bank, a car again; and again, silence.

She stood still. The flesh-warm air was like a caress on her skin. She stooped down and undid her sandals and put them up on the path behind her, with her handbag. Then she pulled down her stockings and took them off. The water was so cold that her ankles were gripped tight with pain. She stood at the edge, a little unsteady, waiting for her feet to get used to it. The song of the grasshoppers and the chanting of that bird behind her seemed to bear down on her, touching her senses as though they were nerve-ends, taut, to be beguiled and stroked, like the strings of a harp. She saw how the water was reflected back on the tree trunks that bent down from the other bank; how light danced, fluid, on the solid geometry of the branches. She saw threads like fine silk stretching from branch to branch and leaf to leaf, blade to blade of grass. A dragonfly hovered like a blue-green flame. She seemed to hear how it moved the air.

It was in a kind of ecstasy that she stripped herself then of all her clothes and placed them behind her on the bank. She stood in the water, throbbing with excitement and fear and with a strange kind of exultation that she had never known before. Never in her life had she done anything like this. She waded into the water, wanting to scream aloud with the pain and cold of it on her groin and her belly, wanting to faint with excitement. She watched her reflection as her breasts met with their image, and then she brought up her arms and began to swim. She closed her eyes and headed towards the bend, her face tilted up from the water. Was this what giving birth was like, she wondered; a swimming away from one's other body?

And then she swam round the loop of the river to where Gordon was sitting. She clambered out of the water to him, laughing at his surprise, her hair loose in long wet strands across her body, a mermaid rising from the sea, laughing and holding out her arms to him.

But she did not do this. For a moment a cloud closed over the sun. A dog barked.

Rose turned on to her back before she ever reached the loop of the river and kicked rapidly back to the bank, rubbed herself quickly with her underskirt and pushed it into her bag. Then she dressed, brushed her hair, and put her make-up right in her little mirror. The sun soon dried her hair. She fastened it back again, the way he liked to see it. Then she did up her sandals and went back up the path to Gordon.

TWENTY-ONE

'And he was asleep, of course! You triumphed over him, Rose. What a fish he would have caught! What a magic fish!'

Rose had needed to tell her story to Helena. As soon as Gordon went to the village that afternoon she went to Paedric's house. She hesitated, not expecting to see him in his kitchen. Already she always imagined him now in his candle room, with his hair loose and his long fingers playing with the strands of his scarf. She sat awkwardly while he started to make coffee for her.

'I've really come to see Helena,' she said. It seemed very natural then, just as though Edmund had said to her, 'Let's play that game now.'

She followed him upstairs, and told her story of the river straight away, even laughing a little as she retold her fantasy. She had stopped being afraid of Helena, she realized. So when Helena, for all the world Helena, said, 'Can I tell you, now, the story of how I told Paedric I wanted his child?' she said yes, she wanted to hear it. She was reminded then of sharing Barbara's bed, and of whispering secrets into the dark.

'I had to wait for the right moment, just as you must. The chance came like a magic sign, the way the jar of snakes had been a magic sign. It seemed to exist not just for itself but as a kind of signal. When it happens you can only wonder at it, for what it is, and afterwards you think, yes, that's why I did what I did just then, at that moment in my life.'

'So this really happened,' said Rose.

'We were in the north of England, and it was winter. It

was a stricken north, and we were in a house that smelled of woodsmoke and mice. The fields were dead, the earth was dead. There seemed to be a hiatus in the natural rhythm of things. We talked about petrifactions and hauntings. The north is haunted by itself – it has its black coffin dogs and its boggarts, its will-o'-the-wisps that lead travellers astray, its witches and giants. Whether you believe in them or not, they're there. That's the thing.'

Outside, Rose could hear Gordon's familiar, repetitive whistle. He had come straight back. He would be looking for her now.

'So there was a kind of enchantment, but the earth was barren. It was not the kind of enchantment that creates energy and flight: it was the enchantment of sleeping princes in underground caverns, a waiting for the green man kind of enchantment.'

'Sleeping Beauty,' said Rose. The door to her house opened and closed. She was aware of Gordon going up to his room.

'And Paedric and I had quarrelled. I can't even remember what it was about now, and yet the fact that we had quarrelled is significant in this story. You know how weary you feel after quarrelling with a lover; sapped. I was glad he had gone out and yet I was bereft, at that moment, without him. I went to look out of the window and I saw what appeared to be smoke gushing from a tree. I went down to the kitchen to prepare food. I had it in my mind that when Paedric came back I would have the house smelling of garlic and lemons, and that after we had eaten we would make love and we would forget about our quarrel. When he came back in I pretended not to hear him. That's what we do.'

'Rose? Are you there?' She could just make out Gordon's voice from next door. It was like the tension of a fine strand.

'And Paedric called out to me, "Helena. Come out and look! There's a tree on fire!"'

Rose relaxed again. The house sounds began to swim away from her.

'I had to run to catch up with him. He wasn't ready to forgive me yet, I realized. By the time we reached the tree it was blazing properly, smoke gushing from its hollow centre. It seemed to be full of window-holes and chimneys, and as we watched the flames found their freedom and leapt up through them. There was a chattering inside, bickering goblin noises. The heat from it was intense. We stood in silence watching it, as separate from each other as we'd ever been. He had his hands deep in his pockets. I had mine clasped in front of me. "You look as if you're praying," he said to me. "Do I?" He put his arm across my shoulders and we walked back to the house, but it was not a companionable silence and I didn't feel at ease with him then. The meal wasn't at all as I'd planned it. I'd lost my appetite, anyway. It annoyed me to see him eating so doggedly. "Nice," he said, when he pushed the plate away at last. "No it wasn't," I said. "The sauce was like cat's pee." "That's how I like it." When I laughed he reached across and took my hand in his. "So," he said. "What's it all about?" And that's when I told him. That's when I knew what the quarrel, whatever it seemed to be, was really about. I want a baby. It was such an easy thing to say, after all. I could still hear the whispering of the tree flames in my head, jittering there.

'He spread out his hands. "When do you want to start? Tonight?" "Tonight would be out of the question." "Why would tonight be out of the question?" His voice was a little mocking, a little anxious. "Because I'm not in love with you tonight, Paedric."

'Paedric read for a little, and I went on up to bed. He

didn't look at me as I went past him to the stairs. When I went to my window I saw that the tree was still burning. I felt a kind of shame for forgetting about it, such a mysterious thing. It glowed in the darkness like a tree cast in bronze, putting out the light of the stars. "Isn't that beautiful?" I asked Paedric when he came up. "An enchanted tree." "We'll go down to it if you like," he said.

'The heat was intense. It gave out little glowing pulses. White flakes trembled away from it like moths. I wondered that it could still stand. I think if we had breathed on it it would have fallen. I held out my hands to it, watching how they glowed. "Shall we go to bed?" Paedric asked me then. "You go," I said, perverse as ever. "We could make love." But I shook my head. It was not the right moment.

'When I was cold I followed him back to the house, but I didn't go up to the room. I couldn't sleep for the images of the tree, its arms spread wide, brazen in the night. The next day it still stood, a white tree of ash, still somehow holding itself up, its heart of flame glowing. I couldn't leave it. Like a child I stayed with it, guarding it. Again through the night I watched it. There was still heat from it. I kept going down to watch its last glow. "Don't die," I kept urging it. The day was so cold that our breaths smoked together, mine and the tree's. "It won't last much longer," Paedric told me. He kept going away and coming back. He couldn't stay through my vigil, yet he couldn't leave me alone with it.

'When I went up to the house to eat he'd made bread for me. We had it with wine. It was a communion. He was in love with me, I knew it. I was beginning to be in love with him again. Yet I couldn't leave my tree.

'"Can you see it?" I said, gazing through our window. "It won't last long now," he said. "Come to bed." He didn't understand me. How could he understand me? I hardly knew myself what was happening. He turned away from me and for a long time I lay in the dark listening as his breathing deepened into sleep. I pulled a blanket round myself and squatted by the window. From across the fields a half-imagined glow told me that my tree was still alive.

'I was brought awake in the early morning by the cold of the window-pane pressing down on my forehead. I opened my eyes to see white ashes drifting in the air outside. It was as if my tree was spreading itself across the earth. I ran outside, and only then did I realize that it was not ashes I was seeing but tiny flakes of snow. I ran to the tree. The snow's stealth spread across the ash-pile, making it shudder and sink down. A slow spiral of smoke rose up from it. Ash upon ash, ice upon embers.

'I wanted Paedric to know. I ran back to the house, my feet skidding away from me, my face turned up to the ashes of snow. He was still asleep. I stripped off my clothes; I was cold to the bone. I ran my hands over his body, rousing him, and as he opened his eyes I levered myself up till I was straddling him. There was snow in his hair and his eyelashes. I wanted him.'

TWENTY-TWO

They were both startled by Gordon's voice. He had tapped on the door, unheard, and finding it unlocked, had come in. Now he stood at the bottom of the stairs and called up, 'Paedric? Are you there?'

Rose blushed as if she had been caught out in an act of mischief. She ran downstairs to him.

'Rose?' He was bewildered.

Rose was confused herself at her own dismay and guilt. 'I was talking to Paedric about Helena,' she said.

They had reached their own door before he spoke to her again. 'I didn't expect to see you there. I couldn't think where you were, Rose. I just wanted to ask him if he'd seen you coming back.'

'Well, you found me, so it's all right.'

'I don't like him. He's peculiar.'

Rose let him sulk. Anything she said would confound her in guilt. Gordon told her he had abandoned his fishing because he suddenly felt he wanted to be with her and to go for Edmund after all. They left immediately for the train. She walked a little behind him, not able and not willing to catch up with him. She felt she was being towed along by his anger.

Edmund had grown leggier, and had lost some baby teeth. He was resentful with them for leaving him so long, and at first refused to talk to them. He played in her mother's garden while the three adults sat and watched.

'He's going to be a big man,' Mrs Waterhouse said. 'Though his father wasn't big, was he, Rose?'

'Not at all,' said Rose quickly. 'William was a slight man.' Her mother had never referred to him in front of Gordon before.

'Does the boy know . . . ?'

'I don't think it would do him any good to know,' said Gordon. 'He thinks he's my son. I'd like to leave it like that.'

Rose said nothing. She could see nothing of William in the boy. Now that his face had lost its babyness he no longer had that look of William around his eyes. If anything he resembled Gordon. He had adopted many of the man's mannerisms: the downward cast of his head when he was thinking, his listening way of watching people, even the tuneless, repetitive whistle.

'And goodness me, you're not big, Rose! You'd blow away in a wind!' her mother said.

'I don't know where he gets his build from.'

'But your father was a big man, don't forget.'

Rose stood up quickly and ran over to Edmund, joining his game by kicking a ball through a makeshift croquet course. She looked back at her mother and Gordon talking pleasantly together, white heads bent forward. 'I wish he'd go to her,' she thought. 'Then he could truly think of me as his daughter.' The fancy did not displease her.

On the way back home they had to change stations in town. Gordon and Edmund walked ahead of her, hand in hand. She lingered behind and paused to look at a theatre hoarding advertising oncoming shows. At the end of the season there was to be a variety show. One of the artistes was William. She was astonished at the pleasure and dread she felt at the sight of his photograph. It showed him with one foot resting back, a cane supporting one outstretched arm, a top-hat in the other. His face was in profile. It was a young, good-looking face still. 'William Tip-Tap' she read. She reached up and touched the face with the tips of her fingers.

She caught sight of Gordon and Edmund waiting for her on the other side of the road and ran across to them. 'Edmund!' she shouted. 'Race Daddy!' She caught his hand in her own and ran with him ahead of Gordon till the child shouted to her to stop. Panting and laughing, she picked him up, swinging him round and round in her arms until Gordon caught up with them.

'Happy?' he asked her.

'Yes! Yes! I'm happy to have my family back with me again!' she laughed. 'It's been a wonderful day today.'

That night, when Gordon was putting Edmund to bed, Rose combed a little perfume through her hair and changed her blouse. She opened the window so the curtain shifted in whispers. She looked at herself in the mirror over the fireplace and decided the blouse was too sedate. She undid the top two buttons and folded back the collar. She undid the third and loosened her hair.

When Gordon came down she was half-lying on the bed, pretending to read. She held out her hand to him.

'He wanted the magic fish story,' he said. 'But I don't know it, so I read him Rupert instead. I love Rupert.'

She smiled. 'He's pleased you're back,' she said. 'And so am I. You don't know how much I've missed you.'

'I've missed you.'

She kissed his hand, his little, bent finger, the palm of his hand, the veined back, the hairs that curled from under the cuff of his shirt.

'I love you,' she said.

'I love you,' he told her, instantly, without moving.

She unbuttoned the cuff of his sleeve, rolling her finger along the hairs of his arm. 'I wish,' she said, searching for the right arrangement of words, the right tone, 'that you would let me come to your bed tonight.'

She watched his silence. He was a fish that would not bite.

'It wouldn't be right,' Gordon said at last.

She sat up, exasperated and humiliated by him. 'Then you don't really love me.' Yet she knew it was William she was yearning for. She pushed Gordon's arm away and went outside.

The air was soft. The stars were just out. All the lights were on now in the Merlins' house. She could hear the chatter of their radio, their silly tittering. She saw the light going on in Gordon's room, his curtains being pulled to. Across the fields she could hear the barking of a fox.

Then she heard Paedric's voice, and his door being opened. He came out into his garden, a mug of tea in his hand. He was not aware of her. He stood as she had done, breathing the silence, tuning his senses to the night.

'Paedric!' she called to him softly. He pushed his way through a gap in the bushes and came over to her. He squatted by the pond, nursing his mug in his hands.

'I see you have your family back,' he said. 'Your little world is whole again.'

Again she was aware of the resonance in his voice, the rich singer's quality.

'It's good to have them back,' she said softly, knowing how their voices would carry.

'Is it?' He sipped his tea. His breath spiralled from him. 'Marriage is such a stultifying thing. It's like a thief, snatching away from you your real self.'

'I don't think mine is a proper family,' she said.

'What is a proper family? Who knows what goes on behind all those closed doors and windows over that embankment there? What goes on in your locked heart, Rose, when you say yours isn't a proper family?'

'I don't know.' Gordon's light flicked off. The garden was

in darkness now. The stars took on their own light. 'Paedric. Did Helena have your baby?'

Far away on the line a train was gathering itself for the long haul. This late express never stopped at the local station, but thundered past the terrace, rocking the houses, taking them with it for its brief second. Just before it reached them Paedric stood up and tipped the dregs of his mug into the pond. He turned to watch the train, drawn away from her, and when its full roar came he went back to his own house, as if he had forgotten who she was.

TWENTY-THREE

When Edmund came down the next morning he pushed open the door to her room before she was fully awake and ran straight in. He stopped, confused, seeing the bed there and Rose still in it.

'I thought you'd gone away!' he said. 'I looked in your room and you weren't there, and I thought you'd gone away.'

'With my bed tucked underneath my arm!' she laughed. She reached out for her dressing-gown and sat up, pulling it around herself. 'I just decided to sleep in this room for a change, and Paedric helped me to carry my bed down. Don't you like my new room?'

'It's all right.' He gazed round it, taking in her displayed treasures. 'It's an upside-down house now.'

'It would be if we had the kitchen upstairs,' she agreed.

'And the bathroom downstairs. Can we, Mummy? Can I ask Daddy to bring the bath downstairs?'

'No, silly.' She slid out of bed and hugged him. Her breasts were soft against him underneath her gown. 'Don't wriggle away from me. You're not so big now you can't have a cuddle, are you?'

'Your things hurt,' he protested, arching his back away from her. 'Your spiky big things. Why are they so big?'

She released him and he wandered round the room, picking up the bits and pieces that she'd put on display on the mantelpiece and the shelves. He ran his finger round the frame of William's photograph and then turned away from it, crouching to open and close the roof of a little wooden chalet, a musical cigarette box that played 'Greensleeves'.

'Who's that man?' he asked. A thread of saliva dribbled from his mouth as he bent over the chalet snapping open and shut its roof.

'Don't now, you'll break it. My brother Desmond gave me that when I was your age. I've had it sixteen years and it's never been broken. I don't want it breaking now, Edmund.'

'Is that man Desmond?'

'No.' She stood up and rummaged in some drawers for her underclothes, which she pulled on underneath her gown, her back to the boy. 'He's a friend of mine. He's a dancer.'

'Pooh,' said Edmund. 'I don't like dancing.'

'I know you don't. But it's not the sort of dancing you do at school. He makes his feet sound like little drums, tip-a-tap, tip-a-tap. He wears shiny bright shoes. You'd love them! And they go pitter, patter, pitter, patter, they're never still for a minute. You should just see him!'

Edmund laughed with her, trying to imitate in his stock-inged feet the sounds she was making, exaggerating the rapid foot movements until he made himself fall over. He squealed with laughter.

'Don't be silly. He dances on the stage, in a big theatre in town. I thought I might take you to see him, Edmund.'

'Would Daddy come?'

'I don't suppose Daddy would like that sort of thing.' Rose frowned.

'But we can ask him, can't we?'

Gordon didn't want any of them to go to the show, but Rose told him she was taking Edmund, and he had to agree. She didn't tell him about William. If he picked up the boy's references to him, he said nothing. Rose and Edmund talked about the coming show for weeks, delighting in their shared excitement at the thought of going. She bought a dance record and together she and Edmund improvised steps in the kitchen. At first it amused Gordon to watch them, and he would whistle along to the music and tap his fingers on the table-top. After a time it annoyed him, and he would bring out things to do, deliberately, Rose thought, to tempt Edmund away from her. His main interest now was in wood-carving, particularly since he had come back to them. He kept the tools, which had been his father's, in a little rolled-up green felt pouch. Each tool had its own pocket. Edmund wasn't allowed to touch them, but when Gordon brought them out he would stop whatever he was doing and go to stand behind him at the table, watching the carved figures peel out of the wood. The shavings of naked wood were like curved shells. Edmund would gather them up or catch them before they fell, and nurse them in his palm. He loved to smell them.

Gordon took to bringing out his carving tools as soon as the dance records went on, and Edmund would run to watch him.

'Come on Edmund! Dance with me!' Rose laughed, catching him by the hand and pulling him away from Gordon. 'Don't you love to dance now!'

When it came to the night of the show, Edmund was far more interested in the theatre itself than in what was happening on stage. He was amazed that there were so many people there. He spent much of the performance wriggling round in his seat, trying to kneel up on it so he could see over the heads of the people sitting behind him.

'For goodness' sake!' Rose hissed. She was tense with the thought of seeing William again. 'I wish I hadn't brought you now!' She knew she would never have found the courage to come on her own. 'Little boys half your age are behaving better than you! Look! Tip-Tap's next!'

Edmund sat still. He glanced at Rose. She took his sticky

hand and held it in both her own, but she didn't return his look. Her eyes were fixed on the stage. He heard what sounded to him like the clopping of horses' hooves; a drumming, insistent, exciting sound. Rose squeezed his hand and smiled.

And on swaggered William with a team of beautiful long-legged girls, all stepping high. The girls didn't do much dancing but draped themselves round the stage, smiling widely and showing off their thighs. William tapped his way from one to the other of them, and each in turn flirted with him. Rose couldn't take her eyes off him. She thought she had never seen him dance so well. She burned with pride for him. He was a beautiful, dragonfly creature. She knew she was in love with him all over again.

When his act was finished she had no heart for the rest of the show. Edmund wriggled in his seat again and she did nothing to restrain him until the woman behind tapped on her shoulder and suggested she should leave. Rose wondered whether William would be appearing again.

'If you behave yourself, I'll take you backstage to meet the tap-dancer,' she whispered to Edmund. 'Would you like that?'

'No,' he said.

All the same, they went. Rose had half-promised herself that she would, and then had told herself that she would not. Now she knew that she couldn't leave town without speaking to William again. It might be her last chance. Besides, she wanted him to see Edmund.

When they came out of the theatre it was raining. The air was bobbing with black umbrellas, all gleaming under the streetlamps. People were hurrying past to their homes, and Edmund clicked his tongue in imitation of the sound of their hurrying feet. He had never been out this late before, and he was unused to town crowds. He stumbled along at Rose's side, wide-eyed with tiredness and thrill.

'Can we see William Tyrone?' Rose asked the man at the stage-door. Nervousness caught her throat and made her husky.

'Tip-Tap Tyrone!' Edmund shouted.

'He's gone,' the doorman said. 'Left an hour ago.'

Rose was deeply disappointed now.

'He a friend of yours?'

'Yes, he is.'

'Well, that's what they all say, but I'll believe you.' The man laughed. 'He's in theatre lodgings down the next street. I'll write it down for you. But don't tell him I sent you. They all want to speak to Tip-Tap.'

He scribbled an address down and gave it to Rose, and passed a wine gum down to Edmund. 'And don't get drunk!' he warned him.

Rose wasn't sure what to do now. The last train would leave in just over half an hour. As it was, they were late. Gordon had asked them to try to leave the show early and catch an earlier train.

'Should we go straight to the station, do you think?' she asked Edmund.

'I want to see Tip-Tap.' His voice was croaking with tiredness.

'Come on then!' Rose agreed. 'Just for five minutes!' They began to run, laughing as they splashed through puddles. 'He might be a bit funny with you,' Rose said, just outside the house. She crouched down, smoothing Edmund's hair, dabbing rain off his cheeks. His face was white and his eyes huge and dark. She hugged him. 'He knew you when you were a baby. He won't expect to see such a big boy.'

She pushed open the door, and began to climb up the stairs.

TWENTY-FOUR

'Here you are, Mother. The cup of tea you've been waiting for.'

Rose hauled herself out of her sleep and struggled to sit up. She blinked as Edmund switched on the light.

'What time d'you call this?'

'I call it six o'clock, Princess. What time do you call it?'

She sank back on to her pillow. 'Is that all?'

Edmund put the tray down on her bedside table. It was more cluttered than usual. She had moved things from the mantelpiece during the night. He picked up a photograph in a silver frame and blew the talcum powder off it. He held it out at arm's length.

'I remember you taking me to see him.'

'Do you?'

'What did they call him now? Tap. Tip-Tap. That was it.'

'His name was William.'

'That was it. William. Tip-Tap Tyrone.'

'How old were you then?'

'I don't know. Six or seven maybe.'

'You don't remember that.'

'I do. We had to climb a lot of stairs. You laughed a lot. You wouldn't stop laughing. And then you cried. I remember it very well.'

He replaced the photograph, and there he was, a tired child clutching her hand, excited and bewildered by her animation. The wallpaper was greasy, he remembered. The man at the top of the stairs was laughing down at them, holding out his arms to them as they came up. He looked smaller than he had done on stage. His eyes were dark and wet and laughing, his mouth open and noisy like a dog's. Rose sat down on the stairs, too weak with laughter herself to carry on. Edmund had nearly fallen. He clung on to her hand, beginning to cry. She wasn't looking at him. She was looking up at the man, at his shiny, laughing face, at his eyes that were like bubbles of rain. And then a woman in a brown petticoat with straps slipping down her arms and her pink legs bare had come out of the room at the top of the stairs and put her arms around the tap-dancer's neck and nibbled his cheek. She shouted down at them, shouted and shouted into screams until Edmund and Rose had half-tumbled down the stairs and out into the streaming rain.

'It was the day Paedric went away again,' said Rose, her eyes half-shut.

'Was it, Princess? I don't remember that.'

'No. You wouldn't remember that. It was all a long time ago.'

'It was.' She looked old and tired today, he noticed. Old before her time. 'You stay in bed today,' he told her, his voice soothing. 'You've had a rough night.'

'I ought to get about more. You spoil me, Edmund. You treat me like an old lady. But I'm not.'

'No, you're not. You're the princess in the tower.'

'I thought I might go round to see Paedric today.' She smiled up at him.

'No, you don't. You know how it upsets you.'

Edmund opened her window a little and came over to kiss her. She lifted up her face to him like a child.

'Edmund, is he well?' she asked.

'He is. He's quite well. I'd tell you if he wasn't.'

'Would you ask him to come and see me?'

'No.' He went out of her room, closing the door behind him.

'How's Molly?' she called.

'Molly?' He put his shoes on, picked up his mac and checked that his gloves were in the pocket. 'Molly died, Mother. Twenty-five years ago.'

When the front door closed Rose opened her mouth in a silent cry of grief, but the grief was not for the dead girl Molly, because she had never met her, if she had ever existed. The grief was for her dead self, for the ghost of thirty years or so. 'Oh, the ghost of myself is old,' she thought. 'But I am not an old woman, whatever he says. He has locked me in a tower of darkness.' She swung her legs out of the bed and looked down at them. 'I am not old. These are not the legs of an old woman. Somebody stole my youth away from me, a long time ago, and they never gave it back. Do you hear that, Paedric?' she shouted. 'Are you listening, you old sorcerer?'

She picked up William's photograph and turned it face downwards on her table.

TWENTY-FIVE

By the time Rose and Edmund arrived home from the show it was nearly midnight. Gordon met them at the station, angry with Rose for keeping the boy out so late. He carried Edmund home on his shoulders, the child's head slumped against his own. Rose walked just behind him, too full of grief to speak. She would drive William out of her mind. Gordon didn't ask whether they had enjoyed the show. He took Edmund straight up to bed, saying on the way up the stairs, 'Your friend's gone, by the way.'

'My friend?' She went dull inside herself.

'He brought the key here this evening.'

'He's gone? How long for?'

'Who knows, with Paedric?'

Rose undid her hair so that it fell in damp strands around her face. She took off her wet coat and draped it over the back of a chair near the fire. She crouched down, trying to coax life from the white embers, blowing into them. She was too tired to go to bed. The ashes yielded nothing. She went to her room at last. The rain ran in folds down her window. She could hear it tipping down the chimney, spitting on to the hearth. She imagined the house next door, a hollow, empty place full of shadows.

Next day she kept to her bed, and the next, feigning sickness. When Edmund came in to ask her to take him to school she lumbered out of bed towards him, her breasts loose and swinging under her opened nightdress, alarming him. 'God,' she said, 'is it day again? Another bloody day?' He backed away from her embrace and ran to Gordon. He loved his father best.

At last word came from Paedric. It was a postcard, not signed or even properly addressed, and had gone astray on its journey. On one side was a picture of the mountains of Tibet, the Himalayas: Lhotse, Everest, Makalu, Chomolonzo, the white ghostly line of them set into a holiday blue sky. On the other were the scrawled words, 'The power of rocks elevates my soul.' Gordon turned the card over, puzzled by it.

'It can't be for us,' he said.

Rose said nothing. She took the postcard into her room, exploring Paedric's fine, untidy writing.

'I should like to see some mountains,' she told Gordon later that day. He had come out to her when she was working in the garden. He watched her as she struggled to uproot a sprawling bramble patch.

'We're a long way from mountains here,' he said. 'The nearest we've got to them is the place I took you to before we were married. Don't you remember?'

'I do remember.'

'And you didn't like it there.'

'It was the caverns I didn't like. Being smothered in that darkness. That's what I hated. But I loved the hills. Can't we go back?'

'Tomorrow, if you like,' he told her. 'I'm fishing today.'

But the whim had gone, as soon as it had come. She knew it would spoil everything to go to the mountains with Gordon. He was rooted to the earth.

'Do you remember that story?' she asked him.

'No,' he said firmly. He took from her the spade she had been working with and drove it into the soil, easing it back and shaking free the strands of root.

She leaned back against the house wall, her arms folded behind her head, looking up at the sky. The clouds reminded her of rocks tumbling away from each other, being born out of each other.

'The story of the sleeping giantess, and the lonely giant.'

'No,' said Gordon. 'I don't remember that story.'

She moved away from the wall and spiralled in a slow, full circle, her arms spread wide, her head tilted back. Above her she could see the canopy of Paedric's tree, with its leaves already unfurling from the buds.

'Come back,' she whispered. 'Wherever you are, come back!'

That night when Gordon had gone to bed Rose found a writing pad and a pen. She was not at all tired. She felt nervous and excited. She lit the fire because the evening had grown cold, and sat on the rug with her pen poised in her hand.

'Dear Helena,' she began. 'Once upon a time.' The house creaked. The night wind moaned like a breath in the chimney's throat. 'There was a beautiful woman, a giantess.' She read aloud as she wrote, imagining the sound of Helena's voice and the vocabulary she used. 'For thousands of years she slept, and the wind made soft sounds around her hair, the birds flew over her. Sleeping near her was a giant. And he too was alone. His limbs were like rocks. His flesh was as brown as the earth. One day the giant awoke. He heard for the first time the sobbing the giantess always made in her sleep, like the moaning of the wind. He rose up out of the earth, and boulders thundered away from him. He saw the giantess and he fell in love with her. When she awoke her eyes were as blue as the sky. Her breasts and her belly were like small hills. Her forest places were mysterious. She opened out her arms to him and he came down to her. She spread apart her thighs to him and he entered her. And there was never such gentle loving, such rising of sap and rivers, such flowing of air and limbs.'

Rose read through what she had written. She had never done anything like it before. She felt disturbed by it. She went out of her room and stood in the hallway, wanting for a moment to take the story up to Gordon and read it to him. From where she was standing she could hear his heavy breathing and the quick, lighter sighs that Edmund made.

'I have no husband,' she said aloud. 'I have no child.'

She went on out through the kitchen and into the garden. She was cold, but she was unwilling to go back into the house, into its breathing web. She remembered the time she and Paedric had sat out late like this. He had betrayed her friendship in the same way as Gordon had betrayed her marriage. The moon drew the clouds over itself and shook them away again as if they were garments. Her small pond took on the reflection like a winking eye, a knowing, secretive, lunatic thing. Her tininess appalled and frightened her. She felt as if her substance had slipped through her shadow, and that she had become nothing; not atoms, not dust, not senselessness, but nothing.

She hurried back into her room and put a small log on to the fire, coaxing up the flames until it was embraced by them. The heat was a benediction. She picked up her pen again.

'The giantess cried out for more, and the giant wanted more. She cried for more than he had to give, and he took more than she had to give. They forgot each other. They tore and wrenched. They bellowed out for more. So loud were their voices that the one could not hear the other. Love fled like a small bird. More! they cried. And more! till he forced himself into her gaping cave so hard and so deep that he ripped her apart.'

The log cracked in the fire and Rose started. She looked

again at what she had written and was ashamed. She could not remember Helena's voice, nor Paedric's.

'The two halves of the giantess rolled away from each other and clung to the earth on either side of her. Boulders rolled down on to her hips and lodged there. They buried her thighs. Huge crags piled up on her sides, layer upon layer. Coarse grasses spread across them, and where she had been lying there was only a long snaking trail. And that became the mountain pass.

'But what became of the giant? He stood up in grief and dread at what he had done, at what they had done together. He touched the sides of the pass but they yielded nothing to him. He stumbled across the earth shedding tears like stones, and at last he returned to look at her again. A weariness like death came over him. He slept at last, and as he slept his spine turned to stone, his limbs to stone, his head to stone. His flesh was hard earth, hard as stone.

'From time to time across the years a memory comes to him through the tiny caverns and rills around his bones, and he shudders in sorrow. And that is why he came to be known as the shivering mountain.

'And from time to time down the long tunnel of the pass there is heard such a wailing, such an unearthly and solitary wailing, that listeners shudder and tell each other that no wind on earth could make that sound.'

Rose folded up the letter and put it into an envelope. She went out immediately, pushed it through the letter flap in Paedric's door, and ran to her room. Then, overcome with weariness, she fell into a long, deep sleep.

TWENTY-SIX

Joan Merlin had three children by now. Soon after she had the third child she became pregnant again. She broadcast this fact proudly to Rose across the gardens, as if she was talking about a new crop of vegetables she had sown and was waiting to harvest. The third baby was an unpleasant, sickly child. She used to wheel him out in the mornings and plant him in the middle of the lawn as though sunshine was the only thing that was needed to make him grow. The other children played around him noisily, and when he grew old enough they carried him round, worrying him and loving him alternately, discarding him when they grew tired of their game. Rose felt sorry for him. Edmund kept well away from all of them. He used to watch them from his bedroom window, his pale face pressed against the glass. Sometimes Pete Merlin would come outside and shout at the boys for the noise they were making, but Joan would come to him, laughing, and tease away his bad mood with kisses. This behaviour fascinated Edmund. He had never seen Rose and Gordon behaving like that. Rose watched them too, and was jealous of their intimacy. Through the months she watched how Joan's belly plumped to fullness.

'It's disgusting, isn't it?' she said to Gordon, wanting a response of any kind to her remark. 'They're little better than animals, producing at this rate.' But Gordon had no thoughts on the matter, it seemed.

One evening Pete knocked on the door. When Rose opened it to him and invited him in she realized it was the first time he had been in the house since the incident with the eel. She was embarrassed, and called Gordon down immediately. Pete stood, big and awkward, his head bowed a little as if he felt himself to be their inferior. Rose despised him for that.

'I've just popped in to tell you that Joanie's had a girl,' he said.

'I'm very pleased for you,' said Rose. Dismay bloomed unbidden.

'Again?' said Gordon, startled. He took so little notice of his neighbours that hardly anything that Rose told him about them registered.

Pete grinned and scratched his head. 'We're fast workers, Mr Doran.'

'Would you like a drink?' Rose asked him.

Pete rubbed his hands together and, unexpectedly, Gordon offered him whisky. The man perched on the edge of the settee, rounding himself over his drink, with his legs apart and his freckled forearms resting along his thighs. He held the glass between his palms, his hands outstretched as if in prayer. It was obvious from the way he drained it back, slack-mouthed, head tilted, that he was more used to drinking beer. Gordon offered him a second.

'Melanie, she wants to call her. Sounds like a fruit to me, but there you are.'

His large pink presence unsettled Rose.

'Are the boys all right on their own?' she asked him.

'They're at Joan's mother's for the week. I'm my own man now, till they come roaring home.'

'A bit of peace and quiet for you,' Rose murmured.

'I'm counting the minutes till they come back. Place is like a morgue without them.' He leaned back, pushing out his legs, fully relaxed now. 'You'll know that yourselves, how it is when the boy's at his grandmother's. Mind you, he's a quiet boy, not like mine. He takes after his dad.'

Gordon refilled his own glass and offered Rose one. She

shook her head. She was hoping the man would leave, but he held out his empty glass.

'Go on, force me,' he said. 'I think I could grow to like this stuff.' He let out his huge laugh and wiped his mouth with the back of his hand. Gordon excused himself and went upstairs with his drink. Rose knew that he would not come down again until Pete had gone. Their neighbour looked set for the night. He loosened his collar and eased himself against the cushions, spreading out his pink flesh. He beamed at Rose, hazy-eyed.

'Wouldn't it be nice for young Edmund to have a brother or sister,' he said. 'Can't be much fun for him, an only child.'

'You may be right,' said Rose. She sat stiff-backed, trying to show him by her unease that she wanted him to leave. She was disturbed by the way he stared at her.

'You're a lovely-looking woman,' he said. 'D'you know that?'

She drew in her breath and looked down at her hands, clenched on her lap.

'Don't get me wrong, like. I'm not being improper.' He laughed in his coarse way. His lips were sloppy and wet. 'It might be the whisky talking. But you are. In that blue. You look very nice.'

She bowed her head. 'I can't think what Gordon's doing, upstairs so long.'

'I hope he knows how lucky he is, that's all. Having a lovely young woman like you for a wife.'

'You're embarrassing me, Mr Merlin.'

'Pete. Now Joanie, she's a wonderful woman. She's a wonderful mother to my children.' He reached for the bottle and filled up his glass. 'And she's got a fabulous smile. Have you noticed? A fabulous smile. But it breaks my heart to see her arms. How fat they've gone. Why is it that when women have babies their arms go so fat?'

'I don't suppose they all do.'

'Joanie's have.' He hiccoughed. 'Don't tell her I said that, Rose. She's a lovely woman. But she's got fat arms. It'd break her heart ...' His eyes filled with tears of melancholy.

'I think perhaps you should go home to bed now,' said Rose. 'It's getting late.'

He drained back his glass like an obedient child and staggered to his feet. 'It's a lonely place, bed,' he told her and sang out in a whining, Country and Western voice, 'I got the empty bed bluehoos.' He allowed himself to be propelled to the door. 'Goodnight, Mr Doran!' he called. 'I want to say goodnight to my host.'

'I'll tell him you've gone,' Rose promised. She opened the door and stood with him on the doorstep. 'Look at this,' she said. 'It's snowing. And we'd never even noticed.'

Pete tilted back his head. 'Great fat white lumps of snow!' he chuckled. 'Like bloody great swans dropping out of the sky. Kids'll love this, when they see it. I'll tell her to call the baby Snowflake. I never did like melons.'

Rose closed the door on him, and then went through the house to the back, to her own quiet garden. The snowflakes whispered down to her in a ceaseless, mothy fluttering. She lifted up her hands to them. The melted flakes trickled in runnels down the inside of her collar, down the blue wrap-round dress that Pete Merlin had told her she looked so lovely in. She undid the belt so it hung loose from her. The shock of the cold splashes on her flesh made her gasp, made her burn warm inside herself.

She went up to Gordon's room. He was lying in bed, his eyes wide open. He didn't turn his head when she came in to him. She stood by his bed, shaking off her dress, laughing as the cold flakes made him cringe. She took off the rest of her clothes and drew back his sheets. She was ice-cold against him. She drew herself down to him and straddled him, stopping his mouth with kisses until neither of them could breathe. Then she felt down and pressed him inside her. He was trembling as much as she was.

'Now,' she urged. 'Now, Gordon. Now.'

TWENTY-SEVEN

The next morning the houses were shrouded in freezing mist. Rose and Edmund walked briskly to school, hand in hand. Their voices were hollow and isolated. She walked back along the farm lane that divided the canal and the river. In the fields the cows were looming shadows, dark bulks that had no reality. One beast lumbered out of the mist towards her. Even with the wall between them she felt alarmed. The cow strolled forward head down towards the gate, where a drift of snow had piled up during the night. Its pink bell of swollen teats swayed. When it reached the snow drift it put down its head and began licking it in a slow, concentrated sort of way, its tongue rasping along it. It seemed to Rose that the cow was not licking the snow but shaping it, as though there was something hidden within it to be discovered in the way that a sculptor discovers form in stone or marble. She half-expected something living to emerge from it, born from the ice and the beast's warm breath. She couldn't take her eyes away from it, and the beast was oblivious to her, and lost in its ponderous and determined licking.

'Rose!' Someone shouted her name from the lane behind her, startling her. A hunched figure loomed out of the grey.

'Paedric! Is that you?' she shouted. She ran towards him. 'Oh Paedric! Welcome home!'

She turned back briefly, wanting to show him, but the cow had lumbered away, and had left behind it only a mess of trampled snow.

In Helena's upstairs room Rose told the story of how she had raped her husband on the night the snow fell.

'And what happened?'

'He pushed me away from him,' said Rose. 'I'll never go to him again. Not like that. I cheapened myself for him. For his child.'

'Edmund is not his child?'

'I told you. He's neither mine nor Gordon's. As a matter of fact I stole him.' After all these years it was such a simple thing to tell. 'I had to take him away from his grandmother. She didn't care. Neither did his father. I had to take him. Anyway, I wanted him. I loved him. Was that such a terrible thing to do?'

'I know of a woman who stole her own son, because she loved him. She lifted him out of the earth, where he was dead and buried. She dug him up in the night and scurried over the fields with his skeleton bumping across her back.'

'Stop it! I wish you wouldn't tell such gruesome tales!'

'I don't see it as gruesome. She must have loved her son a great deal, I think, to have stolen him out of his grave.'

I am in a room with a madman, Rose thought. What am I doing with this man with his scarves and his candles and his woman's voice? She stood up abruptly.

'I don't want to talk this way any more, Paedric.'

He was totally silent. Like the very first time she had come into the room, Rose was afraid.

'I don't mind the stories,' she said. 'I like the stories, Paedric. But this . . . it's daft. It just seems a bit daft to me.'

She went downstairs and stood in the kitchen, over-whelmed with the same kind of sorrow she had felt on the day she had stood with Barbara Gleadall's father in his kitchen and had recognized herself to be a woman. Outside she could hear the grating of rain with sleet in it. The sun through the window was a low-slung, sallow globe tipping behind the embankment. Soon it would be time to go back for Edmund. She was afraid to go without speaking to Paedric. She was afraid that she might never see him again.

She heard movements upstairs. She went to put the kettle on and realized that her hands were shaking. Paedric came into the room behind her. He had taken off the coloured scarf and tied back his hair again.

'That's better now,' said Rose.

'I live in an ugly shell,' he said. 'It won't release me. Nothing will set me free.'

She made a drink for him and set it in front of him. 'I like you,' she said, shy. 'I like you as you are. I missed you when you were away, Paedric.'

He drank his tea, saying nothing to her.

'Thank you for the card you sent me,' she said. 'I still have it.'

'I love mountains. When I touch rocks I feel as if I'm in touch with myself. I don't know if you understand me.'

'Oh, I do!' Rose laughed. 'Once Gordon took me to some mountains, and I felt so free and wild! I wanted to fly!'

'You wrote me a story about mountains.' He indicated the envelope on the table.

'I'd forgotten about that. It was months ago. It's a bit . . . I don't know what came over me that night!'

'I want to ask you something.' He rocked himself off his chair and went over to the window, tracing patterns on the condensation, making jagged runnels. His hands are beautiful, she thought. The dredge of the rain outside was like a beating pulse. 'I want to ask you if you will have a child with me.'

TWENTY-EIGHT

As she ran past the field of cows on the way to Edmund's school Rose went over and over in her head the conversation she had had with Paedric.

'It would be our secret, this child,' he had said into her shocked silence.

'But where would we keep a secret child?'

'In our hearts.'

TWENTY-NINE

The rain had driven away the fog and had melted down the last of the drifted snow. It was a drenching and exhilarating rain, splashing under her feet as she ran, beating against her cheeks and making her gasp. Edmund was cautious about coming away from the shelter of the school porch into it. He peered out at her as she ran up to him. He was worried about getting his feet muddy and his socks spattered. She took his hand and ran with him deliberately through puddles, laughing at his timidity.

'Stop it, Mummy!' he shouted, putting his free hand over her wrist to try to pull himself free of her. 'I don't like rain! I hate it, you know I do!'

'I love it! I love it!' she laughed. She stopped and crouched down to him and cupped his wet face in her hands. 'And I love you, Edmund!'

That evening she and Gordon were like strangers to each other. He was courteous to her, and she was embarrassed. When Edmund was in the bath and Rose was tidying his room Gordon came in to her and stood watching her.

'I suppose we should talk,' he said.

She looked up, surprised.

'About what happened last night.'

At that moment Rose had been so absorbed in her own thoughts that she wasn't sure what Gordon was referring to. Last night, her shame, all seemed a lifetime away. When she remembered she was shocked with herself.

'Look,' she said, 'these lovely drawings of Edmund's!' She stood up to show him. 'He will draw trains though – all the time it's trains!'

Gordon took the picture from her and sat down on the bed. 'Don't you want to talk about it?'

'No,' she said. 'I don't think I do. There's no point any more, is there?'

She didn't want Gordon's bleakness to interfere with her happiness. He could leave her, if he wanted to. She didn't care any more. He couldn't hurt her now. She took his hand and kissed it, then hurried away from him to see to Edmund.

All the time now she was thinking about Paedric's suggestion. His voice haunted her; the words danced in her mind. A child of her own. A secret child. A child of her heart. For the first time she began to love the house and to think of it as her own. She saw it not as a grey shell confining her but as a living membrane which was about to glow and expand. She watched the children next door and enjoyed their vitality. The new baby was brought home from hospital and lay cosseted in its blankets in the winter sunshine. She went round to congratulate Joan and was invited to hold the child. For the first time in her life she held a tiny new-born baby in her arms and felt its frailty and warmth, smelt its particular smell. Edmund was a huge, lumpish thing. He always had been. Unaccountably he resembled her own father with his stocky, firm build, and Gordon in his precise and laboured mannerisms. Much as she loved him he was not a child of her heart, she knew that now. The bond between Gordon and Edmund was unbreakable. She saw their heads bent over board games at the kitchen table and felt for them both a new wave of tenderness. They were both cuckoos in her nest, unwieldy fledglings demanding care. She knew that she could never push either of them out. They were her security. But Paedric was her nourishment, and his vigour would breathe life into her child.

She never went inside his house now. His Helena embarrassed her. She liked to meet him out of doors, where she felt completely at ease with him. She took to listening out for his leaving the house and then she would abandon whatever she was doing, pull on her coat and follow him. He had found odd jobs to do in the area, gardening and walling mostly. 'It keeps my hands busy and my head free,' he told her one day.

'What do you do with your head, when it's free?' she asked him, amused.

'I let all sorts into it. Wild things. I couldn't do a job where the people who paid my wages owned the thoughts in my head, now could I?'

'No, I don't suppose you could. I was thinking I must find a job myself, Paedric. I'd like that.'

'But Gordon doesn't want you to, I suppose?'

'No. He doesn't want me to.'

They reached the canal bridge where they usually parted company.

'And what wild thoughts will your head be busy with today?' she asked him.

'Our child,' he said, not looking at her but at the smooth and nutty water below.

She turned away from him, her face burning.

'It will happen,' he said.

'Tell me what happened to Helena's child.'

He spread out his hands then in a helpless gesture. 'Helena will tell you,' he said, his voice cast high and whimpering.

'Then I won't ask you again,' said Rose. 'Not if you won't tell me yourself.'

She walked away from him, deliberately choosing a long and unfamiliar way home. She walked briskly. As she approached a barn at the end of a farm lane she could hear a kind of popping, as if someone was shooting an airgun in there. She paused, listening. The popping became more of a banging. There was something inside that was desperate to get out. She felt suddenly afraid. She walked on quickly and then looked back as the banging started again. Grey wisps were seeping from the barn. The thudding became frantic. Rose ran up the farm track towards the house, then heard someone on horseback coming from the other direction. She ran back to the lane.

'Do you know who owns that barn?' she shouted to the rider.

'We do,' the woman called back. 'Why?'

'I think it's . . .' Rose began, and a sudden spurt of flame leapt up from the barn behind her.

'My God! The horses!' the woman screamed. She flung herself down from her own horse and looked around, distraught. 'Hold him!' she shouted to Rose, and ran off to the house, screaming, 'The barn! The barn!' A man ran from the house. Before they had reached the massive door of the barn it splintered, kicked down from inside, and through the black billow of smoke reared a horse, nostrils flaring and eyes bulging, and behind it another, stepping high and whinnying in fear, all white rolling eyes and pink fleshy gums, snorting and rearing and stamping, and behind them gushed blue smoke and the intense rush of flame, and at last a third horse billowed through, turned wild with terror. The man and woman ran the horses away past the house to a paddock. Now the barn was a cracking, gushing thing, a spiral of gold and red and black. The man ran into the house and the woman came sobbing to Rose, took the reins from her and led her horse in a wide sweep away from the fire. It shied away, sidestepping with an alarmed clatter of hooves, while the woman urged it on.

With every few steps Rose turned again to watch as the

flames took hold of the bulk of the barn. She could hear their roar, like the sea. In the distance she heard the clamour of fire engines. She climbed the embankment and looked back, and it was as if the whole of the landscape was focused in on this fury with its red core, the whole sky blackened with it, the air burnt raw with it. She saw again the horses rearing out of the smoke and flames.

She dropped down to the terrace. When she opened the door of her house it was like walking into a cave of silence. She found a piece of paper and wrote a note to Paedric.

'I have conceived.'

THIRTY

Through the weeks that followed Rose barely knew how to contain her secret. She was glowing with it, and she knew it made her beautiful. She became more tender and affectionate towards Edmund, though he resisted her embraces and was often alarmed by her excitement. He found comfort in Gordon's steadiness. Gordon was cautious himself of Rose's new laughing mood. He was highly suspicious of her friendship with Paedric. He couldn't understand what she saw in this odd, twisted, shambling man, and yet he felt threatened by him. He took his own comfort from Edmund.

Rose watched and waited for spring. It came to Paedric's garden before her own, fattening to burst the buds on his tree.

'My baby is three months inside me,' she told him.

'You're glowing with it,' he said.

She did feel as if new energy was running through her. She was in love with everybody and everything. Even the Merlins appeared in a new light for her; she loved them because of the way they nourished their babies. She loved the roughness of their children. She watched the mothers at Edmund's school as they handled their younger children in their pushchairs and prams. She was beginning to share their secret, the power of their wisdom.

'I know I said I wouldn't ask again,' she said to Paedric. 'But please tell me about Helena and the baby.'

'Come to my house,' he said. 'Let Helena tell you.'

'I can't.'

'Then I can't give you the story.'

'Gordon hates me to go into your house.'

'It's nothing to do with Gordon, is it? It's to do with you and Helena.'

'I suppose it is,' Rose said. She was too joyful in her secret to be afraid or jealous now. She decided she would go, and waited for the chance when Gordon and Edmund would be away from the house. She didn't have to wait long. Together with Edmund's friend Simon they were constructing a series of model railway stations based on the local network. Every weekend they went by train to a different station to do their research. Gordon had bought Edmund a camera, and Rose supplied them with sketchpads, crayons and a picnic lunch. On this particular day they were to travel to the end of the local line. It was a return journey that would take them most of the day.

'Why don't you come with us?' Gordon suggested to her the evening before.

'I won't, thank you. I've got things to do.'

'What will you be doing?' Edmund asked her, surprised.

'I'm going to see a friend.'

Gordon stopped packing the rucksack. He was immediately suspicious. He knew that she had no friends, though she occasionally mentioned mothers of children at Edmund's school when she was reporting local gossip. Since Joan's new baby had been born she was often round there, gloating over the child. She never lifted it out of the pram but could be seen turning back the covers, peering down at it, letting the baby's small fingers caress her own. Gordon watched her sometimes from the bedroom window, and was made uncomfortable at the sight of her. But she always protested that it was the baby she went to see, and that she couldn't stand Joan.

'Who?' he asked.

'I told you. A friend.' Rose smiled at Gordon. He was

angry with her happiness these days. She knew that. He didn't understand it, and it excluded him.

'Paedric?' he asked.

She shook her head, still smiling.

'I've asked you not to go round there.'

'I've told you. It's a woman friend.'

'It's all right,' said Edmund, anxious to restore peace. 'I don't want Mummy to come. She's bored by trains.'

At last Gordon turned his gaze away from Rose. She continued to watch him, her confident smile full on her face. He hated her like this. He fumbled with the bag, dropping apples on the floor, cursing. Rose had never heard him swear before. It made her laugh. She put her arms round Edmund, smothering him with kisses.

'Look at this boy, too big for kisses now!'

She took Edmund up to bed that night, and later went in to his room to find his light still on. He was reading a book on model-making, and protested when she took it away from him and drew up the sheets to his chin.

'You need to sleep now, Edmund,' she told him. 'You've a big day in front of you tomorrow.'

'But it's important research,' Edmund told her. 'I need to look it up before I go.'

'Then you can look it up first thing, while I'm making up a flask for you. I'm putting off the light now, and I don't expect to see it coming back on again, mind.'

She repented, seeing his eyes darkening. 'But I'll tell you a story instead. That's a much nicer thing to go to sleep on, isn't it, than a book about glue and bits of wood and paper?'

'It's about ideas, Mummy,' Edmund wailed.

She switched off the light and sat on his bed. 'Shall I tell you a story now?'

'What kind of a story?'

'A fairy story.'

'Pooh,' he said, turning over away from her.

'It's one Desmond used to tell me when I was a little girl, and I'd forgotten all about it till now. It used to frighten me so much that I couldn't get to sleep after it, but you're a big brave boy and you'll love it.'

He didn't answer. She could hear him stroking the pillow with the back of his hand.

'Well now. A mother goat was going away for the day and she was very anxious about leaving her seven little kids behind. She was anxious because they were so young and so silly, but she had to go without them so that was that. And she was very, very anxious because the big bad wolf was prowling around the woods these days, gobbling up little kids whenever he had the chance, because they were so tender and so tasty. So, "Promise, promise, promise," she begged them, "that you won't let anybody in but me!" And, "We promise, promise, promise!" the seven little kids all said.

'So off she went with her scarf around her head, and the seven little kids closed the door behind her. Now, who should see the mother goat go hurrying through the woods but the . . .'

'Big bad wolf!' chuckled Edmund.

'Exactly. And Mother Goat was in such a hurry to get there and back before dark that her scarf fell from her head and she didn't even notice. The wily old wolf crept after her and picked up the scarf and tied it around his head, so his snout was covered up and only his eyes could be seen. And off he went to the mother goat's house, and he could smell the tender little kids, and his mouth watered. He knock, knock, knocked upon the door and instantly the kids stopped their chattering. "Who can it be?" they asked. "We mustn't let anyone in," they said. "But it might be Mother," they said. "But how can we tell?" they said.'

'By her voice. They'd know her voice,' said Edmund.

'They would! That's just what the cleverest little kid said. And the big bad wolf, with his ear squashed up against the door, heard him, and he said in a light happy voice that was just like their mother's, "Let me in, little kids. I'm home!" So they let him in, but the cleverest little kid looked at the clock and said, "It's too early for Mother to come home." "But it is Mother," the other kids insisted. "Look at her scarf." The wolf set to work preparing the tea, but the cleverest little kid looked at the clock and said, "It's too early for tea." "But smell the beautiful cakes!" the other kids said. "We'll know if it's Mother," the cleverest little kid said, "by her white hooves." But the wolf in the kitchen heard him say that and quick as a flash he dipped his brown paws into the bag of flour. He carried the plate of cakes into the room and the kids munched them down.'

'Even the cleverest one?'

'Even the cleverest one, who loved cakes more than any of them. "Did you enjoy your tea?" the wolf asked, and the seven little kids chorused "Yes!" "Well, that's good," said the wolf, showing off all his lovely yellow teeth. "And now I'm going to enjoy mine!" And he whipped the scarf away from his snout and gobbled up the seven little kids one by one – all except for the cleverest little kid, who hid himself inside the clock. Well, the big bad wolf couldn't count, and was very, very full, and when he had six little kids inside him he sat in the rocking chair in front of the fire and fell fast asleep.'

Edmund was very quiet. Rose could tell by his breathing that he was just awake still, his face now half-turned towards her. 'And what did the cleverest little kid do?' he whispered, knowing the story could never end there.

'Well, he waited and waited till at last he heard a knock, knock, knock! upon the door and his mother's voice saying, "Let me in, little kids, I'm home!" He ran to the door and flung it open and hugged his mother. He didn't need to tell her what had happened. She could see for herself the big bad wolf fat with sleep and the cottage empty except for one little kid. "You promised, promised, promised me!" she wailed. "But he had a voice like yours and his paws were white and he made such lovely cakes," the little kid sobbed. "Well, he's not having my little kids!" his mother screamed, and she picked up the carving knife and she slit open the wolf's big fat belly and out tumbled all her six little kids, all alive and wondering where they'd been. Then she found six stones from her garden and she put them in the wolf's belly and sewed him up again, and she and the kids huffed and they puffed and they shoved and they pushed until they'd got the wolf out of their cottage and the door shut fast against him. And,' she bent down and kissed her sleeping child, 'that's the end of the story.'

She paused, with her hand on the door. 'I don't think it's quite the way the brothers Grimm told it,' she said. 'And now I come to think of it, they must have been wrong about the big bad wolf. Only a she-wolf could eat up somebody else's children.'

'Are you sure you don't want to come, Rose?' Gordon asked her the next morning. She knew he was still anxious about Paedric, and the thought of his jealousy pleased her.

'You go,' she said. 'You'll have a lovely time. And,' she added wickedly, 'I will too.'

'Come on then.' Gordon picked up the rucksack and

opened the door. 'If she doesn't want to come with us, then that's that.'

'But I didn't even want her to come!' Edmund protested.

When they had gone Rose felt like dancing around the kitchen. She was jubilant with release. She stroked her stomach, wondering whether at this stage she could expect it to be rounded, losing her waist perhaps. She wanted to look pregnant. She went to her room and found a looser blouse than the one she was wearing. She wore it over her skirt instead of tucking it in, so it hung like a smock. She laughed at her reflection. It transformed her. She looked good, nothing like the neat person she always presented to Gordon. She loosened her hair, sure that her face looked fuller that way.

She could hear sounds now from Paedric's house. She went to an upstairs room and watched for him to come out. He went down the garden to his outside toilet and she could hear him singing in there. She smiled to herself. When he came out he inspected his flowers, crouching down to them, snapping off dead pansy heads. He went back into the house and she knew that he had left the door open for her. He was ready.

She was pleased to see Helena's room again, dim in its dance of candlelight. The scarved figure reclined on the cushions, waiting. Again, Rose felt a tremble of nervousness. She sat in her usual place, on a long cushion just under the curtained window.

'Tell me about your child,' she said.

'There was a woman who wanted a child.' The voice had changed. Rose hardly knew it. It had become a dull monotone. 'She conceived on a night of frost and fire. In the dark cave of her belly she carried the fruit. And she grew great with the fruit, and months passed while it fed upon her. But when the day came at last for the woman to give birth she laboured in vain. She toiled and sweated through a night when there were no stars, but even at the coming of the dawn there was no deliverance for her. For inside her womb the fruit was dead. Like a river bed in drought she had run dry, and her child was a stone within her.'

Rose had been unaware that while she was listening with growing dread to Helena's story she had been nursing her belly, her hands spread out across it like the spars of a cage. She felt ill.

'I know a fairy story a bit like that,' she said, a catch of horror in her throat.

'It's not a story. It's true.'

'Paedric, why do you always tell such horrible stories?'

'Because life is horrible,' said Paedric in his own voice. 'Life plays nasty tricks, and brings ugliness where beauty should be. Life turns babies into stones and living things to dust.'

'Is Helena dead then?'

'She turned to stone.'

'Did she die giving birth?'

'I turned her to stone.'

Rose stood up and drew back the curtains. The sky was white. Its brightness hurt her eyes. She could hear the dull throb of an approaching train. It was no longer a solid thing but a mass of living particles, splinters of flint and metal, water drops, sparks of flame and soot. Soon the particles would separate out from their mass and stream into the air and would disintegrate, would scatter as rain across the earth. She pressed her head against the glass. She no longer knew what was real and what was imagined. There was nothing solid to touch.

When she turned round again she saw that Paedric was

asleep. She took Helena's shawl from his shoulders and folded it up, lifted down the scarves from the walls, blew out the candles and bundled them together. She saw now that the room was thick with dust and that the curtains were filthy. She took them down and sat unthreading the hooks from the tape while she watched Paedric. In his deep sleep his face had the pallor of death. She went into another room and found a blanket, which she laid across him, pushing another against him to stop him rolling off his cushion pile. She didn't want to leave him. From time to time shudders shook his body. She brought her own cushion across from the window and lay down beside him, not daring or even wanting to touch him, but needing to give warmth to his body. She lay taut, watching him, breathing his breaths. At last he sat up, gazing round the room, hardly able to take in what he was seeing.

'What have you done?' he asked in the hollow voice of sleep.

'They're dead, Paedric.'

THIRTY-ONE

Rose went back to her own house, glad to see the familiar clutter of the breakfast dishes. She made as much noise as she could clearing them up, found a music station on the radio and turned it up loud. When her chores were done she walked briskly down to the village to do her shopping. She needed to be near the busyness of people. She saw the mother of the boy who had gone out with Gordon and Edmund and on an impulse suggested they should have coffee together. The woman was surprised; she hardly knew who Rose was. They went into a café together, each a little shy of the other. Rose took her time. She had no wish to go home yet.

'I hate to be in the house on my own,' she explained to Simon's mother. 'And I don't expect them back until late afternoon.'

'Hungry as wolves,' the woman laughed. 'I don't know why it is, but when any of mine go out for the day they come home and raid the larder as if they'd been starved for a week. And the funny thing is, I love to see them doing it. I love to treat them.'

'I think I'll make mine a cake,' said Rose, surprising herself. She liked the idea of the treat. She was pleased to have a good reason for going home early. She deliberately didn't look at Paedric's house as she passed it, dreading the thought of seeing him standing at the bare window of the room that had been Helena's. As she creamed together the butter and sugar and the mixture grew pale under her fork she thought of her father, who had always done the baking when she was a child, and of how his breath used to come thick and heavy when he worked, and how she would hang about near him ready to run a sly finger round the bowl when the creaming was done. She stopped, with her fork held up, and felt a pang of grief for him. She thought of her mother, reproachful, watching in the background, saying nothing. Her mother had been gentle and calm at the side of her father's mercurial swoops of temper. Now what Rose saw was her mother's coldness. They had nothing to give each other; husband or wife, child or parent. Rose had tiptoed between her parents' separateness. She had blamed herself for their differences, and for their indifference to her. They had not loved her enough because she had not been lovable. They had not loved her because they had lost their son. That was what she had always believed.

She measured flour, milk and eggs into the mixture and beat them together rapidly. Chemistry would heal the morning's wounds. Gordon and Edmund would come home to a house that smelled deliciously of love.

She guessed rightly the time of the train and decided to meet them at the station. Simon's father was there too, and he and Gordon talked together briefly. Edmund ran to Rose, showing her the sketches he'd made, excitedly pulling out of his rucksack pencils and scraps of paper, spilling them in his eagerness. Rose scooped them up for him.

'So you had a good day?' she asked Gordon when he joined them.

'Perfect,' he said. 'And did you?'

She hugged her stomach as she walked. It was a new habit that puzzled him. 'I had coffee with Simon's mother. And I've made us all a special tea. And I'm so happy to see you both again!' She whirled round, arms spread out.

'You're a lovely girl!' Gordon said to her, surprising them both.

That night Rose felt weary and complete. She scribbled a note to Paedric. 'Today I felt the baby move.' She took the note round and paused at his door. The house was in darkness, and completely silent. She thought of him somewhere alone with his grief and knew she had no way of consoling him. But it was his grief that had made her whole. She pushed the letter through, let it go, and ran home. In her bed she hugged herself and laughed out loud.

When she next saw Paedric he had cut his hair. He had not done it well, but in a random, bunched sort of way that made his face look chubby and comical. He knocked on her kitchen door with a bunch of flowers from his garden, and hung about oafishly in the doorway, dangling them at his side, while Gordon glowered at him.

'Come in, Paedric!' Rose was pleased to see him, remembering her note, wondering how he had reacted to it. 'Gordon and Edmund are just going out fishing, but come in.'

'I'd like you to come with us, Rose,' Gordon said.

She lowered her eyes, unwilling to respond to him. She wanted to talk to Paedric. 'All right.' She turned to Paedric, clapping her hands. 'It's a beautiful day. You should see the place where they fish, Paedric. I love to sit there and daydream.'

Paedric's flowers still dangled at his side. He pushed them towards her and she took them with both her hands, burying her face in them to smell them.

'Do you eat the fish you catch? Or do you throw them back in?' Paedric asked Edmund.

'They only throw them back if they're magic,' smiled Rose. 'And if they've granted my wish.'

Edmund frowned up at her. 'That was that story, Mummy. Ishy wishy. You used to tell me that story.'

'I did. The woman who always wanted what she didn't

have, isn't that right? And she never wanted what she did have. So her wishes were no use to her after all.'

'It was a silly story really,' said Edmund. 'She was a stupid woman.'

'Paedric, you've made a terrible mess of your hair,' Rose said. 'Were the hedge-clippers so blunt?'

'You're very familiar with him,' Gordon said later, as they were walking down to the river together. 'Quite the little flirt, aren't you?'

'When I feel like it. The man has been ill, if you must know. I was glad to see him looking so much better.'

She skipped ahead of him, teasing Edmund by threatening to tip him into the water. As they were setting up their tackle she chattered gaily, oblivious to the peacefulness which she loved so much about the river. She was restless. She wanted to stay with Gordon and Edmund and she wanted to be with Paedric. Now she had seen him again she wanted to talk to him about their secret baby. Her mind was fluttering. She lay back on the grass and tried to be still, tried to succumb to the river's silence and to concentrate in on herself, to her secret centre. She closed her eyes and drew darkness down inside herself. She imagined a fish twisting and spiralling inside her. She thought of it as a golden fish in a warm red sea. It was a lazy, flickering, gleaming fish, sinewy and calm. She folded her hands across her belly and smiled.

'I think I'll go back now,' she said after a time.

Gordon frowned across at her. 'Why? Stay here with us, Rose. We like to have you with us, don't we, Edmund?'

'I suppose so,' said Edmund. 'But sometimes when she doesn't come with us she makes a cake.'

'Once!' Rose laughed. 'Only once, Edmund.'

'I'd like you to stay,' Gordon said.

She knew how anxious he was. He would be fancying all sorts now, recognizing how excited she had been to see Paedric that morning. 'It doesn't matter then.' She made her voice dreamy for him, yawned and stretched in the sun. 'I'm quite happy here.'

She lay with her eyes open, listening to the quiet noises of the river and watching the slow dance of clouds. Four swans flew over with their necks outstretched like the needles of a compass. They made such a winnowing sound as they flew, such a musical, mourning sound, that it struck sorrow into her.

'What is it that makes that sound?' she asked. 'Is it their wings, or their cries, or air pumping from their lungs with their great effort? I've never heard such a sound!' She ran up the bank and watched their flight, her hand shielding her eyes, till they were well out of view. They were a family, it seemed, and the smallest was trailing behind, straining to keep up. They were arrows set on a sure flight. She could not turn the thought of them from her mind. All that day she could hear their harrowing song and she could see the smallest bird, yearning to keep up.

She went to see Paedric that evening. She told Gordon where she was going. If he cared he said nothing, but kept his brooding silence.

'You aren't thinking of leaving again, are you?' she asked Paedric as soon as he opened his door to her.

'I wasn't. Why?'

'I saw some wild swans. I don't know why, they disturbed me.'

'Our child will be wild,' he began. She loved to hear him say this. It had become their chant, with each of them adding another pretend quality to their phantom child. To Rose the thought of the child had become more real to her than the memory of the solemn-eyed, watchful baby that Edmund had been, or the sight of the lively sweet-smelling baby next door.

'Our child will be wild,' she said. 'And have the flight of a swan.'

'Our child will be wild and will run like a hare and will leap like a salmon.'

They both laughed.

'How long will it take, do you think?' Rose asked. 'Will we have to wait the full time?'

'No,' Paedric decided. 'He'll come when the time is right.'

'How do you know it's a he?'

'I'm sure of it.'

'Maybe.' Rose stroked her belly.

'And we'll find out,' Paedric promised, 'when the time comes. But we'll have to wait until the darker months.'

'Will you stay?'

'Of course I'll stay. This child is for both of us.'

'I'm excited,' she said. 'It will change my life.'

'It has already. Look at you. You've become beautiful.'

They were on opposite sides of the room. He never touched her and she never went to him. She knew instinctively that he would back away if she did, and that any such rejection from him would be worse for her than ever Gordon's or William's had been. Besides, she didn't need him. She had his child within her.

Now she thought of nothing else but the secret child, while she worked in the house for Gordon or walked to and from the school for Edmund, while she lay alone in her bed; she was concentrated in on the centre of her being, the heart of her maze; her cave. She imagined the child crouched there, head tucked down into its supple limbs, awash in the drowning darkness of her blood. She had the sensation that it was herself that was crouched up in there, and that inside that self was another, and another; that she had spent her life waiting to be born. She was deeply contented. She stopped the lively dancing that had so irritated Gordon for the past few months and became calm and withdrawn, ticking to the quiet rhythm that was deep inside herself. At night she tried to cradle Edmund but he rocked himself away from her. He was filling out and becoming ugly to her, like a large bird with no gift for flight.

She took him to see her mother at the end of a long, tedious summer. They went on an autumn day, when the sun was low and the trees seemed to be smoking with mist. She had not seen her mother for some months, and was shocked at the change in her, at how small and frail she seemed.

'I want to talk,' her mother said when she and Rose were in the kitchen together. 'There's something I need to talk to you about.'

Rose felt strangely distressed. 'I was thinking of going for a walk,' she said. 'Wouldn't you like to come?'

'It's too hot for me.'

Immediately Rose felt a sense of lassitude washing through her. Her limbs were heavy, her blood hardly seemed to move in her body. She clutched at the sink.

'Rose? Are you all right? You've gone white as death!' Her mother gave her some water and helped her to sit down, pressing her hand on her forehead. Edmund watched, worried.

'It's just the heat,' Rose gasped. 'I should be better when I go out for air. I can't breathe in here, Mum.'

'Don't go far now. Don't overdo it!' her mother warned. Her hands fluttered to Rose's face. 'Sometimes you look such a child, Rose.'

As soon as she left the house Rose felt better. She had been stifled in there. She walked beyond the village to where the hills began to rise, and stepped out quite jauntily, almost at a run. When she started to climb she walked so fast that she was breathless with the effort. She willed her body to move faster. Her breath grunted away from her. She clasped at tree trunks as she hauled herself up, laughing aloud at her weakness. When she reached the low summit she lay down. Her heart was a fragile, rocking shell. She lay on her back and gazed up at the clouds as they came together and parted, rolled and separated, like waves on an ocean, a ceaseless, restless mass that changed shape and renewed itself, devoured itself and spat itself out again.

As soon as she arrived back at her mother's she fell asleep with exhaustion. Her mother let her sleep for a bit and then woke her up with a cup of tea.

'Aren't you well?' she asked, anxious for her. 'You don't seem yourself, Rose.'

'I'm fine,' Rose assured her. 'Fine, fine, fine!'

'You seem so low to me. I worry about you. I'm glad Gordon's back with you, looking after you. It's a lonely place, where you live. It's worse than here.'

'I've made some friends. And I've got plenty to do.'

'Well,' Mrs Waterhouse said, sorrowing for her daughter. 'You're like me, after all. You'll do nothing with your life. You'll take what it has to give you, and then you'll give it away.'

'I don't know what you mean.' Rose felt panic rising up in herself again. She knew that her mother wanted to talk to her, to spill secrets, maybe, to hand her some precious and fragile thing that she didn't want to take. 'I'm quite happy.' Her secret bloomed in her, calming her. She didn't want the burden of her mother's confidences to shadow her. She picked up the plate of food that her mother had prepared for her and sat out in the garden with it. She could hear her mother and Edmund talking together in the house. She told

herself that the boy needed to have time alone with her. He
didn't see enough of her now.

'Rose, I've some news for you.' Her mother followed her
out and sat down by her. 'I'm getting married again.'

'You!' Rose laughed. She tried to sound pleased. 'Married!'

'Don't sound so surprised. I've been very lonely since your
father died. He's a very nice man. A retired farmer. Very
gentle.'

'I'm pleased for you then,' said Rose. Pain swelled her
throat. She couldn't bring herself to embrace her mother,
who sat stiffly at her side, her hands neat in her lap.

'I love him more than I ever loved your father. I can say
that to you now.'

The two women stared in front of them. Edmund swung
idly on the gate. Rose had to move back to the kitchen. She
couldn't bear the nervous happiness in her mother's voice.
She asked Edmund to collect his things together and called
to her mother that they had to leave for an earlier train.
There was no need for her to come to the station with
them. She ran down the lane, half-dragging Edmund with
her, knowing without turning to look that her mother
would be standing at the gate, her hands red and wet with
suds, her mouth open in a call of goodbye; and that the
elderly man passing them in the lane was her mother's
future husband, going to the cottage to meet his family-to-
be.

'My mother is getting married again,' she told Gordon that
evening. He was reading, his lips forming the words,
occasionally whispering out the sound like someone in private prayer. He glanced up at her, frowning, and laid down
his book.

'Your mother?'

'Exactly! Little did you know she was ripe for picking. You could have had her, you know, if you'd moved quickly enough.'

'Your mother?'

'For goodness' sake . . .'

'I don't know what you're talking about.'

'Of course you do. She's a handsome woman, my mother. You and she are well suited.'

'But I don't want your mother! What a ridiculous idea!' He half laughed, spreading out his hands as if he was laying open to her the pages of her silliness.

'Well, you don't want me, that's for sure.'

'When have I ever said that?'

'I wish I knew what you did want. Goodness, I wish I knew!' She could hear her voice rising into a wail of protest that she couldn't suppress. She could hear how ugly it sounded. She didn't want him to hate her.

He picked up his book again. 'You know very well what I want. I want you and Edmund and my home. I'm a contented man. I've never harboured any amorous thoughts towards your mother. Besides, it would be against the law.'

Rose laughed out loud, wincing as she did so at the harsh magpie sound she made. She was overwrought. She clutched at her stomach and eased herself down into a chair. Gordon was watching her, puzzled.

'Aren't you well?'

'I'm very well, thank you,' she told him.

'You looked as if you had a pain.'

'Not a pain.' She smiled brightly at him. 'I'm all right. I've never felt better in my life, as it happens.'

'You're on edge.'

'Yes,' she conceded, 'I'm very edgy tonight.' And then, unaccountably, she began to cry.

Gordon put down his book again. 'You mustn't worry about your mother, you know. She'll be fine.'

'I know,' Rose sobbed. 'I don't know why I'm crying. I just feel like it. I feel abandoned. I know it's silly.'

'Of course it's silly. No one's abandoning you.' Gordon came to sit beside her, his arm stiff across her shoulders.

'I never talk to my mother. She's so far away.'

'She's only a train journey away.'

Rose sobbed again. 'That's not what I mean at all.'

Gordon shook his head. 'Poor little thing!' He was very tender with her. 'You look tired these days. You're not ill, are you?'

'I've told you. I've never felt better in my life.'

'I'll make us some supper if you like. Would you like that?'

He went into the kitchen, taking his book with him. He decided to make omelettes. As he became absorbed in the task of breaking and beating the eggs he started his familiar, tuneless song. Rose leaned back, her strange grief spent. She felt at ease again now. She caressed her stomach.

'Almost ready,' Gordon called, and sang his tune again. From next door came the sound of Paedric's fine strong singing voice, giving the melody its full worth.

'Dammit,' said Gordon, under his breath. 'Dammit, Paedric, damn you.'

THIRTY-TWO

As the months passed Rose grew more and more anxious and overwrought, desperate now to give birth to the secret in her womb and to know how she must cherish and nourish it. She examined her breasts and decided they were definitely growing fuller.

'Aren't I beautiful?' she said to Gordon one morning, going straight into his room from the bathroom, proud of her nakedness. 'Don't you think I'm beautiful?'

He was shocked. 'What d'you think you're doing, walking round like that? Edmund might come running in at any minute!'

'So what!' She turned round, flaunting herself, hating him. 'What kind of a man are you, Gordon, to behave like this when your own wife comes naked into your room? Laugh at the fun of it, why don't you, or take me in your arms for God's sake? Take my breasts in your hands, caress them why don't you, stroke them, put your lips around them and suck them, bite them, but for God's sake don't just tell me off!'

Gordon was sitting on his bed with his body twisted away from her. She crossed over to him and thrust herself against him. She was warm in her loins and aching and angry with him. He stood up and started shaking her until she felt her limbs would dislocate from their sockets and her flesh flake away from her.

'Stop it! Stop it!' he shouted, his voice a thin wail of suppressed anger. 'You're acting like a whore, like a cheap and filthy whore!' His face was white and taut, a geometry of angles. She had no strength now against his anger. Then

Edmund was in the room and pummelling them both with useless fists, dragging Gordon back and crying out to them both until his high voice made itself heard over Gordon's bellowings and Rose's screams, and silence like the pall of death descended on the room. Gordon let go of Rose and she fell like a doll. He bent down to Edmund and buried his face in the boy's shoulder.

'I'm sorry, Edmund. I'm sorry,' he said. 'We'll go downstairs now. It's all right.'

Rose lay on the floor. Her womb was convulsing. She could hear Gordon and Edmund talking as if their voices were far away, echoes from another time. She heard them having breakfast together and then the door closing behind them as they went out. Only then did she try to sit up. She felt weak and nauseous. She crawled into the bathroom and vomited into the lavatory bowl. She was shivering. She daren't try the stairs. She crawled back into Gordon's room and climbed into his bed, drawing his sheets over her for the first time in their marriage. A train rattled past. He would be on it, going straight to work from Edmund's school. The morning settled into birdsong and, at last, she fell asleep.

When she woke up Gordon had just come into the room. He was standing over her when she opened her eyes. She struggled to sit up, remembering the horror of it all. She felt hysterical with shame.

'Who's been sleeping in my bed?' she giggled. 'I didn't expect you to come creeping home, Gordon. I thought the joys of work would have called you away.'

'I've been walking,' he said. 'I needed to clear my head.' He passed her his dressing-gown. 'It's midday, didn't you know?'

'I've been sick. Then I slept.'

'Well, I'm sorry. I've come to say I'm sorry.'

'It's all right. I suppose I provoked you.'

'You did provoke me, but that's no excuse for me. I told you I was frightened of hurting you.'

'You should get help. I think you need help, Gordon.'

'We all need help.' He sat down next to her on the bed. His face was ashen and lined. He sat with his head bowed, clenching and unclenching his fists so the bones cracked. 'And I've come to pack.'

'So you're leaving again.'

'I'm leaving for good.'

Silence droned in the room.

'You can't just keep running away,' she said at last.

'I can't stay with you.'

'You said you had everything you wanted here. You never talk, do you, about what's wrong between us? You never want to talk.' She felt strong again now, and almost tender towards him in his misery. She fastened the dressing-gown round herself. 'You never tell me what you really think.'

'All right. I'll tell you what I think.' His voice was a low, hollow monotone. 'I think you're carrying on with Paedric.'

'Then you think wrong.' She flushed with pleasure. Thoughts of the secret child warmed her. 'Paedric has never touched me.'

Gordon winced and stood up. 'That's not everything, is it? He's odd, he's cracked. But you think more of him than you do of me.'

Rose shrugged. 'What could I do about that, if it was true?'

'I don't expect you to do anything about it. I think I should go. And I think I should take Edmund with me.'

Rose felt a low, dull throbbing in her head. She thought she was going to faint. She leaned back, gasping for snatches of air. He watched her steadily, saying nothing. He was very calm.

'You have no right,' she said at last. 'He's not even your child.'

'He wants to come with me. I've talked to him about it.'

She shook her head, disbelieving. Her throat ached so much that she couldn't trust herself to speak. The stranger on the bed leaned forward and touched her chin, tilting up her face.

'If you don't want us to go, then stop seeing Paedric.'

Hailstones suddenly peppered the window like a frantic summons. Rose stood up and crossed the room, unconscious of her movements. She leaned out to draw in the curtains and closed the window firmly. The sky was as grey as slate, with a brooding darkness on the horizon. Black against it was the tree in Paedric's garden. Hail dripped from its branches as though it was yielding milk. Her waiting child flexed itself.

'That's something I can't do,' she said. 'Not now.'

She went down to her room and got dressed, and went round immediately to Paedric's house. He was out but she kept on walking, in spite of the sting of hail on her cheeks. It was like a flagellation to her. She felt sure that Gordon would not go. There was no home for him apart from this one. She tried to imagine him camped out in a bleak bed-sit somewhere, and shuddered for him. He would not leave her, because he loved the comfort of his home. It occurred to her that he could turn her out. He had a right to do that. But it was she who had created the comfort for him. They clung to each other simply because they were afraid of swimming alone.

She didn't realize how far she had walked until she saw Paedric coming towards her across the bridge. His hair, like hers, was streaming wet and his cheeks blue with cold. He had the collar of his grey trench coat turned up, and his hands dug deeply into his pockets.

'You look terrible,' he told her.

'I feel it. I feel terrible.' They had to shout to be heard. He turned so he was standing right in front of her, sheltering her from the blizzard. 'You shouldn't be out in this,' he shouted. 'What're you doing, tramping about in this filth?'

'I was looking for you. I've had a bad time. I feel as if something's going to happen soon.'

He laughed, turning his face up to let the hailstones slash at his skin. He held out his arm to show her that they should turn round and head back for home.

'Gordon says I'm not to see you again,' Rose shouted. 'He says he'll leave me if I do.'

'Let him. Nothing he says or does has anything to do with our child. He can't do anything to stop it happening. Unless you've told him?' He stopped, cupping his hands around his face so he could look at her.

'Of course I haven't told him.'

'He is the god who would swallow your child the moment it was born. Look how he swallowed Edmund.'

'You're mad! I think we're both going mad!'

'Maybe. What's madness but the other side of the moon, and what's the moon but the pale echo of the sun? And where's the sun today anyway?' He held up his hands. 'Gordon has swallowed it whole!'

Rose wondered for a moment whether it was possible to be loved by this man. She hated the thought of sharing his attentions with anybody. She knew nothing about him except for what he told her in their brief walks together and in the intimacy of Helena's room. Her old jealousy of Helena sheered up wilfully again.

'Do you still talk to Helena?' She couldn't stall the ridiculous question.

'Helena?' he cupped his hands around his mouth. 'Helena? Helena? Where are you?' he shouted. 'Gone?'

'Don't, Paedric.'

'The goddess of love is also the goddess of death.' He ran ahead of her, his boots sliding on the mud of the path. He scrambled up the embankment, making to plunge across the track to the other side and down to their terrace, when a train seemed to appear from nowhere, its voice drowned under the noise of the blizzard, its bulk splintering out of it. Paedric staggered back, exaggerating his surprise with kicking legs and flailing arms like a comic in a silent movie. Rose ran to catch him up. They were both gasping with the new force of the iced wind. He bent towards her and for a moment she thought he was going to kiss her. Involuntarily she held her face to his. He ticked his head from side to side, crossing his eyes.

'Will you have my baby, sleeping princess?'

'You're not the handsome prince, surely?' she laughed.

He stopped his ticking, suddenly serious. 'Ah, but would you, all the same?'

'Yes,' she said.

He swung away from her. 'Here comes the cuckold, poor old chap.'

Rose turned to see Gordon coming up over the embankment from the other side of the track. 'Go in,' he shouted to her. 'I'll fetch him.'

She had forgotten about Edmund. 'I'm soaked already,' she shouted. 'I might as well do it.'

'I said go in.' He came past her, ignoring Paedric.

Rose bundled herself together and ran past him over the track and down to her house. There was a rush of panic in

her. She lit a fire in her room and draped her wet clothes over
a chair, putting on her dressing-gown. She took from one of
the drawers a tissue-paper package which she had hidden
there some months ago. Inside was a bundle of baby shawls.
She had bought them at a school jumble sale, washed them in
secret, and hidden them away. Now she spread them out
around her, examining them. She picked out one and held it
to her face, enjoying its softness. Then she knelt down with it
on the hearth.

The flames curled slowly at first around the bed of
kindling wood, then took heart and embraced the coals. Hail
spat down the chimney in an urgent and restless dance. The
colours flecked from blue to green to apricot, from warm
peach to poppy. Rose was hypnotized by them. She held out
the shawl to the fire, warming it for the coming child. She
heard Edmund and Gordon coming down the embankment
and the door slamming shut behind them. Edmund scampered
upstairs and changed into dry clothes. Gordon made toast for
them both. She heard the television chattering its way through
a children's programme. In the kitchen a meal was being
prepared. Rose could hear Edmund singing away to himself,
not in his natural sweet voice but in the flat monotone
humming he had adopted from Gordon. He seemed to be
practising a song he had learnt in school that day. Gordon
called out that the meal was ready. Rose ignored him. Theirs
was another life operating on a different plane and at a
different pace from her own. She had lost touch with their
reality. The meal was eaten. Edmund ran upstairs and down
again. The door closed, and the house went quiet. Rose was
almost asleep, crouched on the hearth rug, drawn down into
the pitch of the house's silence. A sudden pattering of fresh
hail roused her into a delirious wakefulness. She saw the tap-
dancer with his lithe, neat body and his white shirt-sleeved

arms dancing like a dragonfly across the coals. Tongues of flame lapped around him. His eyes were black holes flashing with sparks. Still he danced and danced.

She felt herself being lifted up. She felt a cold benediction like a quietus wrapping itself around her. A deeper darkness swam around her eyes. She reached out for the shawl. It had gone.

THIRTY-THREE

Some time later she was aware that Paedric was in the room. She opened her eyes, not knowing what time of day it was or why she was in her bed. Paedric had brought her a drink and sat holding it to her lips while she gulped it down.

'I'm cold,' she told him.

'Rose.' Paedric lifted a bundle of shawls from the side of the bed and placed it next to her. 'Our baby is called Finn. He was surely born out of the flames tonight.'

'Finn,' she murmured. She picked up the shawls, marvelling at their softness. 'It's a good name.'

'And he is the secret of our hearts. You mustn't ever forget that.'

'I won't tell anyone.'

The bundle was a soft and rocking thing, sweet-breathed and warm in her arms.

'You nearly set the room alight with your fire,' Paedric told her. 'It was a good thing I came in when I did.'

'So it was you. I thought I'd dreamt it, being lifted up like that. Did you put me in my bed?'

'I wanted to see you, Rose. I heard Gordon and Edmund going out so I decided to come here. And there you were, fast asleep like a child, and with a shawl singeing and smoking in your hands. I don't know what might have happened if I hadn't come in just then. I dread to think.'

'I was warming the shawl for the baby.'

'I had to throw it out. I took it to my house.'

'Well.' She looked down at the bundle. 'So we have Finn.'

'Our child is as wild as fire.' Paedric crouched down next

to her. 'He is the secret of our hearts. He will die if anyone finds out about him. You know that?'

She nodded, her face still buried in the shawls.

'You have no right, and I have no right, to tell anyone about him. He only lives because he is a secret. You must never forget that.'

'I've told you I won't.'

'I'll go,' he said. 'They'll be home soon. Take care of Finn.'

She didn't look up, but stayed with her eyes closed and the soft fabric pressed against her cheek. As soon as the door was closed she rocked the bundle in her arms. 'Finn,' she whispered. 'Finn, Finn, Finn.'

She was not aware that Gordon and Edmund had come home until she heard Edmund shouting for her. She held the bundle against her breast.

'You haven't had your tea!' Edmund called. 'Can I have it?' He flung open her door and stared at her. Her breasts were bare, her arms folded over some kind of blanket, her face rapt. Startled into awareness by him she opened out her arms and shook out the shawls, pulling them across her shoulders to hide her nakedness.

'Can I have your tea?'

'Not a bit of it!' she laughed. 'Not a morsel, little wolf!'

THIRTY-FOUR

From that day it was Finn who obsessed Rose's thoughts. She stored up stories about him to report to Paedric: how he cried in the night, smiled in his sleep, how he began to focus on things around him – leaves in the trees, the movement of curtains, the sound of Gordon's clock ticking. She left his shawls in her bed but in her thoughts she carried Finn around with her all the time, at her breast, and she would be rocking him or singing to him. To Gordon she had become so closed in on herself that she was unreachable. Sometimes Paedric asked if he could take Finn to his house for a few hours. It was almost more than she could bear. She imagined that she could hear Finn's crying through the walls. She thought of him being carried from room to room in Paedric's house, being held up to look at the movements and colours of things that she could not see. She wanted to know his every response. All the time he was away from her she longed to have him back again. Her head was a house of dark rooms, and Finn was a candle being carried from one part of it to another, lighting up its shadows, making it shine.

When Paedric tapped on her door to bring him home to her she devoured every word about the baby's day.

'Did he cry much without me?'

'Not a bit. He's been laughing and smiling,' Paedric would say. 'And then he slept all afternoon. When he opened his eyes, they were blue.'

'Oh yes,' she agreed. 'And isn't his hair dark and fine?'

'And his limbs are long.'

One day Paedric told her that he had carried Finn up the embankment to see the train go by.

'You never did!' Rose was shocked. 'How can a baby understand a train? It's all noise to him, all loud frightening noise.'

'Not a bit of it! He loved the train. He felt the rush of air from it and he braced himself against it. He felt its power and he put his own power to it. He relished it.'

'He's too young,' Rose protested. 'He'll dream about it, and we'll have no ways of helping him.'

Paedric only laughed. 'He's happiest when we feed his senses. That's the sort of child he is. Give him sweet air to breathe. Give him firelight to watch.'

'I do.'

'Hold him up to the rain. Let it wash over him. He loves anything like that.'

'He loves his bath. You should see him splashing in it!'

'It doesn't harm him to bathe him in the river.'

'He has to be held and comforted after you've had him, Paedric. You frighten him.'

'I sing to him. He likes that.'

Rose laughed at last. 'I know,' she said. 'I've heard you. I like it too. You've a fine voice.'

They were walking together up the lane towards Edmund's school. Soon, at the bridge, they would part. It was Paedric's turn to take Finn home.

'I've found a meadow to show him,' he told Rose. 'There are cowslips there, would you believe, and forget-me-nots? He'll love to see them and smell them.'

'He'll sneeze. And don't you dare take him in there today. See how muddy the lane is still. The grass is too wet for him.'

Paedric shook his head at her. 'You're too literal,' he said. 'The truth only destroys things.'

Rose watched him go. He had his head bent and his hands in his pockets, and he walked in deep concentration in that awkward and rolling way of his. She tried to imagine how he would have to carry Finn. The child would be big enough to sit up, supported. Paedric would not be carrying him on his hip, as she would have done. That was a woman's way. Over his shoulder, maybe. Finn would be looking back towards her, laughing perhaps, flexing his fingers to wave.

Finn was as real to her as Joan's baby next door. He was never out of her mind. She knew what he looked like, even what his voice sounded like. She knew the smell and the feel of him, and the firmness of his round flesh. She and Paedric talked of nothing else. It was all she could do not to mention Finn to Gordon, as casually as she might say, 'Edmund hurt his knee today.' She nearly told Edmund not to slam the door in case he woke up the baby. She hovered around Joan, eager for reports on Melanie's progress. She longed to be able to say, 'Oh yes. Finn cried after his inoculations too. He hated them,' or 'He cried all last night. Would he be teething yet, would you think?' She stored up details of Melanie's baby habits for when Finn was older, so she would be able to share them with Paedric. Rose saw that Joan was a good mother to her children. She would be even better.

Edmund was becoming sulky and withdrawn. He resented the hours she spent in her room away from him. His moods began to annoy her. She saw that he was jealous. When she cared enough she tried to coax him with sweets and chocolates. She no longer wanted to smother him in her arms with hugs and kisses. After all, he had always resisted them. The sweets were a way of telling him that she still loved him. Sometimes he stole money from her purse for them. She knew this was happening and she let him get away with it. She felt guilty for neglecting him. In the end she simply hid her purse where he couldn't find it, and that was when he started stealing from Gordon. He was guileless, as if he wanted to be found out. It wasn't long before Gordon caught him doing it. He marched the child into his room and called Rose upstairs.

She was singing to her baby. She shushed him to sleep and tiptoed out of her room. Upstairs, Edmund was sitting on his bed. He was red-faced and snivelling. Rose looked at him dispassionately, noticing how fat and ugly he had become. His second teeth had come through and were over-large and protruding. His legs were pink and bulbous. He had outgrown his school shorts and as he sat they strained to hold in his fat flesh. Slime trickled from his nose as he snivelled. He was repulsive to her. He reminded her of a slug.

'Why did you steal my money?' Gordon demanded.

'I don't know,' Edmund sobbed. His nostrils bubbled.

'For goodness' sake, wipe your nose,' said Rose. She went into the bathroom and pulled some sheets of toilet paper free for him. She glanced at herself in the mirror. 'The sooner this is over, the better,' she told herself. 'You have a baby to feed.' She went back into the room and held out the toilet paper to Edmund. It hung limp from his hands. He cried on, miserable.

'He says he took the money because he's hungry,' said Gordon, accusing Rose.

'Of course he's not hungry. He's always eating. Look at the size of him. He's enormous.'

Gordon swung back to the boy. 'What do you buy with it?'

'Sweeties,' whispered Edmund. He screwed the toilet paper into a ball.

Gordon had to smile at the childish word. He crouched

down to Edmund, full of tenderness for him. 'Show me,' he said.

Edmund swung out his arm to point to the cupboard and then flung himself sideways across his bed, hiding his face in the pillows. Rose opened the cupboard door. The bottom shelf was strewn with chocolate wrappers, with nibbled bars. Little piles of untouched bars were arranged according to make and size.

'You disgusting child!' said Rose. 'You fat little pig!'

'Shush,' Gordon said to her. 'There's no point in getting hysterical. Leave this to me, please.'

'You spoil him!' Rose shouted. 'That's why he behaves like this. You spoil him.'

'Go downstairs. You're doing no good here.'

Rose was ashamed of herself. She ran downstairs to Finn, cradled him, sang to him, rocked him in his sleep, pressed his softness to her. The children next door were shrieking over a game. 'Shush!' she whispered, burying her face in the shawls in her arms. 'Shush, oh shush my baby. Everything's all right.' She did not want to know what was happening upstairs.

THIRTY-FIVE

Next day she was determined to be nice to Edmund. They walked in the rain, and she put his mac on him, letting him drape it over his head the way he liked to wear it, so it hung like a cape behind him. His legs were scarlet and mottled with cold.

'I'm planning a treat for you on Saturday, Edmund,' she told him. 'We'll go into town and I'll buy you some new clothes. And maybe if you're very good we'll go to see a film, if there's something suitable for you to see. Would you like that?' She wondered whether she would take Finn. It would be a new thing for him to see the shops and the traffic, and all the lights if they stayed on into the evening. He'd love the experience. He'd be so tired after all the excitement and the travelling that he would sleep through the film. He'd be no trouble at all.

She became aware of Edmund's voice rising to a wail of protest.

'I don't want to go to town on Saturday. I want to go out with Daddy.'

She stopped and stared down at him. His eyes were bubbling with tears again. 'For God's sake!' she snapped.

'Daddy promised me,' he pleaded. 'And you could easily get my clothes without me.'

Rose walked away quickly, dismissing him. She took the turning down Cow Lane, despite the rain and the mud. Edmund always hated it. She preferred to take it when she was on her own. Cows walked down it twice a day to be milked, their hooves churning the lane to slurry whenever the weather was wet. Half-way down it a spring rose up, staining the track like blood when the earth was dry, gushing down it at other times. She walked on quickly. She could hear Edmund lolloping behind her gasping out his compaints. She ignored him. He hated mud. He was a finicky, unnatural child. She walked faster. Finn was on her hip, snuggled into her, warm and uncomplaining.

'Mummy, I don't like it.'

'Come on. We'll be late for school.'

She started to run, her feet sliding away from her in the mud. She loped along at a steady pace, half skiing. Finn would be chuckling at the motion. 'Stop blubbering.'

'Wait for me!' Edmund whined behind her. 'Ah. Wait.'

She could feel Finn's breath warm on her cheek. His hands clasped her as she jogged. At the end of the lane she turned round. Edmund was heavy-limbed and red-faced, panting. His feet skidded away from him with every step.

'Run!' she shouted.

'I can't! I'll fall over!' He flung out his arms as if he was giving himself up to her, and tripped face down into the mud.

She waited. He was crawling to her on his hands and knees. Her baby was asleep again. When Edmund reached her she did not bend down to help him. He struggled to his feet. From the knees down he was caked in mud. His hands were balled with mud. His face and his hair were spattered with it, cobs of mud in his eyelashes. 'Look at you!' she said. Finn murmured. She shifted him to her other hip. He slept again. 'Just look at the state of you, child.'

Edmund gazed down at his spread hands. He was crying out loud now. 'I want to go home.'

'You can't go home. You're going to school.' She turned away from him and walked on. He sobbed behind her.

216

'I can't go to school like this, Mummy. Don't make me.'

'What nonsense! Tell Miss Mallory you fell over, that's all. She'll wash you down, surely.'

She could hear children clamouring in the schoolyard, their voices high as birds'. It was a sound that she loved. Sometimes she lifted Finn up so he could see the children playing. She wondered what it would be like for her when he was old enough to join them. How could she bear to be without him all day? The bell rang, and the clamouring stopped as if someone had closed a door to shut out the sound.

'Go on,' she ordered.

Edmund's eyes were dark and beseeching, and she ignored them. He sobbed away from her, dragging his feet with every step until he reached the school gates. He turned to her again, sorrowful and wretched, and she turned away. She walked off briskly. Now she and Finn could spend the whole day with Paedric.

They spent it walking together, in spite of the rain. They followed the river as far as the track would take them, then went up into the nearest hills. Paedric talked non-stop in his eager, vibrant way. She loved every second she spent with him. He excited her with his ideas. As she walked back to school for Edmund her head was spinning with words. She nursed the things Paedric told her till she was alone, and then she would open them up and explore them, trying to understand them and to make them her own.

'I want Finn to have a mind like yours,' she told him. 'I want him to be full of such exciting notions that he will dazzle people, like a firework show. Children like Edmund are trapped in such workaday thoughts. It's a shame.'

Paedric spread out his hands and then folded his arms across his chest, nursing himself. 'If his mind can fly free, he won't be trapped in a frail house. I would like him to be beautiful, all the same.'

'He is,' said Rose quickly. 'Like you are, to me.' It was a hurtful thing to say, after all.

'He'll be a great child, all right. A great man. A dreamer and a traveller.'

'I think he'll be a musician or painter,' said Rose, conscious of Paedric's fine hands.

'He'll be all of these things. Whatever we want him to be.'

'He'll show us what he wants to be. We won't stop him.'

Later, as they were walking back, she said, 'What will he be, solemn or happy, d'you think?'

'Oh, happy. We both know he's happy.'

'But he won't be frivolous.'

'Not a bit. He'll take life seriously. He'll take nothing for granted. He must know that every moment is a gift from us.'

'Does he have to earn it?'

'He has done already.'

Rose nodded. Would they ever tire of this, she wondered, when Finn was old enough to marry and leave home and have children? Would they still wonder so much about him then? Where would their control of him stop? 'We mustn't think about his future yet, must we?' she said. 'We must take every moment of his present and cherish it before it goes away.'

'Our child is wild and loves the light of the sun,' Paedric began to chant. 'I'll tell you something, Rose. He loves to lie underneath my tree and to watch the leaves dancing.'

'I can't wait for him to be walking!'

Paedric put his finger to his lips.

'No, but I can't. And I can't help wondering what his first word will be.'

'We'll be together when he says it,' Paedric told her. 'And we'll both see him stand up.'

'I think that will be soon.'

'When the harvest moon is full,' Paedric decided. 'That will be a fine time for Finn to stand up on his legs without help and to utter his first syllable.'

It was then that Rose remembered Edmund, crawling on his hands and knees to her that morning. She was full of remorse for him. 'We must go back,' she said. 'I mustn't be late for Edmund.'

'Then run ahead. Leave Finn with me. I have a fine story to tell him.'

Rose had to run to get to school on time. As it was, by the time she got there the playground was empty. Guiltily, she hurried towards the schoolroom just as Miss Mallory was leaving.

'I don't see Edmund,' Rose called out to the teacher, a sudden catch of alarm in her throat.

'But he wasn't at school today.' Miss Mallory's welcoming smile turned to concern.

'He must have been.' Rose looked round, distraught. 'I left him at the gates.'

The teacher came up to her, smelling sweetly of the fresh face powder she had just dabbed on her cheeks. 'He didn't come, Mrs Doran. I thought he must be ill.'

Rose felt weak with shock and helplessness. She went to the gates, as if standing there would bring Edmund smiling into view.

'Should we contact the police, my dear?' She was hardly aware of the teacher's voice, of the cold touch of her hand on her own. 'Mrs Doran?'

'No!' She roused herself. 'No, I'm sure there's no need for that.' Panic was making her breathless. 'Let me think. Where would he go? What about Simon? Was he at school today?'

'As a matter of fact, he wasn't.'

'Then he'll be with Simon. He's his only friend. He's bound to be with him.' All the time she was speaking she was looking distractedly from side to side of the yard, expecting at any moment to see Edmund coming out of hiding towards her.

Miss Mallory did not remove her hand. 'Simon has been away for most of the term.'

'But he'll be with him,' Rose insisted. She knew he wouldn't be. Edmund hadn't mentioned Simon for months. Not since the birth of Finn, she realized.

Miss Mallory returned to the door to check it was closed, then rejoined Rose. She opened the gate for her. 'Of all the children in this school, of all the children I've ever taught, I would say that Edmund was the least likely to play truant. He loves school, Mrs Doran.'

'I know he does.' The voice of the teacher was a distant buzz in her head, like a telephone ringing in a different room.

'I don't want to alarm you, but I think this is a very serious matter.'

'I think I know why he stayed away,' Rose volunteered. 'He fell over on the way here. It's such a silly thing. He got himself into a bit of a mess. I think he thought you'd be cross with him.'

'Is that so? I didn't know I was such a tyrant. All the same, I'd like to come to Simon's house with you.'

'There's no need.' Rose walked quickly away from the teacher, drinking in breaths of air. She broke into a half-run until she reached the village. 'This is to punish me,' she thought to herself. 'And what if it was Finn who did this to me?'

She wasn't sure which house was Simon's. It had always been Gordon who went to collect Edmund, in the model-making days. In the end she had to ask someone, and as she went up the drive she felt weak and afraid again. What if he was not there? It was better not to ask. Of course he would not be there, not at this time of day. Simon's mother would surely have made him go back to school. But perhaps he had hidden somewhere until school was over and then gone to Simon's to play. That was a possibility. And yet Edmund was not a devious child. Still the spark of hope hurried her on. Besides, she had been seen from the window. Before she had time to knock, Simon's mother came to the door.

'I've come to collect Edmund.' Rose forced brightness into her voice.

The woman's face was a crushed rosebud mouth and painted violet eyes. Rose had never liked her. Her eyebrows were thin quizzes, arched in surprise.

'Edmund? He's not been here for months.'

'Then I've come to the wrong house. I'm so sorry. I know where he'll be.' At the gate Rose stood with her hand to her mouth. Fright like a trapped bird plunged inside her lungs. 'This is what it is to lose a child,' she said aloud. 'Oh Finn, don't ever leave me like this. Don't ever, would you?'

She could not go to the police. To go to the police would be to admit that something terrible had happened to Edmund, and that it was her fault. It was not her fault. It was William's fault. She had to try everything else first, before she went to the police. Where would he go, if he wanted to hide from her? She remembered the spot where he and Gordon liked to fish. Yes, it would be there for sure. He would have gone there to wash himself. He would be sheltering under the trees even now. Oh let him be there. Please, please let him be there. She began to run, made strong in her sense of purpose.

The river banks were deserted. They were still with a weight of silence.

'Edmund?' she called. Her voice was a querulous, pitiful thing, pitted against that silence. 'Edmund?'

From along the banks there came the clatter of ducks in alarm. She called again into the silence. Dismayed now, she followed the path round. There was a black mound in the reeds by the bank. No, she told herself. It was not a child's shape. He had not been wearing black, only something dark. Dark, yes, but not black. Water soaks to black. With dread she edged herself forward, noting as she went how the thing ballooned and bumped against the bank, how with its weight it resisted the pressure of the sway of the reeds and had its own purpose and momentum. The air around her was moist and heavy. There was no room for breathing in it. There was no heat in the day, only a cold clamminess which did not feel like air at all, which felt like a skin that was tight and unyielding. And still on her hand she felt the ice-cold touch of Miss Mallory's sympathy.

It was not the boy. It could not be, not that shape, and the colour was wrong, and yet she must look at it. She knelt down at last on the bank and strained forward. It was something like sacking, that bulged and sagged again, bulged and sagged. She fumbled around her for a twig and poked it at the sacking again and again until at last she had purchase, and then she twisted the stick round with all her strength, with both fists burning, until it had scored a hole. Black water blistered through. The fabric flattened and spread. Its bulk was exhumed.

Rose sank back. She was exhausted, absorbed and frenzied as she had been in her task. Her hands were muddied from the stick, and now her coat and her skirt would be caked in mud too. She didn't care. She was shaking now. 'Edmund!' she shouted. 'Edmund!'

She knew she must go home now. She had no idea what time it was. 'The baby!' she thought. 'I hope to God the baby's all right.' Paedric would have told him some tale and would have talked him off to sleep. 'But he must keep him warm,' she thought. 'That's his trouble. He's probably outside with him now, on a damp night like this, waiting for the stars to come through.'

She began to run, taking the cow lane. It was little drier than it had been that morning. She was so muddied now that she no longer cared what happened to her. She loped along, recalling every detail of Edmund's distress there. Again and again she remembered that last hopeless appeal he had made before he fell, the way he had held out his arms to her, how she had stood and watched him fall, her hands in her pockets, and had watched him crawl to her. 'I will remember that every day of my life.' At one time she would have held out her arms to him, crouching down to his height, laughing to reassure him, lifting him free of the danger that threatened him. That would not have been long ago. But how could she have done that anyway, if she had held a sleeping baby on her hip? Perhaps by now Finn would be in a pushchair. It was not Finn's fault though. It was nothing to do with him. She would go home now and hold Finn in her arms and pour out to him her sorrow and her grief.

She would have gone straight to Paedric's house, but as she came over the embankment she saw that the light was on in her kitchen. Immediately she thought of Gordon's shock. He had no knowledge yet that the boy had gone missing. How could he not know when she had known so long, when she was heavy and weary with knowing, when it was already part of her life?

He was watching out for her. He opened the door as she

approached. 'What's going on?' he called out. 'Where've you been?'

The full gravity of the situation drained over her. Gordon loved Edmund. He was a father to him, and Edmund was his son. She gasped to calm her breath.

'Gordon, I've been looking for Edmund. I can't find Edmund.'

'Edmund's in the house. In bed,' he told her. 'It's you who's been missing.'

And only then did Rose begin to cry. He put his arm round her shoulder and steered her through into the house. She ran upstairs to Edmund. He was sitting up in bed, his face and his hair shining. He was sweet-smelling in clean pyjamas. He had been playing chess with Gordon, and the board was still balanced across his knees. He smiled at her. He is all-forgiving, she thought. He is so stupid he has forgotten the distress of this morning. He is punishing me with his forgiveness.

'Where do you think you've been hiding all day?' she demanded. She had not meant to say that. She was angry with him for his forgiveness. It was a triumph over her. He still smiled, half-closing his eyes and tilting back his head to peer at her through dark slits. 'I've been worried about you, Edmund. I've been out of my mind. I've been combing the village looking for you. Why weren't you at school?'

He shook his head at her, secrets glinting through the slits in his eyes. She wanted to fold him in her arms and tell him she was sorry. She wanted to shake him.

'I even went to Simon's looking for you.'

Edmund picked up one of the chess pieces and moved it. 'Simon! I haven't played with him for years! Don't you know I don't like him any more?'

In a fury of relief and shame and anger Rose tipped the

chessboard off his knees. The pieces skittered across the floor, clattering and rolling in all directions. It was a set that Gordon had carved, and that Edmund had helped to rub down and varnish. The pieces were beautiful. It had always angered Rose that she didn't know how to play and that Gordon had never tried to teach her. Edmund dived out of bed after the pieces, shouting at her. 'There was no need for you to do that! You've chipped one of the knights. You've *chipped* it!' He held it out to her.

'Don't you dare shout at me! Have you no word of apology to me for all you've put me through today?' Rose was shocked at her unreasonable wrath. 'I thought you were dead! I thought you'd fallen in the river and drowned, that's what I thought! Look at me! How do you think I got like this? I've been in the river nearly, poking round for your drowned body!'

Her voice was rising to a higher and higher pitch. She hated the sound of it. She desperately wanted to make him cry in the way that he had cried that morning, so she could take him into her arms and rock him and say, 'I'm sorry my baby, I'm sorry, I'm sorry,' but he was beyond tears now. He was afraid of her. His fear made him hysterical. He giggled as if she was playing a game with him. The more he giggled the more she shrieked. She was just aware of a high keening from Paedric's house. Not till Gordon intervened did she realize that she had been shaking Edmund, that he had been lolling his head backwards and forwards, laughter glinting in his eyes at each upward roll. Gordon held her by the shoulders and stood her at arm's length. He looked down at her in sorrow and disbelief.

'What's happened to you?' he said. 'I don't know you any more.'

She stared back at him, and at Edmund, white-faced,

half-smiling still in his shocked terror of her. She backed away from them both. She went into the bathroom and filled up the bath. She wanted to sleep in it. She could hear Edmund and Gordon talking together. She was resentful of their closeness, and she was deeply ashamed of herself. The Merlins' radio was switched on for the evening entertainment. She sank back, grateful for the idiot clamour of voices as the drama of pretend family life was played out. As soon as she had had her bath she would go to Edmund and tell him she was sorry. She would stroke his hair and tell him a story and she would watch how his eyelids fluttered down and his breathing steadied into sleep. She refilled her bath and lay half-dreaming. At last she let the water go and put on her dressing-gown. Her clothes lay in a muddy pile in the corner. They were the remnants of a nightmare.

When she looked into Edmund's room he was already asleep. She closed his door and tiptoed downstairs. She was relieved. Tomorrow they would go to school the long way round because Finn would be in a pushchair. She hurried to her room to dress. Finn would be awake and screaming now for sure, lonely and needing her. She wanted him back. When she came out of her room Gordon was standing outside her door. His presence was ominous.

'Where do you think you're going now?' he asked. There was an edge of authority in his voice. She was aware of the faint smell of whisky on his breath.

'I just need to go round to Paedric's for something.'

He watched her levelly, not moving. 'There's nothing you need to go round to Paedric's house for at this time of night.' He chose his words with great care. 'Nor at any time. This is your home.'

'Did I say it wasn't?'

'Your family is here.'

She tried to pass him. Without using any force at all he blocked her way. He was a big man. She would have to push to get past him. He leaned against the door, and behind him the glass sparked with rain. She was glad of the rain. She imagined it gushing from Paedric's tree. She thought of the trees bowing down to the river, rain streaming from their branches. She saw again the bulge of sacking bloated with her guilt, rain pitting the water around it.

'I'll be five minutes, that's all. I'll come straight back.'

'No.'

'You've no right to keep me here.'

'You're my *wife*.'

She turned away, helpless, back into her room. She sank down on to her bed. Gordon stood in the doorway watching her.

'You've been drinking,' she said.

'I was worried about you. I didn't know what had happened to you.'

'I told you. I was looking for Edmund.'

Gordon came into the room and sat on the bed next to her. He held her hand. It was his way, she knew, of controlling his emotions. It anchored him. She did not draw away her hand, nor did she respond to his touch.

'When I got off the train this evening Edmund was waiting for me at the station. He was covered in mud and he was very cold and very hungry. He was also very distressed. He said he'd been back to the house several times during the day but that you had not been here. Joan had seen him and offered to take him in but he had refused. You know how timid he is. He had tried Paedric's house but there was no one there either. He had no idea where you might have been.'

Rose stared in front of her. 'He should have been at school.'

'He thought you had run away.'

'What nonsense!'

'Where were you?'

'Looking for him. I searched the river for him.'

'Before you started looking for him?'

'Does it matter?' She let anger override her guilt. She was ashamed of herself. She had no right to be angry with Gordon. He didn't demand anger. It would have been easier if he had. 'The fact is the child took a day off school. That's what matters.' His hand tightened on hers. She saw the blue veins, the curl of white hairs.

'Were you with Paedric?'

'I can do what I like. Surely to God I don't have to give an account of my day to you.'

'I'm your husband.'

'No, you're not!' Anger flashed again. 'What kind of a husband are you? No woman would live with you and call you husband. I clean your house and feed you. You are not Edmund's father. You have no claim on me or my time whatsoever. You don't own me, Gordon.'

'I own the house you live in.'

'Yes,' she conceded. She stroked his hand. 'You are a good, kind man.' Finn had nothing to do with him. She thought of him now, crying lustily for her, his face red with anger, his fists clenched in small rage. Surely Gordon could hear his screams. They filled the caverns of her head.

Gordon made a sudden movement and she flinched away from him, startled. He reached across her and picked up the bundle of baby shawls. He stood up, shaking them out of their bundle.

'What's this supposed to be?' There was grief in his voice.

There was no answer she could give him. She walked out of the room and into the shock of rain. When she returned from Paedric's the house was in darkness.

THIRTY-SIX

Edmund spent most of the summer holiday with Rose's mother and her new husband. When Rose went to collect him she felt estranged from her mother. The old man cared for her as if she was a child, and they spoke together in quiet whispers that excluded Rose. Her mother seemed very tired, and it was obvious to Rose that Edmund was too much for her now, that he had been bored at her house.

'He's a strange child,' her mother said. 'I didn't know he could be so moody.'

Rose longed to tell her mother about Finn, who was sweet-tempered and loving and who now had a lively interest in everything. 'Finn is different altogether,' she wanted to say. 'You'll love him.' She wanted to tell her about her friendship with Paedric, but she knew this would distress her mother unnecessarily. And now that her mother was settled into this quiet, caring relationship with the retired farmer she would have liked to talk about her own father, to rouse him from the dead and let him account for himself. But Mrs Waterhouse was closed away from her. She responded to her husband's solicitousness with tired smiles. She seemed to have lost touch with her past, and it was as if her future was to be a quiet turning down of lights.

Early in October Rose had a dream which frightened her so much that she went immediately to see her mother. In her dream Edmund had come running to her to tell her that her mother was leaving. Rose had gone out of the house and found her mother lying on rocks. 'I want to come with you,' she had said. 'No, you can't come,' her mother said, though her lips weren't moving. 'It's too cold for you. Besides, you don't have a passport.' 'I do. I'm sure I can find one.' Rose ran back to the house and was feverishly searching through drawers and boxes when Edmund ran in. 'Gran's going now,' he said. 'But she can't. Not without me.' She ran with him to the door and there was her mother, wrapped in white and lying on a sledge which was moving slowly down the ice road outside her house. Rose would never forget the cold sheesh of the blades on the ice, or the chill which crept over her dream.

When she arrived the next day at her mother's house the old man confirmed what she already knew, that her mother had died in the night.

'We knew she was dying,' he said, trying to comfort Rose, 'when we married. We knew we only had a short time together.'

'Then why didn't she tell me?'

'It made us very close,' the old man said, shaking his head at her, troubled by her despairing anger.

'I'll never know her now!'

She longed to get back home to Finn. He was all she had now. All the way home on the train she tried to summon up grief for her mother, but could find nothing. She tried to bring her back from her past, and could remember nothing but vague images that drifted across each other: a fold of hands, a tilt of head, an anxious, still look about the eyes. It seemed that wherever she looked her mother was in a shadowed background; while other things were going on, she was a silent watcher. And now her mother had slipped away into a blackness that was all silence except for the sheesh of blades on ice. Not all the shimmering heat of that autumn day could take away that chill.

And again these days there was a restlessness inside herself that she could not name. It was like the days just before the birth of Finn, when she felt feverish with waiting.

'Finn will be talking soon,' she said to Paedric. 'He'll be standing up and taking his first steps.'

'In his own time,' said Paedric lazily, and she hated him for it. He was the sorcerer. He knew all the spells. 'When he walks he will be taking steps away from us. And language will give him power over us. Think of that.'

And yet on the day of the full moon she felt sure the time had come. The sky was ripe and full. That evening she took her time over preparing the meal. She followed Edmund up to his room and sat on his bed.

'Would you like a story?' she asked.

'A story?' He was surprised. 'I've got my book.'

'Put away your book. I want to tell you a story about a poor farmer and a witch.'

Finn was in the corner of the room, watching her. The story was for him.

'There was a witch,' she said, 'who stole milk from the farmer's pails, and eggs from his barns, and grain from his stores. He knew she was doing it, but she was such a clever witch that he could never catch her at it. This is what she would do. She would steal into his milking sheds and lift up two pails brimming with milk and walk away down the lanes with them. He would turn around and see that his pails of milk were gone. "Have you seen an old woman carrying two pails of milk?" he would ask, and people would point and say, "That's the way she went." He would see her away in front of him but as soon as he caught up with her he would see only an old woman with two white geese at her side. And the same when she stole his eggs. He would be told by people that they had seen an old woman hobbling along with a basket of eggs but as soon as he caught up with her he would find that the eggs had become a brood of hens and chickens, pecking round her feet as she walked.

'But he was most perplexed when he found his sacks of grain were going missing. Whenever he counted the sacks in his store the number was always the same, and yet he was forever being told that an old woman had been seen hobbling away from his barn, bent double with the weight of a sack of grain across her back. "Next time you see her, tell me," he ordered, and sure enough his daughter ran into the barn one day and said "I've seen her, I've seen her, and she has a sack of grain right now." He turned to the sacks and counted them and they were exactly right, yet he ran out and down the lane, following the old woman's steps in the mud. When he came round the bend all he could see was a brown hare, leaping away from him.

'Next time he was bagging grain he heard a scuffle in the barn. He counted the sacks and they were just right. He took a fork and drove it into the sacks one by one, and from one after the other grain spilled out, but from the last of all there came a spill of blood. "Ha ha!" said the farmer. "I have her! I have her!" But no, his daughter ran in and cried, "I've just seen her, but this time you're sure to catch her. She can hardly carry the grain because there's a wound in her leg and she limps so badly." So he picked up his gun and ran after her, following the drops of blood. When he rounded the bend he saw only an old hare, but the hare was slow, dragging a leg behind itself. It paused for a moment at the top of the hill, with the red moon like a balloon of blood behind it, and the farmer aimed his gun and fired. The hare fell, but as soon as the old man ran forward to collect his prize a hawk rose up into the air from the very spot where the hare had been lying. As he raised up his head to watch, down dropped the hawk, down and down, and stole the very eyes out of the farmer's head.'

Edmund was silent in his bed, staring out of the window.

'I don't like it,' he said at last. 'It's not supposed to end like that.'

'I didn't know when I began the story that it was going to end that way,' said Rose. 'It just took that turn in my head. But don't you think it was a happy ending? After all, the witch got away.'

'I just felt sorry for the poor old farmer,' said Edmund. 'Why did the witch have to win?'

'I'll give you one of your books to read,' said Rose. 'You know all the ones that have happy endings – you can read one of those to cheer yourself up.'

'Ask Daddy to come,' he called after her as she went downstairs.

Rose gave Gordon the message. 'I'm just going out,' she told him.

'Are you going to see him?' he asked, nodding his head towards Paedric's house.

'I am.' Through the window the moon was glowing and golden. She was restless with excitement.

'I can't understand you,' Gordon said. 'There must be more to him than I can see. All I see is an ugly gnome.'

'That's all there is to see,' she smiled. Nothing would spoil her mood of joy now. She went to her room to find the shawls. She felt sure they would be part of the night's ceremony.

THIRTY-SEVEN

Paedric was in Helena's room. Rose went straight up without switching on the lights. He had lit the candles and had them surrounding a mirror. He had painted his face white and with a blackened cork was filling in huge rings around his eyes. His face changed shape, a grotesque and beautiful thing. He blackened his lips and streaked his cheekbones. She sat on a chair and watched him, the baby shawls in her arms. He turned round to look at her.

'I don't recognize you!' she laughed.

'Now you.'

'I don't think I want to.'

'That doesn't matter. I want you to.'

She moved to the chair by the mirror and sat with the shawls spread across her knees and her eyes closed. A moth kept up a steady drumming on the window, drawn by the candles. Rose surrendered herself to the deft touch of Paedric's brushstrokes.

'What am I becoming?' she asked him. 'A demon?'

'I want to bring out the goddess in you,' he told her.

She succumbed to him. The stroke of the cork and brush on her skin were soft and sweet. Not once did Paedric's fingers touch her.

He stood back for a moment, regarding her thoughtfully. 'Would you undress?' he asked her. Like a child she obeyed him, turning her back for him, lifting her arms, lifting her breasts while he drew out his patterns and lines. She knew he was seeing her body as a canvas. 'A tiger in the rushes,' he said. 'A snake in sunlight. You're rising out of clay into light and shadow. You are becoming night and day, the year half-turned.' His voice purred beneath her consciousness.

'I told Finn a story tonight,' she told him. 'What did you do with him today?'

'He cried a little, for you. He laughed a little. I took him to the river. I held him out over it so he could see himself there. He held out his hands towards himself. Our child is wild . . .'

'And then he slept, before you brought him back to me?' She lifted up her arms as the cork nosed into the hollow pits darkening the fuzz of hair. 'If he's going to be awake tonight he needed sleep.'

'He did sleep. He slept in a bed of rushes.'

'Oh, Paedric! You will drown the child one day.'

'A long time ago,' he soothed her with the strokes the brushes made, 'there was a child sleeping in a bed of rushes in the river. "Oh, but he's not safe there!" his mother cried. "I'm always safe, as long as I'm not seen," the baby told her. "As long as I'm a secret, I'll be safe." But one day the baby's step-brother came down to the river. He was intrigued because his mother spent so long there instead of being at home with him. He didn't know about the baby. Nobody knew. As he came down to the river he heard his mother singing and he knew by the sweetness of her voice and by the faraway rapt look in her eyes that it was a baby she was singing to, even though there was no baby to be seen. The step-brother was weak with jealousy, but he kept it locked in his heart. Then, one moment when his mother wasn't looking, he crept to the rushes and saw what was hidden there. In a sudden rage the jealous step-brother cut away the rushes that formed a bed for the baby. He ran to hide again, with gladness and fear chock full in his heart. Now his mother would love him best.'

'Would you stop the story now?' Rose asked him.

'It's too late for it to be stopped. The mother looked back and she saw that the rushes had been cut away. She saw the baby floating in its bed of rushes down the river, and she ran along the banks, screaming out loud. She plunged into the river and she was furious with grief. Her skirts were floating in a swirl around her and nobody could hold her back or restrain her passion as she tried to reach her baby. But the current was too strong, and he was swept away from her.

'"I've lost my baby! I've lost my baby!" she wailed, and in that very instant of her cry what did the baby do but turn into a fish, a magic green and golden fish, and was soon lost to sight in the green and gold of the river?

'"My baby is drowned!" the mother cried, and in that very instant of her cry what did the step-brother do but become a heron? And with his huge grey wings paddling the air he loped above the surface of the water until he spied the fish, and he lifted it up and up, streaming green and golden pearls out of the river and back to it again. He flew to the mother and dropped the fish into her arms. "Now my mother will love me best," he thought. But the mother did not recognize the fish as her baby. She threw it back into the river. The heron flew down again, calling out to her that it was a magic fish and she must take it, but she had no ears for the voice of the heron and did not understand its language. She did not recognize her step-son. He dived again and brought up the fish into the air, and came to her with it, and she was afraid of it and ordered the heron to be shot. And when that happened, he dropped the fish on to the earth where it writhed and gasped until it too died.

'So because the mother loved too little and too much, she lost the two things that meant most to her in all the world.' Paedric put down his brushes and stood back. 'Now you are a goddess,' he said. 'The goddess of darkness and light.

Our son is coming to life. He is a living thing now, born out of the darkness of our minds and into the shock of light.'

He took the shawls from her hands and shook them free from their bundle. He swirled them round. 'I have seen Edmund dancing with these in your garden.'

Rose shook her head. 'Surely not! He doesn't know, Paedric.'

'Look at yourself.' He held up the mirror to her. 'Enter the moonlight.'

'Like this?' But already Rose was not herself. She was enchanted by her own reflection and its dazzle of curving stripes. She was the snake on the forest track.

'The moon is full,' Paedric told her from the window. 'And the moon is kind to women.'

Rose followed him downstairs and outside. His garden was rich with the patterns of night, slanting shadows and silvery casts. Paedric placed the shawls under his tree, which was a web of silver and black, sinewy twists of insubstantial light and shadow. Rose touched the trunk to establish its solidity, put her arms round it, pressed her cheek against its rough bark. She spiralled away and held up her arms to the canopy of leaves and began to spin slowly round, watching how the same lights and shadows blurred into the solidity of her painted flesh.

'Dance!' whispered Paedric. He began to intone a whistling nasal song, and Rose held up her head and closed her eyes and danced. She felt as if the darkness and light were flooding into her limbs and entering her. He began a slow clap, clap, clap and his song rose and fell, rose and fell, not song at all but the drone and buzz and piping of birds and insects. It was for Finn that she was dancing. He was lying at her feet in the whirl of air. He could see the night's flashing sky and the glimmering between dim branches and the dark reeling of her limbs. At the end of the dance he hauled himself up with one of those ropy twists of light and stood for the first time. Rose bent down and scooped him up, lifted him above her head and high up towards the tree, and now through the geometry of branches came the clear warm flood of light, the ice of the night's sun. 'Moon!' he cried. Both his hands pointed up to it. 'Moon!'

'Finn is the baby is the child is the man, is love is life is death itself,' chanted Paedric, and louder, 'Finn is the baby is the child is the man is love is life is death itself . . .'

'Stop this madness!'

Someone had come into their garden. Rose began to tremble. She couldn't stop herself. It was as if the surface of her skin was pricked by millions of separate impulses, would flake away like the ashes of a fire, papery and cold. She was weak. Gordon came up to her and picked up the shawls from the grass at her feet. He wrapped them around her shoulders. She heard herself whimpering like a child.

'There now, there now,' he said. 'We'll go home.'

Her feet were cut and bleeding. She winced as she tried to walk.

'Would you like me to carry you?'

She shook her head. The night was spinning away from her.

Paedric ran up to them, moaning and holding out his long hands. 'Don't stop now! Don't go away now!'

'Leave her,' said Gordon. 'She's nothing to do with you.'

Paedric snatched at the shawls but Rose clutched them to her, hiding her face in them, willing the trembling to stop.

'You're taking away my son.'

'You have no son,' Gordon told him. 'Go back, Paedric. Go inside where it's warm.'

'You have no son,' Paedric whined after him. 'You have no son.'

Rose half-turned her head towards him. He was standing with his hands still stretched out toward her. He moaned again, giving a baby's sob. She let the shawls slide away from her on to the ground.

THIRTY-EIGHT

Gordon took her upstairs, filled a bath for her and lifted her in. Already the stripes on her body were smudged and blurred. He washed her down with tenderness, lathering up soap with his hands and stroking them across her, soaping and soaking her. At last he wiped her face, helped her out of the bath and towelled her down. He kissed her.

'Now I would like to make love to you, if you'd like that too,' he said.

'I would.'

They went down again to her room and with the same careful tenderness he made love to her, and with the same shy tenderness she responded to him.

'I don't understand myself,' he told her then. 'I've done you great harm. I'm sorry for all the hurt I've caused you.'

'I'm sorry too.' She thought of Paedric reaching out for the bundle of shawls that was their baby. She wanted to weep for him. 'I don't understand anything any more.'

Paedric's voice could be heard still, keening.

'Will you tell me about those shawls?' Gordon asked her.

'I can't.'

'Why not? They're just a bundle of shawls, Rose. Rags. That's all they are.'

Paedric's keening had become louder. With a start Rose realized that he was standing at her window looking in on them. They could make out the white moon of his face peering through, the pale bundle in his arms. Gordon went to the window and pulled the curtains across. He stood with his back to them.

'You know that man is mad. Not simple. He's mad, Rose. He's a lunatic.'

'If he's mad then we all are.'

Paedric's keening had turned into the high wailing of a small child.

'Listen to him. The man is ill.'

The door was pushed open and Edmund came in, clutching his pyjamas to him. 'Make him stop. Please make him stop.' His face was white and his eyes deep and dark. He stared at Gordon and Rose, naked together on the bed.

'Up you go,' said Gordon. He pulled on his shirt and took Edmund's hand, leading him upstairs. 'It'll be all right.'

Rose went to the window and lifted back the curtains. Paedric held out his hand to her as if the glass did not exist and she could simply reach out and touch him. He was whimpering still, his face puckered like a small child's. 'Our child is wild . . .'

'Go home. Please go home.' As Gordon came back down she let go of the curtains. He sat on her bed and she went to him.

'You have to tell me what's going on, Rose. Edmund has been through enough, you know that, don't you? He wants you back.'

Paedric was hammering on the kitchen door now. 'Go away!' Gordon shouted.

'Let him in,' said Rose, weary. 'He'll never stop now.' They went together into the kitchen and Gordon opened the door. The stripes on Paedric's face were smeared and running in a peculiar jagged line, as if his face was peeling away. Gordon indicated to him to sit down but he ignored him. He couldn't take his eyes off Rose. He held towards her the bundle of shawls. She shook her head.

'I let you in because Rose asked me to,' said Gordon. 'But I have to tell you that I don't want you in my house. You're intruding on my home and on my family.'

'What family?' Paedric jeered, still not looking at him. He pitched his voice again to the high moan of a child. 'You have no son.'

'Don't, Paedric,' Rose begged. She wished he would go. She couldn't bear the sight now of those shawls, blackened as they were with streaks of cork, trailing like tattered rags from Paedric's arms.

'Once upon a time there was a man who had no son. And he put his hand in a pond and drew out a frog and said, "This will be mine, I will have him for a son." '

'Edmund is our son. I wish you'd go home.'

'Once there was a woman who did not have a son. She plucked a golden apple from a tree and said, "Ah, this will be mine, I will have him for a son."'

'Stop, Paedric. You have no right . . .'

'What's he saying, Rose?'

'It's just nonsense.'

'Oh, his son and heir is only a bubble! Fancy that!' Paedric laughed, rolling his eyes at Gordon.

'I know Edmund isn't my son. Go away. Go on.'

'Once there was a woman with a belly full of stones.' Paedric covered up his face and laughed.

Rose stood up and took Gordon's hand. She stood side by side with him, facing Paedric, speaking slowly. 'Edmund is not my son. I don't even think he was William's. I don't know who he is.'

Gordon let out his breath in a long, slow sigh. She could feel his hand growing limp in hers. When she turned to him he had the face of an old man. 'But he is our son, all the same,' she urged. 'We have taken him as ours.' She pressed his hand, urging him to look at her, but he refused. He sat down heavily at the kitchen table and slumped forward so his head was buried in his arms. She kneaded his shoulders. 'I love you and Edmund.'

Paedric gave out Finn's whimper again.

'Go home now,' she told him. He offered her the shawls again, and again she refused. 'He's yours.'

'No, he isn't,' Paedric moaned. 'He's ours.'

'He's a bundle of rags. He does not exist. I don't want him.'

Gordon raised his head and stared from one to the other of them. Paedric began to sob and stumbled out into the garden.

'He's dying,' he wailed.

Gordon put out his hand to Rose but she ran out after Paedric, suddenly afraid for him. He was scrambling up the embankment. From the near distance came a rumble to the lines, a buzz and a hiss, a frantic singing; and out of that taut wail of sound came the beast's roar as the train bellowed towards them. Paedric had reached the tracks, his small twisted frame tensed to the yellow rush of the train's eye. Rose screamed, desperate to reach him. Paedric stepped forward, his legs apart, his arms scissoring out. And out of the shadows under the tree came Edmund. He flung himself at the man and with all his child's strength hauled Paedric back from his willed darkness.

The white shawls spread out like the wings of a huge bird, soared and plunged across the track, and under the thundering wheels.

THIRTY-NINE

'Our son is dead.' She hears it forever. She hears it in every moment of her waking and every night of her dreaming.

Edmund lies awake remembering his father's leaving, though he has long given up watching out for the train that could bring him back again. After all, he is an old man now. Perhaps he is dead.

Paedric has forgotten his secret child. In his walking dreams he follows the steps of his nightmares, knowing nothing. He is consoled by Helena, and he knows he is safe with her.

Rose Doran lies naked as a peach on top of her bed and watches the moth that flutters its dark and dusty wings down the wall. Maybe, she thinks, Paedric will hear its whispery strumming between her room and his and think of her before sleep takes over. She closes her eyes and imagines the moth's lips brushing like velvet along her flesh.

AUTHOR'S NOTE

The stories of the Fisherman and his Wife, Yggdrasil, the Seven Little Kids, the Farmer and the Witch and the African Snake are all based on traditional tales.